About Thyme for Love

"A romantic mystery full of twists, turns, fancy cooking, a hunky hero, and a heroine who doesn't take no for answer. A true delight for romance readers everywhere."

CYNTHIA HICKEY, author of the Summer Meadows Mysteries and *Unraveling Love* (A Barbour novella)

"Auhhh, springtime in Wisconsin! April Love finds more things smoking than just the steaks on the stovetop grill at the *Rescate de Niño*. Great food and a murder are all the rage today for *haute* cuisine. I'm looking forward to more adventures for this character! The clock is ticking! Do you have *Thyme For Love?*"

BONNIE S. CALHOUN, Publisher of *Christian Fiction Online Magazine,* author of *Cooking the Books*

"Fresh, clever, witty, and real, *Thyme for Love* is that rare romance that leaps to 3-D life, snatches you by your apron bib, and keeps you enraptured—and guessing—until long past the dessert in the oven has burned to carbon. This is one book I'll be recommending to my family and friends."

TAMMY BARLEY, award-winning author of The Sierra Chronicles, Executive Editor of WorldTalk international Christian books and *Destination: Earth* magazine"

"*Thyme for Love* is a compelling romance with unique characters, including a rogue parrot named Pedro, that will live on in your hearts long after you turn the last page. A delightful debut book from Pamela Meyers. I'm looking for a sequel."

ANE MULLIGAN, Sr. Editor, Novel Rocket; http://www.novelrocket.com

ON THE ROAD TO LOVE
PAMELA S. MEYERS

Thyme for Love
BOOK ONE

❧❦

Love Will Find a Way
BOOK TWO

❧❦

Love's Reward
BOOK THREE

ON THE ROAD TO LOVE
BOOK ONE

THYME FOR

PAMELA S. MEYERS

OAKTARA

Waterford, Virginia

Thyme for Love

Published in the U.S. by:
OakTara Publishers
P.O. Box 8, Waterford, VA 20197
www.oaktara.com

Cover design by Yvonne Parks at www.pearcreative.ca
Cover images © www.shutterstock.com: sunset on the river/Nadiya_sergey;
curly blonde woman with smile and pearls/Darryl Brooks; ©iStockphoto.com:
young male portrait/drbimages

Scripture quotations marked NIV are taken from The Holy Bible, New
International Version®, NIV®. Copyright © 1973, 1978, 1984 by Biblica, Inc.™
Used by permission. All rights reserved worldwide.

ISBN: 978-1-60290-302-9

Thyme for Love is a work of fiction. References to real people, events,
establishments, organizations, or locales are intended only to provide a sense
of authenticity and are used fictitiously. All other characters, incidents, and
dialogue are drawn from the author's imagination.

Printed in the U.S.A.

Acknowledgments

First and foremost, I must give thanks to God Almighty, who called me to write, even before I knew Him as my Lord and Savior. He has been faithful to me through many years of learning the craft and developing stories. He has blessed me indeed as I've grown spiritually and a writer.

Thanks to Lois Fleming, my writing professor at Trinity International University, who told me I had what it took to be published. The seed was planted. Lois, it took awhile, but here is the fruit of what you saw when I lacked the vision.

Thanks to American Christian Fiction Writers who, over the years, has provided me with all necessary to achieve writing success. ACFW—you guys rock! Thank you.

Thanks to Karen Wiesner, who took this fledgling author under her wing when this story was only a figment of my imagination and taught me how to write a mystery. Karen, your patience and encouragement during those months are now paying off. Thank you!

An author is only as good as her critique partners. Thank you to Tammy Barley, who took the time to edit this story just when her own editing business was taking off. And more thanks goes to my dear friend and writing buddy, Ane Mulligan, who critiqued a later version of this story and helped me take it to the next level. Love ya, girlfriend!

Thanks to my final readers: Kimberli Buffalo, Chandra Smith, and Michelle Shocklee. You blessed me so much by stepping to the plate at the last minute and giving me your undivided attention.

Thanks also to my agent extraordinaire, Terry Burns, who took me on and works tirelessly to get his clients placed.

Thanks to Jerry Steinke of Steinke Funeral Home in Lake Geneva, Wisconsin. Jerry spent a chunk of his day explaining to me the procedures that would be followed in Wisconsin around a suspicious death. Your explanations helped tremendously, Jerry. Thank you!

✌ 1 ✍

The kitchen door opened, and I came face to face with a ghost. Not a Scrooge's Christmas Past kind of ghost. More like the Ghost of Long-Lost Love. Bronze complexion, espresso-dark eyes, and hair as black as licorice, Marc Thorne looked as gorgeous as he had when he walked out of my life the day before college graduation.

Limp as overcooked pasta, I gripped the island's granite counter, its rock-solid support my only hope of not toppling off my three-inch, too-tight heels. Why now? I opened my mouth to speak, but a vise-like grip on my chest had squeezed out every ounce of air.

He stepped toward me, and a whiff of his citrus-like aftershave tickled my nose. Thankfully he wasn't wearing the spicy fragrance I'd always liked. One sniff of that stuff and I'd have been transported back to a time I preferred to keep dead and buried.

"April? What are you doing here?"

What was I doing here? I forced a ragged breath into my lungs. "I'm waiting to interview with...Mr....Gomez for the chef position."

"Galvez." His voice cracked.

"You're right. Galvez. Ramón Galvez." How many times had the man's name run through my head recently? As many as the number of restaurants I'd interviewed within the past two weeks. If I'd been taken straight to Mr. Galvez's office, I might not be facing this flash from my past that I'd tried for eight years to despise. And what was Marc doing back? He was supposed to be in California working with His Helping Hands Ministry. At least that was his plan. His carved-in-granite plan.

Like mannequins in a department store window, we faced each other with set-in-plastic smiles—his features, tanned by his Argentine heritage on his mother's side, and mine, no doubt pasty white from shock. His gray slacks fit his build as though tailored for him. The navy and red striped tie coupled with the crisp button-down shirt exuded business, while the sleeves rolled up to reveal strong forearms gave the right touch of casualness.

I gulped. Where was his jacket? If he were here on business, he wouldn't be in his shirtsleeves. Did he work here? I pulled my eyes away from my personal version of *Back to the Future* and mentally said good-bye to Rescaté de Nino's made-for-a-chef kitchen: granite counters all around, a pair of microwaves, commercial-sized dishwasher. They'd done a wonderful job bringing the century-old mansion's kitchen up to date.

My gaze rested on the six-burner stove I'd been drooling over for the past fifteen minutes. A dull pain filled my chest. None of that mattered anymore. Not if Marc worked for Rescaté. Day after day I'd be reminded of how I'd lost him to something else. *Good-bye, chef job.*

I faced him. "Why are you back in Wisconsin?"

His puzzled expression dissolved as his stare bore into me. "Didn't your aunt tell you my news?"

My back stiffened. "What does she have to do with anything?"

"I've been in Canoga Lake going on a year and working here since last summer when Parker Montclaire willed the mansion to Rescaté. It's been good to be back home." He flashed the smile that used to send me soaring to the moon and back. "As the assistant director, I'm in charge of corporate sponsors." The left corner of his mouth twitched. "Whoever gets the chef job will be working with me."

My portfolio hit the floor, scattering its contents across the terracotta tiles like autumn leaves. Marc squatted and gathered up the papers while I stood by like an inert lump of dough, my face heating. In less than one minute the man had managed to discombobulate me. I needed to get a grip.

He straightened, and I reached for the papers, expecting him to hand them over. But he was too busy reading my résumé. My stomach sizzled. He gave up his right to my personal business eight years ago. I cleared my throat, and he looked up.

His face colored. "I, um...sorry." He placed the documents in my hand, his fingers brushing mine in the exchange.

Was that my tremble, or his? "Am I...to interview with you?"

Please, Lord, no.

"Not this round."

His comment jolted me back to reality. Mr. Galvez could walk in any moment, and here I was, acting like a twit. Not much of a professional image. If only on principle, I had to go through with the interview and not let Marc's presence unhinge me. I wanted to leave in the worst way, but I wouldn't.

I laid the papers across the island counter. Résumé first, then the photos of my best culinary creations, followed by the letter of recommendation from a chef at Canoe, one of Atlanta's finer restaurants. Last, the letters from my instructors at the Atlanta School of Culinary Arts. I gathered them into a stack.

"I came to tell you Ramón is running late and to show you the way to his office in…" Marc checked his watch. "Two minutes. Let me help you with that." He gripped the papers.

"Thanks. It's okay." I pulled against the force of his grasp.

"We need to get going."

"That's why you ought to let go," I said as politely as possible through my clenched jaw.

He released his hold, and an awkward silence hung in the air as I slid the documents into the portfolio's pockets. I faced him. "Ready if you are, Dr. Thorne."

Color drained from his complexion, and he lowered his gaze. "It's just mister."

Just mister? No PhD? Fire returned to my gut. If I couldn't have influenced him to change his carved-in-stone plans for a doctorate, what—or who—did? I shot a mental prayer to God for control and forced a smile. "That's quite a bombshell."

He jammed his hands in his pockets, but not before I noticed his ring finger was as naked as a plucked chicken. Not good. He should be married and unavailable. "So, no PhD, no Helping Hands, no California, and no wedding ring. Fill me in."

"Still nosy as ever, I see." He jingled his coins. "I've asked your aunt about you several times. I thought she said you were a CPA in Atlanta. Odd she didn't mention to you that I'm back in Canoga Lake and working here."

I ignored his reference to my penchant for knowing details about my friends' lives. I always called it caring. Marc had called it nosy, but in an endearing sort of way. At the moment my concern was more with my Aunt Kitty who had always been more girlfriend to me than aunt. Wouldn't even let me call her "Aunt." Seemed she was playing matchmaker. Again.

Funny how she "happened" to tell me about this job opening, making it sound like a perfect opportunity. So perfect I drove all night from Atlanta not to miss out. No wonder she had me make a curious promise before she left on an overnight jaunt that no matter the outcome of my interview, I wouldn't leave until she returned. Anyone but my aunt, and I'd be on the road back to Georgia faster than an ice cube could melt in a microwave.

I ran my tongue over my lips, certain the color had long been eaten off. "Kitty may have mentioned you were here and I forgot." *Yeah, right. Like I'd forget my aunt telling me that my former fiancé worked next door to her house.* The house that always welcomed me like a warm cozy quilt and a cup of chamomile tea whenever I came to Canoga Lake. The house I'd no longer be able to visit with the mansion next door harboring a ghost from my past.

"Well, she didn't mention you were applying for the chef job either." He rocked back on his heels. A mannerism he always manifested when he was uneasy. The notorious left eyebrow twitch wouldn't be far behind. "So what's with the chef gig?"

I shrugged. "Corporate takeover. You have fifteen minutes. Here's a box. There's the door. Two weeks later, Kitty told me about Rescaté's chef position. Dad's pushing me to work for him again in Chicago, but slaving under his thumb once was enough. Not to mention I'm trying to ditch the numbers game." Unable to bear Marc's probing stare, I turned my attention back to the stove. "When Kitty told me about the chef job, I decided it was time to chase my dream."

"Did you prepare the food in those photos?" He indicated my folder.

I lifted my chin. "Of course."

"I don't remember you wanting to be a chef."

That hurt. How many times had I said...

"I mentioned it about a hundred times. Actually, catering is my goal. Maybe call it Lovin' Spoonfuls from April Love."

His eyes creased at the corners. "What about 'Somethin' Lovin' from April Love.'"

I couldn't help but chuckle. "That's a good one."

"Guess it's a good thing I didn't give you my last name after all."

My spine stiffened. "I still could have used my given name. At least my aunt didn't forget my aspiration. She's my biggest cheerleader."

"Same here. Without her character reference, I doubt I'd have gotten the job. She's one of Rescaté 's major donors. Supports three kids in Chile and one in Guatemala."

With the jerky motions of a robot, I picked up my portfolio. Marc or no Marc, the scenario had cleared. The interview with Mr. Galvez was a favor to my aunt, a mischievous 70-year-old with more energy than a room full of preschoolers. If only she'd channel that energy into something else besides trying to resurrect something that was better off dead and buried.

We stepped into the wood-paneled hall and turned right. Although we didn't say another word, the silence was anything but comfortable. How could it be when the only man I ever loved, the man I'd tried unsuccessfully to loathe and forget, had turned my dream come true into a nightmare?

We came to another corridor and stopped. Marc settled his dark-chocolate gaze on me. "I'm sorry for what happened with your papers back there. Ramón's suite is that way at the end of the hall." He pointed down the passageway to my left. "I think you can find it okay."

I fought my way out of the irresistible lure of his stare. Was this good-bye already? But he did say he was to show me the way, not take me there. Just as well. He probably no more wanted me as a coworker than I wanted him. Maybe he was sent to the kitchen to feel out the candidate first, then phone Mr. Galvez his thoughts before the interview.

"I'm sure I'll find it." I turned toward the office suite at the end of the corridor and began my best imitation of a dead woman walking. "Good seeing you again."

"April?"

I pivoted.

A hint of a smile teased his lips. "I don't forget everything. Happy birthday."

If I'd been born on any other day except Christmas, I'd have been impressed. But rarely does anyone forget when you're born on April Fool's Day and your name is April.

"Thanks." Today was turning out to be some kind of big 3-0. I'd rather be dining on grubs.

"Maybe we can go out sometime and catch up."

"Maybe."

"I'll call you."

I nodded and returned to my solitary walk. Call me? If I were smart, I'd be on my way south before the phone had a chance to ring. But my traitor heart told me if he called, I'd be there. Hopefully, he wouldn't.

I had only the time it took to walk the approximate 50 or 60 feet to Ramón Galvez's door to gather my sensibilities. I slowed my pace. Wasn't this chef gig, as Marc called it, the open door from God I'd thought it to be? How could something sound so right and be so wrong so fast? Surely God didn't intend for me to work under the man I'd been trying to forget for eight years. I'd be polite with Mr. Galvez, say how worthy Rescaté de Niño's mission to support needy kids was, and withdraw my name from consideration, beating them at their own game.

I glanced at several of the black-and-white photos lining the corridor wall. Faces of the kids Rescaté supported through its individual donors. A few of the children managed toothy grins, but most projected serious expressions, reflecting the hardships of their young lives.

A lump of guilt pressed against my heart. What happened to the joy I'd felt at the opportunity to use my cooking skills for such a worthy endeavor? This wasn't about me or Marc. It was about those kids. If I wanted this job and the door of opportunity still beckoned, what was to stop me? Marc Thorne didn't control my life anymore. And that was all the more reason to pursue the position. With shoulders back, I continued my walk. I couldn't wait to put on my spanking new chef coat and whip up some empañadas.

Arriving at the carved wood door to Mr. Galvez's suite, I gripped the brass handle and pulled. The new April Love was back. Gone were calculators and spreadsheets. Hello, sauté pans and chopping knives.

The administrative assistant's desk stood empty, but who needed a formal announcement when one was expected? My footsteps fell silent on the plush carpet as I crossed toward the open office door—the gateway to my dream come true, the first day lived as April Love, in-house chef.

A voice called out, "Well, it's about time."

Had Marc detained me longer than he should? I picked up my step.

"If the money isn't in Rescaté's account by next week, all bets are off."

I stopped short.

"I'm not afraid to blab."

A string of anger-laced Spanish filled the air. Words probably best left in a language I didn't understand. I glanced over my shoulder at the outside door. Overhearing the private conversation was accidental, but staying to hear more was wrong.

"Your threats don't scare me."

At the icy tone, I flinched.

"I'm only going to say this once. If any harm comes to me, my people will know who's responsible. You'll pay, *mi amigo.*"

My stomach quivered. Was I in the right place? I tiptoed closer to the man's door and read the nameplate. Right place, wrong time.

A loud crack sounded, and I visualized a phone receiver slammed into its cradle. What was I doing? I couldn't be found lurking here like a spy in a Tom Clancy novel.

Moving faster than I ever thought possible on three-inch heels, I darted for the hall and clutched the door handle. One more moment and it would be as if I'd never been there. Maybe I wasn't. Maybe I'd wake up any second now and still be in Atlanta working for Keystone Financial. Still trying to get through one whole day without thinking about Marc. Still dreaming of becoming a chef.

"Ms. Love, I didn't realize you were here. Please come in."

~ 2 ~

I followed the rotund man into his inner sanctum, certain my face was red as tomato salsa, and feeling more like *I Love Lucy* than Tom Clancy.

He paused at a massive oak desk and indicated a visitor's chair. "Please sit."

I lowered myself onto the upholstered seat cushion and clasped my hands in my lap. Pleasant smile, polite command in accented English. Was this a tease before he showed me the door? While he circled his desk and wedged himself into his leather seat, my gaze settled on one of the colorful tapestries that warmed the large area. What had this room been when the Montclaires lived here? A parlor?

A loud creak jerked me out of my reverie, and I drew my attention to the other side of the desk. Mr. Galvez leaned back at a 45-degree angle, his head inches from the window behind him. I prayed the chair didn't implode.

He wove his fingers together and rested them across his belly. His body language wasn't that of a man involved in a hot-tempered phone conversation, or one ready to lower the boom on a would-be chef with big ears.

I relaxed. Maybe I misunderstood. Wouldn't be the first time.

A smile filled his flushed cheeks. "So you had an opportunity to inspect our kitchen. Were you impressed?"

I crossed my legs and leaned forward. "Oh, yes. I love the stovetop grill. That's essential for creating a smoky flavor."

He patted his stomach. "You are a woman after my own heart. I've tried out that feature a few times since we remodeled the kitchen. Nothing fancy. Steak, a few burgers. I'm looking forward to sampling what a chef can create."

I shamelessly grinned. He would be a joy to cook for. But could I develop good low-fat recipes for enchiladas?

The director sat forward, his chair snapping into position with a *thwap.* "May I see your credentials?"

I handed him my portfolio.

Extracting my résumé from the folder, he slowly skimmed it, the space between his brows creasing.

I ran my palms over my skirt and pushed down the sensation of sitting in front of my dad's huge desk while he looked over my latest report card.

The director turned to the section that detailed my recent culinary history. My shoulders sagged. No one else wanted to hire a perpetual cooking student with a knack for financial reports, so why would he? Through the window over his shoulder, Canoga Lake glistened in the early spring sun. I'd always wanted to live here. Summers at Kitty's were never enough.

But what was to say I couldn't? Maybe one of the restaurants over in Lake Geneva needed a *sous* chef.

"Rescaté's motto is 'Rescue the Children and Save the World.'" Mr. Galvez's face lit up. "We're already in Central and South America. Now it's on to Mexico. We're looking to add corporate sponsors to our individual supporters to accomplish this. The drive begins with presentation dinners of a Spanish influence." He caught my eye. "Is this something you can handle?"

I nodded so vigorously I must have looked like a bobble-head doll. "Absolutely. I've already researched recipes indigenous to Mexico and have created several that are a notch above the usual Tex-Mex cuisine." I clasped my clammy hands in my lap to still the tremble.

He pulled out the photos and sifted through them, his gaze lingering on the *paella*. "Looks so good I wish I could taste it."

I released the breath I'd been holding. "It would be an honor to prepare it for you."

He flashed a smile. "Your aunt is a very high-spirited and dear lady. I was more than delighted to interview you as a favor. Never did I expect to find your culinary training to be so impressive. Holding down a full-time position as a CPA while attending school is to be commended. Even so, you've had little hands-on experience outside the classroom. Tomorrow, you'll prepare a Mexican lunch for my brain trust and me. The meal will be served at 11:30 sharp."

An urge to leap out of my chair and do the Mexican hat dance pulled at my heart, but constraint won over. "Of course. Do you want to select the menu?"

"You choose the entrée and make enough for four men. Before you leave, stop in the kitchen and make out a supply list, then drop it with Kim, my administrative assistant."

My heart rate running double-time, I mentally counted backward from 11:30. For the *paella* I needed more than a couple hours. "I'd like to come in early tomorrow morning to familiarize myself with the kitchen. Is someone here by seven?"

Mr. Galvez ran a hand over his gelled black hair. "Not usually, but perhaps I can arrange it." He picked up his phone and pressed a button. "Marc,

I have the chef candidate with me. She needs access to the building tomorrow morning at seven to prepare us an audition lunch. Can you plan to be here?"

Mr. Galvez nodded and said, "Uh-huh," then nodded again. My euphoric heart crash-landed in my stomach. Was Marc telling Mr. Galvez that he'd known me from the past, and I wasn't worth considering? Wasn't it enough that he'd dumped me in favor of a parchment on his ego wall?

Mr. Galvez switched to Spanish and continued to speak. The only word I recognized was my name, which he said like "Ahb-reel." I should have felt insulted, but concern over my dream job evaporating before it even began was stronger. What was he saying? Why hadn't I taken Marc up on his offer years ago to teach me Spanish? I reached for my purse. On second thought, maybe this wasn't my dream job. As soon as he hung up, I would be out of there.

"I see." Mr. Galvez switched to English. "Small world. If you vouch for her, I guess that's okay. Have Taryn bring me the card."

Card? Vouch for me? Great. Marc must have told him I was his ex-fiancée.

Mr. Galvez hung up. "My assistant director informs me you two knew each other in college. You should have said so."

I forced my mouth into what I hoped was a pleasant smile. "I didn't want that to influence your decision. Until he came to the kitchen a few minutes ago, I didn't know Marc worked here."

"Good. I like that." He rested his elbows on the desk and leaned on them. "Marc has a breakfast appointment in the morning, so I'm assigning you a key card. Something I wouldn't do without your connections through your aunt and Marc." He pulled a handkerchief from a pocket and blotted his forehead. "I suppose you're quite familiar with Canoga Lake since your aunt lives here."

"Yes. I spent my summers here up through college. I've been thinking, and I need to tell—"

A knock came at the door, and Mr. Galvez gave a verbal beckon.

I turned. Marc's gaze immediately went to me. As much as I wanted to look away, I couldn't. Not with his piercing stare wrapping itself around my heart and giving my deadened emotions CPR.

"I brought the security pass myself since Taryn is in the copy room. Wave it over the pad by the front door. It's configured for tomorrow only." He handed me a plastic card along with a form. "You need to sign this."

Without removing my focus from his dark-chocolate gaze, I grasped the keycard. Our fingertips brushed, and a warm tingle filled my stomach.

"Thanks, Marc." Mr. Galvez's voice broke our trance, and Marc looked away.

I glanced at the items in my hand. Now was the time to say I'd changed my mind. Why couldn't I get my mouth to move?

"If that's it..." Marc rocked back on his heels. "I'll be on my way."

The men's voices faded into the background while I feigned interest in the form. Reason told me to flee, but the remaining flutters in my stomach screamed, "Stay." Marc left, and sensing Ramón Galvez's impatient eyes on me, I scrawled my signature.

Mr. Galvez gripped his chair arms and pushed to his feet. Wincing, he rested a hand on his chest. "The alarm automatically shuts off at 6:30 a.m., so you shouldn't worry about that. It was a pleasure meeting you, Ms. Love. I have another appointment, or I'd escort you back to the kitchen."

I made my way out of his office on legs so rubbery I thought I'd end up facedown on the floor. An attractive brunette looked up from her desk. I nodded her way without stopping and made a beeline for the kitchen.

❧❧

The next morning, I grabbed my leather jacket from a hook by Aunt Kitty's back door, then checked my belongings a final time—my purse, chef jacket on a hanger, and duffle containing an iPod & speaker dock, recipes, and the knife set Aunt Kitty had given me for culinary school graduation. All I needed for a successful audition, if I didn't count a heavy dose of assurance and a guard around my heart regarding one Marc Thorne. It was only 6:30, but Kitty's rambling house was lonely without her. As it was, I'd hardly slept with the mantra *Remember what Marc did to you* running through my head.

Outside, icy pellets peppered my face on a wind strong enough to straighten my usually stubborn curls. Yesterday's warm temperatures were fast becoming a distant memory. Such was springtime in Wisconsin.

I ducked my head and set across my aunt's lawn, taking the path through the copse of pines that separated her estate from the old mansion. A minute later, I emerged onto Rescaté 's sprawling property. About a hundred yards ahead, the large building stood like a fortress.

Taking a moment, I soaked in the surroundings. Other than the parking lot where an English garden once stood, little had changed. The wooded area that acted as a shield between the main building and Shore Drive remained intact. To my left, the lawn sloped to the lake. Through the early morning twilight the vintage boathouse's outline stood out against the calm waters. I unmoored my thoughts and pushed off. Too many memories associated with that place, especially the boathouse's rooftop screened-in gazebo, where Marc had proposed.

At the main walk to Rescaté 's entrance, I peeked at the darkened second floor windows where I'd been told Mr. Galvez kept an apartment. Was he still asleep? Suited me fine if he were. I intended to enjoy coffee from the espresso machine and begin the meal prep without interruption. I could almost smell the freshly ground beans.

As I stuck my hand in my pocket for the keycard, a loud click came from the lock.

The door flew open.

A hard body crashed into me.

I stumbled backwards and landed on my bottom. Never before had I been so glad for extra padding. Who needed coffee to wake up when someone plows into you with the force of a Mac truck?

Shaking off my confusion, I caught sight of a guy hoofing it across the parking lot, a half-zipped backpack hanging from his shoulder. Or was it her shoulder? Hard to tell with the orange baseball cap. Something white popped out of the pack and rolled across the pavement.

"You dropped something," I called.

He trotted to where it had come to a stop and scooped the white thing up in his fist before sprinting toward the road.

"You're welcome." I brushed a strand of hair out of my eyes and pushed to my feet. If I got the job, I'd have to ask for accident insurance.

കൈൗൎ

I lifted the ceramic tureen of tortilla soup and settled it on the stainless-steel serving cart next to the *paella,* then checked my watch. Eleven-twenty and still no sign of Marc or Mr. Galvez. Did I dream about the audition? Had plans changed, and no one told me? Surely someone would have. Having spent the morning chopping, sautéing, and baking without interruption, I managed to forget about the strange encounter with the orange-capped person. A sure sign cooking was what God had called me to do. If the audition didn't work out, I'd find a kitchen somewhere else.

I'd already laid out a yellow tablecloth and colorful Fiestaware across the conference room meeting table, giving the austere space the ambiance of a Mexican café. Now all that was needed was the food and four hungry men. After checking the mirror in the pantry to make sure my feisty curls remained captured in the claw clip I'd inserted hours ago, I pushed the cart into the reception area, the mansion's former entrance hall. Rosemary, the grandmotherly receptionist who had been my guinea pig throughout the morning, greeted me with her ever-present twinkling eyes.

"Last trip. Are the men in the room yet?"

"All but Marc and Mr. Galvez. Marc just went upstairs." She indicated the staircase to her left and sniffed the air. "It smells divine. If you're not hired, I'll be mighty—"

"Get to Rescaté ASAP, Doc!"

Footfalls pounded above our heads. I pivoted toward the staircase.

Marc slid his cell phone shut and thundered down the steps. He came to a stop several feet away, a zoned-out stare plastered across his face. The expression I remembered so well from the day he learned his dad had died in a car crash.

Back then I'd comforted him with hugs and kisses. This time, I reached out and touched his arm. Not wanting to ask, but knowing I had no choice, I forced the words through my mouth. "Marc? What is it?"

"Ramón is dead."

"**R**amón is dead?" I sounded more like Minnie Mouse than me.

"Yes. I can't believe it." He shook his head.

"Marc. Is it true?" A man double-timed across the Oriental rug. Short, with a rim of fuzzy gray hair circling his shiny dome, his eyes darted from Marc, to me, then back to Marc.

"He's gone, Bob," Marc croaked.

Bob pushed past us and started up the stairs. "Are you sure? Did you do CPR?"

"No need."

"You didn't call 9-1-1?" The man's voice was at a near shriek.

Marc tensed. "Why? He's gone. Doc Fuller will know what to do. He's the only doctor Galvez saw."

The man reached the top of the steps and turned. "I'll stay with Ramón. You wait for Fuller."

Marc's left eyebrow twitched as he stepped toward the stairs. "He's gone."

I finally found my voice. "Maybe he's right. We can sit over there until the doctor gets here." I gestured toward an upholstered sofa.

Marc's gaze went to the top of the stairs, his jaw muscle pulsing. The other man had moved out of sight.

Spicy aromas from my brimming cart wafted toward my nose and my stomach lurched. I stepped back.

"Is there anyone I should call?" Rosemary held up her phone.

"Try to keep the news quiet for now. We'll be in the kitchen." Marc gazed at me. "Let's go."

I grabbed the cart and pushed it along beside him, hating how the lid on the tureen rattled. "Don't you need to wait for the doctor?"

"I can watch for him through the window."

When we arrived at the kitchen, I shoved the food into the pantry and shut the door.

Marc leaned against the island counter and loosened his tie. "Why didn't I go up there sooner?"

He looked more boy than man. My heart turned to mush, and I took a step toward him, arms opening. What was I doing? I cupped my head in my hands and turned toward the coffee maker. "Coffee. That's what we need. How'd you happen to go upstairs when you did?"

"He didn't come down at his usual time. Kim called and got no answer." His voice was barely above a whisper.

"Kim? His administrative assistant?"

"Yeah. We tried once more, then I went upstairs."

"Did he always start work so late?"

"It's not unusual to get e-mails from him written in the middle of the night. Most days he is...was...at his desk no later than ten." Marc closed his eyes.

I found the coffee and began scooping spoonfuls into a filter. My vision blurred. Ramón had been so proud of this kitchen. I'd known the man no more than fifteen minutes. How could I be so upset? I shoved the basket into position on the drip-maker. "I wonder how he died."

"His cholesterol had to be through the roof. My guess is heart attack."

I moved to the sink and ran water into a plastic pitcher. Loud squeals from outside split the air.

Out the window, a large car zoomed into the parking lot and came to a haphazard stop in front of Rescaté 's entrance.

Mark spoke from behind me. "It's Doc. I gotta go." He strode to the door and disappeared into the hall.

I poured the water into the coffeemaker and hit the *On* button. At least with Doc Fuller on board we'd soon have answers. Curious, I headed for the reception room.

"April, this is Doc Fuller." Marc made the introduction as I approached the men.

The stooped man studied me with watery eyes. "What'd you say your name is, young lady?"

"April Love."

His eyes brightened. He wasn't going to start humming that song at a time like this, was he? The doctor cast a glance at Marc. "Lead the way." They moved toward the stairs, Doc's wisps of snow-white hair standing on end from the wind.

I called out after them, "Marc, I'll clean up the kitchen and head back to Kitty's. There's coffee brewing if you want some."

He turned. "April, please don't leave. Wait for me in the kitchen?"

I nodded. "Sure."

The lines around his mouth relaxed, and he continued up the steps. His softened demeanor startled me. In the past when under pressure, the old Marc

14

usually became more rigid than a fence post. This Marc seemed different. One I could get used to. I chastised myself for thinking such thoughts during a crisis. What did it matter anyway? Without Mr. Galvez, I had no future with Rescaté and no opportunity to see if Marc had really changed since I'd probably return to Atlanta in a few days.

༼ຊໆ

I stood at the kitchen sink window, sipping a triple-shot espresso and staring out at Doc Fuller's car. I'd selected one of the classical albums on my iPod that I used to cook by and set the volume to a moderate level on the dock's speakers. The soothing tones of Mozart were calming my nerves. Since the men had gone upstairs, I'd cleared the untouched food from the cart, stored everything in the stainless steel fridge, and returned the Fiestaware to the cupboard.

Outside the door, the offices remained eerily silent except for whispered conversations as people passed by in the hall. I yearned to talk to someone, rehash what had happened, and draw comfort by sharing the experience. But except for Marc and Rosemary, no one knew who I was. If I were smart, despite Marc's asking me to stay, I'd leave. But how could I with the memory of Marc's pleading eyes asking me to wait? Even if it was only to say good-bye, staying was the least I could do.

I reached for the phone on the wall and punched in a number. My aunt's chipper voice mail greeting filled my ear and I disconnected. I'd forgotten. She wouldn't be home until at least mid afternoon. I considered calling her cell but decided against it. Why upset her while she and her friend were on the road?

Voices filtered in from outside. I stepped over to the window. A black van sat next to Doc's car. A pair of men wearing serious expressions and plain suits stood at the vehicle's rear, hauling out a wheeled contraption. As they bumped the gurney across the grass toward the building, I startled. Although I hadn't seen the son of Canoga Lake's only funeral director since college days when we'd waited tables together, I'd have known Tom Armbruster anywhere.

I refrained from waving hello and made another espresso. I didn't know Mr. Galvez that well, but no matter how he died, he met his end tragically early. He couldn't have been older than 40. Tears formed at the memory of his twinkling dark eyes when he talked about expanding Rescaté 's outreach into Mexico.

"Show me, O LORD, my life's end and the number of my days; let me know how fleeting is my life." Psalm 39's words ran through my mind. Marc hadn't mentioned the man's faith. Was Ramón a believer? I said a prayer for his family, assuming he had one somewhere.

Voices sounded again from outside, and I hesitantly returned to the window, my coffee in hand. Tom Armbruster slammed the van's rear door shut, and both men climbed into the cab. A moment later the van disappeared up the drive toward the road.

"Well, that part's over at least."

I set down my mug and turned. Somewhere along the way Marc had discarded his jacket. He came toward me, resembling more the guy I'd known and less the nonprofit administrator he'd become. My heart won the battle with reason, and I held my arms open for him. Not to hug a friend in his time of need seemed wrong, and sympathy trumped guarding one's heart.

Tucked into his embrace, face pressed to his chest, the scent of citrus aftershave and soap teasing my nose, I'd come home. But not home anymore. I wriggled out of his arms, and looked up at him. "I'm sorry you had to go through this."

He cocked his head toward the iPod dock. "I didn't know you liked classical music."

"The only time I listen to it is while I'm cooking. A habit I picked up from one of my instructors. It relaxes me. What can I do to help?"

Low murmurs drifted into the kitchen from the hallway. Marc's lips pressed into a thin line, pulling the softness from his face. "Do we have any snacks for a break cart? Most people didn't hear about Ramón until after lunch, but a snack might be good. I can't let them leave. They may need to help notify people."

"I saw some chocolate chip cookies in the freezer, and I have the Mexican Wedding Cake cookies I baked for my audition." Grateful for something constructive to do, I started to the large freezer, then stopped. "What was the cause of death?"

"Heart attack." He stepped over to the espresso machine and stared at it. "How do you work this thing?"

I came beside him and turned on the machine to heat it up, then removed the portafilter and opened the canister of coffee beans. I tossed a scoopful in the grinder. "One shot or two?"

"After a morning like this, two."

I measured the coffee I'd ground into the filter, tamped it down, slid the filter back into the machine, then added water to the reservoir and slid a warmed cup under the spigot. Pressing a button, I started the pump action. As rich dark liquid filled the cup, gloom pressed in. Was Mr. Galvez in trouble on the floor right over my head as I merrily made an espresso and got my audition meal prepped? A meal made just for him that he'd never taste? Could I have prevented his death?

"Did the doctor say how long he'd been...gone?"

"He guessed about six or seven hours."

The machine slowed as golden foam formed on the drink. "He could have died while I was here cooking. If only I'd known."

"You didn't, April. And you had no reason to go up there anyway. None of us did. It doesn't matter that you were the first to enter the building this morning. Don't beat yourself up over it."

I turned. "I wasn't the first. Someone was here when I arrived."

"Who?"

"A person stormed out of the building and knocked me down. He took off running across the parking lot and never stopped."

"What time was that?"

"About 6:30."

"What did he look like?"

"Dunno. It was still kind of dark. Actually, it could have been a he or a she."

"Maybe a staff member got dropped off early and went for a run. What were they wearing?"

"Dark sweats and a baseball cap."

"There ya go."

I handed him his coffee and headed for the freezer. "Maybe if you found out who it was, you could ask if they heard anything upstairs. But I guess it's not important." I opened the freezer door. Tucked behind a bag of ice were the two bags of cookies. I pulled them out. Not exactly lovin' from April Love, but with a little thawing in the microwave they, along with my freshly baked Mexican Wedding Cakes, could help soothe some rattled souls.

I placed the bags on the island, opened one, and got the contents thawing in the microwave. Then I went into the pantry and returned with a cardboard box. I pulled out my pocketknife.

"You still have that old thing?" He brought his espresso to his mouth but not before I saw a hint of a smile.

I rubbed the handle of the red knife with my thumb, a gift from Marc our first Christmas together. Another more expensive model sat in my dresser drawer back in Atlanta. One my brother had given me. "Don't think I keep it because of you. It's got a screwdriver, a flashlight, and scissors." I pressed a button, and the blade popped out. "I'll have the cart on the floor in a jiffy."

A shadow of disappointment filled his features before it disappeared behind a mask of indifference. He stood. "At least something I gave you has lasting value."

A vision of an engagement ring worn for all of five months glimmered in my thoughts, and I pushed it away. "I presume once I've run the cart through the office, I'm dismissed."

He furrowed his brow. "You weren't officially hired, were you?"

"No." I fiddled with my apron tie. An hour earlier I'd have given anything to be gone from there, but now that push had come to shove, it was the last thing I wanted. How could I leave? Deaths and funerals always meant the need for food.

"Well, as Assistant Director, I'm hiring you right now."

I turned my attention from the bow I'd retied at least three times. "Really?"

He blew out a breath. "It'll have to be temporary until I talk to the board president. I've got a call in to him in New York. We're going to need you over the next days and weeks."

"But you never tasted the food."

His eyes gentled. "I've sampled plenty of your food, *mi caramela*. How could I forget the way you made an old chicken taste like *coq au vin?*"

With his pet name for me rolling off his tongue, memories of tomato soup suppers, snowy midnight walks, and a pair of tiny diamond earrings tucked inside Valentine roses exploded. I shifted my eyes away from him. "I guess you have eaten my cooking, but if you change your mind and want a taste test, it's in the fridge ready for nuking."

"Maybe later. Thanks."

His tender tone jolted me. Had he, too, been caught up in another time?

With an agreement to reconnect later, we said our good-byes, and I forced my thoughts back to Mr. Galvez.

After nuking my cooled coffee, I moved to the island to make notes on the laptop computer, but the phone rang before I could sit.

❧ 4 ❧

"April, it's Marc. I'm glad I caught you. When you meet the staff, don't say you're the new chef."

The emergence of the old I'm-in-Control Marc begged for a retort, but I kept the snappy answer to myself. "What's that supposed to mean?"

"The board and administrators didn't unanimously agree on hiring a chef. No need to stir the waters since Ramón has, um, passed away."

So his hiring me wasn't a sure thing after all. Thankful Marc couldn't see the tremble in my hand, I asked, "How do you intend to convince the dissenters that I'm needed?" Another unspoken question begged an answer. Was Marc one of the dissenters before he knew I had applied for the job?

"I haven't been able to reach the board president yet. When I do, he'll hear me out."

"How should I introduce myself?" I traced a circle in a sugar spill left on the counter.

"Just say you're helping out for a few days. I'm sure I'll have it cleared up by tomorrow."

"Are you in charge now or not?"

Silence filled the connection.

"Marc?"

"Until we track down the president, your hiring isn't official. But as assistant director, I have to go ahead on some things. So hang in there."

I inhaled. "Guess I'd better start praying." My job wasn't the only thing I'd be storming heaven about.

"We can use some prayer about now. Is the cart ready?"

"Five minutes and I'm on my way."

The H-shaped building had two main corridors. Ramón's office suite sat at the end of the west wing hall and Marc's at the opposite end. The kitchen, ballroom, and reception area made up the bridge between the two corridors. I decided to start in the east wing.

I pushed the snack cart to a stop near a glass door, then stepped inside the suite. A woman with bottle-red hair tumbling to her shoulders hunched over her desk, her acrylic fingernails clacking on her numeric computer keyboard.

When she looked up, hazel eyes ringed with eyeliner flitted between the cart and me. After I offered what I hoped was a warm smile, she stood, revealing the longest legs I'd ever seen. But then with a skirt as short as hers, anyone would look all legs.

"Man, if you aren't a sight for sore eyes. You must be the in-house chef I had to work into the budget." She sashayed over and grabbed a paper plate. "I had the most awesome breakfast this morning and skipped lunch. But now I'm, like, so hungry." She stuck out her hand. "I'm Candy Neer. And you are?"

"April Love. I'm helping out for a few days."

We shook hands; then she moved closer to the cart and turned. "Cool name. It sounds familiar. Wait. I know." Her eyes lit up. In an off-key voice, she crooned the song lyrics about love in April being for the very young.

I forced a laugh. "I'm surprised you know the words."

A grin took over. "That's about all I remember. My mom has a collection of old vinyls she likes to play. So what gives with the name? Is it for real?"

"Afraid so. My mom had a thing for April. She was born, got engaged, married, and had me all in the month of April, and with a last name of Love...well, you get the picture."

She leaned in to select a chocolate chip cookie, and the tiny diamond attached to the side of her nose twinkled in the overhead light. "So your birthday is this month. Happy Birthday." She moved on to the Mexican Wedding Cake cookies and added a couple to her stash.

"Thanks."

My first impression of Candy had been a woman in her early twenties, but on second glance, the lines spidering from her eyes and mouth betrayed her. She had to be pushing 40.

I pulled my attention away and fixated on a bronze plaque affixed to a closed door. "Robert Cousins, Director of Business Operations." The same "Bob" who'd caused Marc's eyebrow to twitch double-time this morning?

"Would your boss like something?"

Candy rolled her eyes. "He's in Marc's office, jousting to see who gets to be king." She filled a Styrofoam cup with hot water, then scrounged through a basket of tea bags. Several packets spilled onto the cart's miniscule workspace, which she ignored. "Good. You have peppermint." She dropped the tea bag in her cup. "I probably shouldn't say this to a total stranger, but I'm, like, so sick of the dishonesty around here."

"Dishonesty?"

"Yeah. To the world, Ramón was generous and caring. Truth is, he was a selfish, overweight man with a heart of stone."

I put my hand to my mouth to make sure it wasn't hanging open. "I only met him once. He seemed all right."

She whispered, "He could charm anyone when he had to." She tossed the napkin onto the cart. "Maybe now, with him gone, Rescaté can finally be the place it makes itself out to be. *If* the right man gets to sit on the throne." She brought her head closer and lowered her voice. "Marc Thorne's the only decent one around here. The only one with a heart. And what's better, he's drop-dead gorgeous."

I felt my face heat. She was hardly Marc's type. Surely he wouldn't be interested in her. Would he? A sinking feeling filled my stomach. What did I know about his type anymore? And what did I care if he and Candy had a thing?

"You just move to the area?"

My shoulders eased. "My aunt lives next door. I came up two days ago from Atlanta."

"So you're unattached." She nibbled a cookie. "It's hard getting to know the single crowd around here unless you hang out at the Apple."

"The Apple?"

"A restaurant on the outskirts of Lake Geneva. It's really called the Red Apple. Maybe we could hit the place together after work some night."

A nice dinner out away from work would be nice. I heard myself say, "Sounds like a plan."

She glanced at her desk. "Cool. I need to get that data entered before Bob returns from his joust. We can talk later."

Back in the hall, I shook my head. Candy sure didn't have much good to say about Ramón. Until then I hadn't heard any unfavorable comments. Kitty spoke well of him, and if Marc had any negative feelings, he'd kept them to himself. Ramón seemed okay to me...the short time I'd known him. Like about fifteen minutes.

A heavily accented female voice drifted into the hall. "It seems funny that Mr. Galvez is dead. I wonder how Ana feels."

"What's Ana got to do with anything?" another woman's voice responded.

✌ 5 ✍

I pushed the cart toward the direction of the voices and entered what appeared to be a mailroom. A pair of middle-aged ladies looked up from where they sat at a long table.

The dark-haired woman set down a stack of brochures and approached the cart. She wore a colorful, flowered top, navy slacks, and a who-are-you expression while gazing at the goodies. *"¿Son éstos para nosotros?"*

Finding the sparkle in her dark eyes irresistible, I offered the one and only Spanish phrase I knew. *"Espanol. Un poco."* I held up my thumb and index finger a half inch apart.

She grinned, revealing a silver tooth. "Oh, that's okay. I speak English good. I say, 'Are these for us?'"

Her plumpish coworker offered a gentle smile as she approached the cart. She looped a lock of her medium-length, salt-and-pepper hair behind an ear. "You speak English well, Rosa."

Rosa bobbed her head. *"Si.* That's what I said. I speak English good." She stifled a giggle. "Sorry. It wrong to laugh when someone just die."

"Sometimes laughter helps ease the sorrow. Help yourselves, ladies. I'm April Love. I hope the warm drinks and cookies will help soften your shock."

"I'm Helen Lubinski," the older woman said. "And this is Rosa Maldonado. Such a sad morning for Rescaté." She eyed the offerings. "Of course, not everyone holds the same sentiment."

I glanced up from reordering the tea bags and caught her eye. "Oh?"

She let out a sigh as she picked up a napkin. "I shouldn't have opened my mouth, but since I did." She nodded in the direction of Candy's domain. "That girl made one mistake, and Ramón threatened to can her until Marc Thorne stepped in. He saved her job."

My insides warmed at her words. At least Marc's good attributes of the past had remained intact. I moved the Earl Gray behind the Lemon Zinger. "No wonder she spoke so highly of Mr. Thorne."

"Candy had a special rider on her health insurance so that her disabled mother was covered, too." Helen picked up a Mexican Wedding Cake. "But Ramón cut her hours back so much she wasn't eligible for medical insurance anymore."

I peered toward Candy's office on the other side of the wall. What Helen had described was downright nasty, but there are always two versions of any story, and I'd only heard one.

Helen gave me a thoughtful look. "I need to ask. Your name...it can't be for that old Pat Boone song."

I rolled my eyes in dramatic fashion. "What can I say? I have a sentimental Mom. She couldn't resist."

A sparkle lit Helen's eyes. "I was a kid when it was popular. I thought it was such a dreamy song."

I had to change the subject.

"Getting back to Ramón." Helen held a ceramic mug festooned with a bright yellow *Grandma's Brew* under the coffee urn's spigot. "Kim's the third administrative assistant Ramón's had in the past year. I guess Marc and Bob will be after Ramón's..." She added creamer to her coffee.

At least we were off what a terrible person Ramón was. "Wouldn't someone be assigned by the Board of Directors to the position?" I asked.

"I suppose so, but that doesn't mean people can't put in for the job. Ramón changed from when he first came here—and not for the best."

"Don't forget his heart for the *niños*." Rosa pressed a palm to her ample chest. "He love them."

"That's true. He did love Rescaté's children." Helen bit into her cookie.

"Too bad he couldn't love the women in his life the same." The baritone voice came from behind me, and I turned.

A short blond guy about my age settled against the doorframe wearing faded jeans, a white T-shirt, and scuffed cowboy boots. He sauntered into the room, his heels *clip-clopping* on the tile floor. I expected him to whip out a lasso and start twirling.

Grateful for the interruption, I stepped back to allow him full view of the snack choices.

He approached the cart and pushed his tan baseball cap back on his head, revealing short-cropped blond hair. "No oatmeal cookies?"

Rosa rested a fist on her hip. "Karl, you no say hello to April."

Karl angled his head back and laughed. "Rosa, you're a hoot." He turned my direction. "Karl Murray, Rescaté's resident handy guy. Pleased to meet ya."

"Same here."

"So where are you off to this weekend, Karl?" Helen sipped her coffee.

"Heading for Missouri tonight. Got a competition just south of St. Louis."

Helen shot him a disparaging look. "I bet your mama's on her knees every weekend."

"Mom gave up on me years ago. After I finally convinced her I belonged in the Little Britches rodeo."

I stared at him. "Rodeo?"

"Bull riding." He puffed his chest. "I'll miss tonight's performance, but I've got two tomorrow," he said around a mouthful of chocolate chip cookie. "I wonder if Isabel will even show up at Ramón's funeral."

"Of course she will," Rosa said. "She's his *hermana.*"

"A sister who doesn't have much use for him." Karl added at least six packets of sugar to his coffee.

Curiosity got the best of me. "Why didn't they get along?"

"That's the million-dollar question. No one knows." Karl pushed a cookie into his mouth and washed it down with coffee. He scooped up another cookie and settled his blue eyes on me. "Mind if I take one more? I'm in the ballroom boxing up brochures. May as well keep at it till we get word to go." He waggled his brows. "Maybe I'll get to leave for Missouri early."

My nod didn't matter because he'd already wrapped the treat in a napkin. Either he wasn't affected by Ramón's death, or making jokes was his way to handle shock. Perhaps he was too excited about the weekend's rodeo.

After Karl left, Helen caught my eye. "Don't pay him any mind. Ramón did have some conflicts with his sister and Candy, but that's all."

"Don't forget his *novia prometida,*" Rosa said.

"Not his fiancée anymore." Helen drained her cup. "Those two always quarreled. Come on, Rosa, let's get to work. Like Karl said, may as well make ourselves useful."

❧ 6 ❧

"This all that's left?"

Hearing Marc's shout over the Natalie Grant tune belting from the iPod dock, I set down the coffee server I was scrubbing and lowered the volume.

"I thought you only played classical at work."

"Classical helps me relax. This music helps me remember who's in control. And I need that right now." My eyes went to the half chocolate chip cookie in his hand. "I'm sorry, Marc. You were in a meeting, so I left you alone." He didn't need to know I'd avoided his office like Aunt Sadie's meatloaf. I headed for the fridge. "Should I heat up the *paella* and tortilla soup?"

Mark popped the cookie remains into his mouth. "Sounds great." He yanked his tie loose and tossed it on the island before plopping onto a stool. His legal pad hit the counter with a slap. "Can we talk while you work?"

"Of course." Business talk was safe talk. If only my racing heart could get the message.

I nuked the food, then filled the bowls and plates. The spicy aroma set my stomach to growling. I set his plate and a bottle of peach-flavored green tea in front of him. Last I knew him the new flavored teas weren't available, but he'd always liked iced tea.

So far he hadn't said a word. "Change your mind about talking?"

He opened his drink and took a draw. "Sorry. This is the first quiet moment I've had. I keep replaying it all in my mind. It sounds strange now, but at first glance I thought Ramón was taking a nap on the floor."

I sat next to him. "I think it takes our brains awhile to register when we see something so shocking. I haven't been able to stop thinking about it either."

He glanced at his notes. "Can you have sandwich trays set out for a board lunch on Tuesday? Then we'll need a buffet meal after the memorial service." He studied the paper. "The memorial will be in the ballroom. It's a large enough space that you can set up the meal behind a screen while the service is going on. We could have up to a hundred people."

Was I supposed to salute or something? "No problem. Did you have a menu in mind?"

"Only that it be an American-style meal. Not everyone enjoys Spanish cuisine." He sniffed the steaming plate in front of him. "From what I'm smelling, it'll be their loss."

My thoughts amped up into a full-blown vision of me serving the Canoga Lake mayor or maybe even a state senator. Didn't such dignitaries come to funerals for people the likes of Ramón Galvez? Why didn't I bring my chef's hat with me? My chest swelled with pride. Would Lovin' Spoonfuls from April Love be far behind? Perhaps I could whip up some business cards to set out on the buffet table....

Like a clay pigeon receiving a direct hit, the fantasy exploded into a pile of rubbish better known as guilt. What was I thinking? A man lay dead at Armbruster's while I may as well have been dancing on his grave over the chance to prepare his funeral meal.

"You okay?" Marc rustled the pages on his legal pad.

"I'm fine."

"It's a lot of food to prepare."

Two minutes ago I'd have said Super April was up for the task. "I could use an assistant."

"I'll get one of the volunteers to help. Is Tuesday morning soon enough?"

"Thank you. That works for me."

He put the pad to the side. "Be sure when you order food supplies to include items for a morning break cart. Everyone's saying how much they appreciated the cookies today. I plan to send most people home soon, but we'll be at full staff on Monday. The break cart was Ramón's idea. Seems right to keep it up."

"Sounds like you're the go-to man for now."

His jaw pulsated. "Someone needs to take care of things." He reached for my hand. "Let's pray."

As much as I wanted to focus on his prayer, with my hand snuggled inside his grasp as though it belonged there, all I could think about was how much I'd missed his touch. I wanted to tell him to let go, but how could I?

As soon as he said "amen," I released my grip and picked up my spoon. I was there to cook, not fraternize with the boss. We were different people than those long-ago days in college, and I still didn't know what blocked him from getting that all-important PhD.

Too bad his mom no longer lived in Canoga Lake or I'd ask her. Probably as well she didn't. Seeing the woman who had almost become my mother-in-law again would only resurrect good memories.

26

One bowl of tortilla soup and a generous serving of *paella* packed with shrimps, sausage, clams, and mussels later, Marc set his fork down. "That was the best meal I've ever tasted."

A warm feeling came over me. He'd always said that after he ate something I prepared. "Guess that means I passed the audition."

"Told you I knew your cooking." He draped an arm over my shoulders. "This may seem like an inappropriate time to ask, but…how about we get together tomorrow night and catch up? The Lakeshore Inn has dynamite food and a great view."

Something fuzzy filled my stomach, and it wasn't the *paella*. Talk about a woman getting side-walloped when her guard is down. He could make the suggestion for a night out sound like a couple of old frat brothers trading stories from the past eight years all he wanted, but we both knew what he really meant. For my own safety, I needed to stay as far away from this man as possible.

Still, he'd had a terrible shock, and maybe a night away from this place would loosen his tongue about his time on the coast. I could keep my guard up for a couple hours. As I turned to accept the invite, my memory kicked into gear. "I can't. Kitty and I plan to visit Great Aunt Sadie in Chicago tomorrow."

"What about Sunday? I attend Canoga Community Church, same as your aunt. We could meet there and spend the day together. To bring each other up to date…as friends."

"It'll be like old times going to church together."

"That okay?"

I gathered our plates. "I wasn't thinking of the bad old times, Marc. Going to church together is a good recollection." I needed to focus on the bad memories, so why wasn't I?

We agreed to meet on Sunday, and he left to make phone calls. As I carried the plates to the sink, questions exploded in my mind like popcorn kernels in hot oil. Why hadn't he finished his doctorate? Was he really at odds with Bob Cousins for Ramón's position? I thought God's plan was for me to have this chef job. Was Marc a part of the equation, or was I delusional and none of this was where I was supposed to be?

I needed answers before rekindling our relationship. And wasn't I jumping to conclusions to presume that was what Marc was after? All he'd said was that he wanted to catch up. Yet I'd worked hard at healing from his hurt and had to keep the man at arm's length.

"I'm glad you are still here."

I turned. Rosa stood in the door, staring at her feet.

"Rosa, come in. Want some coffee."

She shook her head and stepped into the kitchen, closing the door behind her. "I need to get back to the work in a minute. I wanted to tell you I'm afraid that someone kill Mr. Galvez."

~ 7 ~

Kill? Killing happened in Bruce Willis movies, not in my life. Telling myself to remain calm, I slid onto a stool and indicated its matching seat. "Sit and tell me why you think that."

She stepped over and pushed her bottom up onto the stool, then regarded me through liquid black eyes. "All that talk this morning. First about Candy hating him, and then his fighting with his sister and Ana. What if one of them…" A sob erupted.

I fetched a tissue from a nearby pop-up box and handed it to her. "Dr. Fuller said he died of a heart attack, and he should know."

"But he so old. Is he…how you say? As good as when he was young?"

I had to give her that argument. The man looked as though he'd been on Social Security for a couple of decades. But surely, as a doctor, he had to be able to tell how someone died, didn't he? "With his medical training, I'm sure he has it figured out. Haven't you been upset with someone at one time?"

She nodded.

"But you didn't kill them."

She shook her head and blew into the tissue. "I know you right. I need to stop watching those police shows."

"Good idea." I stood and pulled her into a hug. "I'm glad you came and talked to me."

She smiled through her moist eyes. "Me too. I almost didn't since we just know each other. But you seem like a friend long time, and I didn't want to say wrong thing to Helen. She would tell me my…how do you say. Imag—"

"Imagination?"

She nodded. "That's it. My imagination is *loco.*"

I gave her another squeeze and released my embrace. "It's common to have our thoughts go places they don't normally go when we've had a shock."

~❧~

I headed for Kitty's. Since the wind had died, maybe a brisk walk on the shore path would counter the stress that had built since morning. My thoughts went to Rosa and her overactive imagination. A perfect example of how impressionable our minds can be if we watch too much television. For years I'd limited myself to one news program a day. After that, it was the food channel or nothing. I circled the mansion and walked down the sloped lawn to the lake.

At the green and white boathouse I halted. The bench where Marc had asked me to marry him remained in place. Remembering a chance remark I'd made about the romantic rooftop porch, he had made arrangements with the Montclaires to let him use the place for his marriage proposal. He joked later that, if he'd known the worst blizzard in a dozen years would hit the area that day, he'd have waited for summer. To me, his kneeling in a foot of snow with snowflakes glistening from his hair like stars against a midnight sky was far more romantic than a 80-degree day without a cloud in the sky.

I blinked at the moisture in my eyes. Were we so in love then that we subconsciously overlooked major conflicts in our relationship? Namely, his rigidity concerning his grad school plans and my contract with my dad to work for him for two years after graduation?

I swallowed a lump the size of my fist and continued walking. Best to recall a time five months later when Marc walked out on me, my diamond ring jammed onto the tip of his pinkie finger. So much for clearing my head.

I entered Kitty's rambling two-story house through the backdoor and went directly to the sunroom that faced the lake. Her favorite spot.

Except for Rosebud and Violet, Kitty's two cats, in their usual sleeping poses, their paws intertwined like pretzels, the room appeared as desolate as the rest of the house. I dropped onto the cushy sofa. Just as well she wasn't home yet. I needed to figure out how to tell her about Ramón, and also make it clear I didn't appreciate her meddling in my love life.

I released my hair from the clip and eased my head back. I'd kept quiet when she'd tried to match me with the new youth pastor at her church several years ago and the elementary school principal after that. But today was different.

"This is one conversation I'm dreading." I said aloud.

"What are you dreading?"

I turned. Kitty stood in the door wearing a rhinestone-studded denim jacket and jeans.

"Telling you the news."

She moved to a cushioned rattan chair. "You didn't get the job?"

"Yes and no." I reached for her freckled hand. There was no other way to say the words than to simply blurt them out. "Ramón was found dead this morning in his apartment."

Her jaw dropped. "How?"

"The doctor says it was a heart attack."

She fell back into the chair. "You could knock me over with a leaf."

"Feather."

"Feather?"

"The phrase is 'You could knock me over with a feather.'"

She tossed me a wave, her silver bracelets jangling. "I can never get those sayings right. Who found him?"

I drew in a long breath. "The person you neglected to tell me worked there."

She rubbed her arms and stared out the window. "I assume you mean Marc. Would you have applied for the job if you knew?"

"That's beside the point. You know how much he hurt me."

She kept her eyes fixed on the lake view outside the window wall. "I'm sorry, April. But it seemed like divine intervention when you lost your job at the same time Ramón announced the position. You've wanted to be a chef for years. With Marc there, the situation seemed tailor-made."

I clenched and unclenched my hands. "He said he's been there almost a year. Why didn't you tell me?"

"I wanted to, but I was afraid you'd never visit me again. He always asks about you, but I've only said you were a CPA in Atlanta." She pierced me with her blue-eyed stare, hitting the soft spot in my heart reserved for her. "People change. Maybe if he's willing, you should give him another chance. You know that old song." She hummed the tune to "Love is Lovelier the Second Time Around."

"Part of me wanted to agree, a large part. But how could I afford the risk? I still didn't know what stopped him from getting the PhD. The very thing that broke us up. My eyes misted.

"I guess with Ramón gone you won't have to worry about seeing Marc everyday anyway."

I faced Kitty again. "Maybe, maybe not."

Her blond brows lifted. "Do you mean you and Marc?"

"No, not that. Marc asked me to stay on to help. I have to prepare lunch for the board on Tuesday and a memorial meal for one hundred on Wednesday. I'll be there at least a week more, and if he's made director, I may have the job."

Her eyes grew round as quarters. "One hundred guests? That's a lot of people."

"I'm getting a volunteer helper Tuesday afternoon."

She slipped out of her jacket and tossed it over the back of her chair. "I could be your soup chef," she gushed. "Remember the time I threw that reception here for Pastor Shay and his wife on their twenty-fifth?"

I remembered it all right. If I hadn't flown in from Atlanta and come to her rescue, the chicken salad would have been too salty and the yeast rolls wouldn't have risen. Aunt Kitty had many gifts, but commandeering a stove wasn't one of them.

"It's called a *sous* chef. Thanks, but no. I need to show the board I'm capable of whatever they throw at me."

"I thought you wanted out once you realized Marc worked there. You're confusing me."

The knot inside my stomach twisted. She wasn't the only one confused. "I do, but they need someone to help with food. I'm not doing this because of Marc."

I ignored my aunt's skeptical expression and changed the subject. "Which leads me to what I need to be thinking about. Can I borrow your computer to look up some information for tomorrow's menu?"

She let out a sigh. "My computer is broken."

The eagerness *whooshed* out of me. I knew I should have brought my laptop with me, or at the very least gotten a smart phone, or maybe one of those netbooks. The Internet and e-mail remained a business necessity as much as a stove in my world.

"I should have gotten it fixed when it broke, but I was spending too much time in those chat rooms."

Even for Kitty, this revelation surprised me. "You go on chat rooms?"

She flashed an impish smile. "Chat rooms aren't only for you young people. There's one I enjoy for senior Christians. Then there's the book club I belong to. Right now we're reading a romantic comedy."

I shook my head. "Maybe that's where you got the idea to get Marc and me together again. One big joke."

"I'll call Roy Nettles from church. He's a computer whiz."

❧ 8 ❧

I wobbled into the kitchen Sunday morning on the four-inch-high espadrilles I'd bought on a whim.

Kitty grinned. "At least the warmer weather can be thanked for your not covering up those gorgeous legs for a change. Marc's going to love seeing you in that outfit."

I counted Kitty's opinion as prejudicial, not rational, and shrugged. "If I look that good, maybe I should change. The last thing I want is to be eye candy for Marc."

"Eye candy?"

"Something good to look at. He doesn't need to be encouraged. We're friends period."

She tossed me a look that said, "Yeah right," and motioned for me to follow her outside.

Ten minutes later, Kitty pulled her 12-year-old Mercedes into Canoga Community Church's parking lot. Marc waited on the sidewalk near the church's front door. My stomach did a cartwheel. Make that two. There ought to be a law against men with olive-toned skin and hair as dark as coal wearing powder blue. Especially powder blue polo shirts that showcase muscular arms. How was I supposed to sit through a church service with Mr. Hunk next to me?

Kitty pulled up to the curb. Marc opened my door and flashed me the crooked smile I'd loved since we met. *He's only a friend.* I sighed. *One very good-looking friend.*

While avoiding his eyes, I took his hand and let him help me out of the car. I looped my purse strap over my shoulder, then toppled off my right shoe and into Marc's chest. Thanks to his good reflexes, he caught me and managed to stop both of us from landing on the pavement. A mix of citrusy aromas from his aftershave assaulted my nose. I wanted to stay there awhile and enjoy the place that had been exclusively mine so long ago.

A nervous giggle burbled. "And for my next act, I'll do a triple flip off the church roof."

He gave a hearty laugh. "Do we want to do that scene over?"

Did he mean so I could land in his arms again? If he did, we were both in trouble. What's more, we were about to go into church. God should be on our minds and not a lame effort at trying to resurrect a bad romance. We couldn't go there. No matter what Aunt Kitty said.

We let my aunt direct us to "her" pew, second row from the front. Certain every eye in the place was on us, the women at least raising their brows and wondering if we were once again a couple, I busied myself by studying my feet.

Settling in our seats, I sat close to Kitty, leaving several inches of real estate between Marc and me. She removed her wrap and elbowed me in the ribs. "Good heavens, April," she whispered. "Give me some space. The man isn't going to bite you."

At the same time, a couple squeezed into the row at the opposite end, causing Marc to slide over. We both aimed for the same spot and collided, his bare elbow brushing mine. My arm tingled. Glancing over, I caught his lip twitching into a smile. He'd felt it too.

The pastor's voice broke into my thoughts. He was praying. How did I miss that? Heat tinged my cheeks as I bowed my head and prayed for spiritual blinders on my heart.

Walking up the aisle after the service, Kitty remarked how much the sermon challenged her. I had to take her word for it because I'd spent the entire hour torn between enjoying Marc's elbow rubbing against mine and wanting to flee.

In the atrium, Marc and I bid Kitty good-bye, and he led me to a side door close to where he'd parked.

"Mr. Thorne, Mr. Thorne, wait up."

We paused at the exit.

A husky dark-haired boy with a buzz cut ran up. "Mr. Thorne, I wanted to come to practice yesterday, but my mom made me stay home. Did I miss anything?"

Marc hunched down and rested a hand on the boy's shoulder. "We missed you, Matt, but I'm sure your mom had good reason."

The boy stared at his feet. "I was grounded for lying."

Marc nudged Matt over to a bench where they sat. They talked for a few moments, then bowed their heads.

I gave in to a sudden need for air and stepped outside. Seeing his compassion with the boy had me wondering why I was so afraid to let things play out. A family hustled past me, the mom holding a squalling baby, while the dad kept a tight hold on a toddler's hand. Would such a scenario ever be a part of my future? Not a good time to dwell on those kind of thoughts.

"I wondered where you got off to. Ready to go?"

I turned. Marc stood a couple feet away, his eyes seeming to hold a question.

"Sure. I'm starving."

∾৻৸∾

We arrived at the restaurant and were shown to a window booth overlooking a bubbling stream. After a short wait filled with small talk, Marc gave the waitress our order for the buffet, and we ambled to the serving table to mound our plates with eggs, ham, fruit salad, and fluffy biscuits.

"So," I said, as I spread butter over a biscuit, "I presume you still went to California right after graduation."

"Yep." Marc forked a piece of ham and put it in his mouth.

I waited for him to continue after he swallowed. Instead, he attacked his eggs as though this was his first meal in days.

"Your appetite sure hasn't changed. How can you eat like that and not look any heavier than when we were in college?"

He picked up his coffee mug. "I run daily and hit the gym three times a week for strength training."

My eyes went to his muscular arms. Forget food. Feasting on the sight would have satisfied me, but I succumbed to my stomach's growl and forked a strawberry. "I suppose while I was paying my dues to my dad those two years, you were getting your master's degree."

"I carried as many credits as possible and finished in a year and a half. Worked as a Teacher's Assistant and began the doctoral program six months later." Marc reached across the table, nearly knocking over his water glass, and grabbed my hand. "Let's not talk about my boring life anymore. I want to know what *you've* been up to the last eight years."

I wanted to pull my hand away from its snare, but he'd managed to knit our fingers together. "I already told you. Two years with my dad in Chicago, then Atlanta as a CPA during the day, and culinary school at night. Back to your eight years. You began work on the doctorate but didn't get the degree." I pinned him with a stare. "Marc, for you that's major."

He released my hand as though it was a hot coal. "The program didn't meet my needs, and I went in another direction. I wanted to call you, but didn't know what to say."

"Sorry would've been a good start." I pushed my plate away.

"I *am* sorry, April."

"You're about eight years too late."

"You're right. But don't you wonder what God is doing? It has to be more than coincidence we connected again."

He had me there, but I wasn't ready to buy. "It's been a long time, and I don't even know if I'll have a job after the memorial service. If I don't, I'll probably head back to Atlanta." I poured coffee from a carafe into my cup and stirred in cream. "No time like the present to start Lovin' Spoonfuls."

"You'll have a job working for me."

I snapped my head up. "Have you been offered the directorship?"

His face tensed into Mount-Rushmore rigidity. "Not in so many words."

"I heard Bob Cousins wants the position."

"Cousins doesn't have a grasp of the overall picture." His left brow twitched. "He's a numbers guy."

"Are you saying anyone good with numbers doesn't have vision?" I squared my shoulders. "I beg to differ."

His jaw slackened. "Didn't mean you. Cousins can't see beyond the costs. Sometimes you need to spend money to gain donations."

I dropped my napkin on top of my cooled eggs. He'd apologized and in some ways did seem different. But his haughtiness disquieted me. "If you're my boss now, it's best to keep our relationship platonic."

Without a response, Marc signaled for the check.

Tension followed us outside and into his SUV. Once we were on the road, I cast about for something to say. Anything to break the silence. "Did you ever figure out who it was that ran me over the morning Ramón died?"

"Haven't given it a thought. What brought that up?"

"Something that popped in my mind. It seemed odd. The place appeared so lifeless. Come to think of it, I didn't see any cars in the lot."

"Like I said, someone could have been dropped off early. Maybe used the extra time to go for a run before work."

"Something else odd happened. Rosa came to me later and said she wondered if maybe Ramón had been killed. Isn't that bizarre?"

Marc jerked his eyes off the road and toward mine. "How on earth did she get that idea?"

"When I took the snacks around Friday afternoon, she, Helen, and Karl were talking about how he didn't get along with some people. I told her just because someone dislikes another person doesn't mean they're going to murder them."

"Good answer. The last thing we need is someone stirring up unfounded rumors. Doc Fuller said heart attack, and he should know. I found out after the fact that he's the county coroner."

It was my turn to jerk around to face him. "Him? He looked older than my Great Aunt Sadie, and she recently turned ninety."

"He's up there, but not that old."

Marc made a turn toward Lake Geneva.

The man had me on a rollercoaster ride. Right then I was on the down loop and I wanted to be home before we reached the top again. "I thought we were going back to Canoga Lake."

"Not until we get some ice cream. There's a new place called Dagmar's."

Our conversation's strange tangent restored some of the earlier camaraderie, but why did he have to show that he remembered my greatest weakness? We drove down the hill into the business district, a mixture of refurbished storefronts holding gift shops and restaurants.

After we parked and got our cones, me with jamocha almond fudge and him, a double chocolate, Marc suggested we walk to the lake. At the lakefront, we found a bench. Across the small inlet sat the Riviera, the building that anchored the boat docks where Marc and I first met the summer before college. He worked for the Water Safety Patrol and I was a mail jumper on the excursion boat that delivered mail to the lakeshore residents.

Was it the beauty of the lake's blue waters on a warm spring day or the wonderful sensation of butterfat-rich ice cream melting on my tongue that caused the last of the tension to dissipate?

He stretched his free arm across the bench back. "Almost like old times sitting here."

I stuffed the rest of my cone into my mouth. "Uh huh."

"I really meant it, April, about being sorry."

I faced him. "Me too, for the way our brunch date soured."

He cupped my shoulder with his hand and squeezed. His gaze dropped to my lips. "Did you really mean it about only being friends?"

"Yes."

He leaned in. "Even when we're not at work?"

I angled back. Little good it did since he came with me, his gaze resting on my mouth. "More so when we're not at work." I forced the words over my dry throat.

"Does that mean I can't kiss you?"

He inched closer, and I felt his warm breath tickling my lips.

"Right here in front of God and everybody?"

"Right here in front of God and everybody."

My lips yearned to link with his. Who cared that we sat out here in the open, where anyone could pass by? Or that the man was dangerous to my fragile heart?

I cared. After wriggling out of his one-armed embrace, I stood. "I can't do it, Marc. I can't let you hurt me anymore." Ignoring his wide-eyed stare, I walked toward the car.

He hotfooted up beside me and matched my stride. "Would it help for me to say I don't intend to ever cause you anymore pain?"

"I'm sure you didn't intentionally hurt me eight years ago, but you did. It's your nature, Marc. Can you take me home now?"

❧ 9 ❧

"You can't go in there."

I whirled around. Puffs of whipped cream flew from the mochas I'd carried from the kitchen. Marc's administrative assistant stood beside her desk. With highlighted hair cascading past her shoulders, she seemed like a sweet girl when we met last Friday. Today, with her upturned chin, set mouth, and arms folded, she'd morphed into a five-foot-high drill sergeant.

"Marc is in an important meeting," she said, her tone full of authority. "He can't be disturbed."

I met her stare. "I think he'll see me." *Especially when he sees my peace offering, he will.*

"I have orders not to let anyone disturb him."

Like an arrow in a bow, a snappy retort sat poised on my tongue. What was I doing acting like a high-school girl? Wasn't I supposed to set an example for younger women? I forced out an "Okay."

"Taryn, is that April I hear?" Marc's voice floated out his open door without a hint of the icy tone he'd used when he'd said good-bye to me yesterday.

My face warmed, and it wasn't from the steam rolling off the mochas. Had he heard our childish exchange?

"Yes, Marc. She's about to leave." Taryn flipped her mane over a shoulder, exposing three tiny hoops lined across her earlobe.

"Have her come in."

It was my turn to gloat, but I quashed the temptation and stepped to his door.

In shirtsleeves rolled to his elbows, Marc sat at his desk scribbling on a yellow legal pad. Some important meeting. Who with? Himself?

He greeted me with a heart-stopping grin.

I held up the mugs. "I come hoping that little squabble we had yesterday is forgotten." I set his mug on the desk and offered him a coy smile before I whispered, "Just remember. No kissing allowed."

His eyes went to a spot over my shoulder. "April, this is Kendall Montclaire, Rescaté's board president."

Kendall Montclaire is Rescaté's board president?

I turned. A man wearing a corduroy sports jacket and khakis stood in front of the bookcase. Feeling like I'd come in from left field, I clamped my mouth shut. I'd lowered my voice so Taryn wouldn't hear, but did he?

His face, the model of politeness, gave me no clue. Still, it was a far cry from the angry glare I received one summer night 20 years earlier when a pair of 10-year-olds spied on him and his college sweetie making out in the boathouse. Today, his ruddy appearance gave only a hint of the angry, redheaded frat boy who had marched us to my aunt's house.

Unable to wrap my head around the idea of Kendall being Rescaté's chief honcho, I set the coffees on Marc's desk and stuck out my hand. "Mr. Montclaire, very nice to meet you."

He pressed my palm in a soft grip. "April Love. Why does your name sound so familiar?"

I gave him my practiced eye-roll. "No doubt the song—"

"Probably because her aunt is Kitty McPiper," Marc said from behind me.

Exactly the information I wanted to avoid. I tamped down my irration at Marc and focused on Kendall. "You may not remember me, but I recall what an accomplished sailor you were. You must have won the annual regatta four years running."

His eyes brightened. "It was only three, but who's counting? Thanks for the coffee." He lifted one of the mugs and sipped. "Of course I remember the little curly-headed girl from next door."

Marc picked up the other mocha and shot me an intense look. He wanted me gone. As if I wanted to stay there? Not hardly.

He took a sip. "Thanks for the coffee. I'll give you a call later. We need to finalize the menus."

I nodded and headed for the door.

"Such a tragic thing, Ramón's death."

At Kendall's comment, I turned. "And so unexpected. Enjoy your refreshments."

Kendall raised his mug in a salute.

I turned to Marc. "You, too."

"Thanks, April," he said, through lips that barely moved.

I all but ran for the door. What a time for my runaway mouth to go into action. Would my comment have Kendall thinking that Marc was consorting with the hired help? In a way he was, but we did have a history.

I breezed past Taryn and didn't slow my pace until I reached the kitchen door.

The scent of banana muffins in the kitchen made my mouth water. They'd still be warm by the time I took the break cart around. That is, if I still had a job. It had been over an hour since I'd left the men. The phone was certain to ring at any moment.

I upped the volume on the iPod dock. Maybe I should have gone with a stronger beat than Mozart to drown out the phone's ring. Oh well, my future was carved in stone no matter what. I gathered my dirty dishes and carried them to the sink. No way would I leave them for the next chef.

A knock came from behind me, and my breath caught. Had Marc come to deliver the bad news in person? I turned.

Kendall Montclaire stood right inside the door.

I forced a smile. "Mr. Montclaire. Did you come for more coffee?"

"The mocha you made was superb. I didn't make my usual stop at Java Junction, so it was doubly appreciated." With a slight smile, he moved toward the island and brushed a crumb off a stool before he sat. "You gave me your own mocha, didn't you?"

"That's okay. I made another." I glanced at the espresso maker. "Are you sure you wouldn't like one more?"

He leaned back and rested both elbows on the counter. "One a day is my limit. Sounds like you have an appreciation for Mozart."

"He's one of my favorites."

"Interesting." His face grew serious. "I couldn't help but pick up what you said before you knew I was in Marc's office. I don't know what your relationship is with Marc away from here, and I don't care. But I told him, and I'm telling you, that we can't have romantic relationships going on between coworkers. I know you're an outside contractor, but the other staff doesn't realize that. Can I count on you?"

What he asked wasn't any different than any other place I'd worked, so why did I feel like a little kid being caught cheating on a test? My breathing quickened. Kendall Montclaire had been a spoiled rich kid who liked to bully, but now he was the boss, which gave him the right to intimidate. I took the stool next to him. "There's nothing going on. Only some friendly banter. No romance."

A timer buzzed from the stove. I grabbed a potholder. "If you want to wait, you can have a warm muffin."

"Sounds tempting, but I need to go. Next time we can chat about the time a couple of little girls spied on me in the boathouse." He chortled as he headed for the door. "Thought I forgot, didn't you? See you later."

I closed my gaping mouth. At least he was laughing, and I still had a job.

Marc arrived in the kitchen five minutes later, bringing along a stern expression and the empty mugs he thudded onto the counter.

"Guess you feel like you were taken to the principal's office same as me, huh?" I folded my arms.

He leaned against the granite, stiff as a pole. "That's a good way to describe it. I assured him you were joking. Hope you did the same."

I nodded. "It bothered me that he called us out, but I guess it troubled you more. I'm sorry I said what I did."

"I'm not. But I am upset over something else Kendall told me."

My eyes widened. "Oh?"

"Seems you're not the only one Rosa confided her suspicions to about Ramón's death. A rumor has been circulating that he was killed."

My mouth dropped open. "I haven't heard anything."

"Me either, but someone approached Kendall the moment he arrived and asked if the police had been called. He wants me to put an end to it."

"How are you going to do that? Call a staff meeting?"

"Yes. But before I do, he wants me to go up to the apartment and look around. Make sure there's nothing to indicate foul play, which of course there isn't. But if I can say the apartment has been looked over, it will support the truth." He bit his lower lip and frowned. "Going up there isn't on my list of favorite things to do right now. The last time I was there, I found his body."

"I can go with you."

He looked up. "That'll look real good after our warning."

"We'll be going as boss and employee. Another pair of eyes."

"Guess that would work, but let's discuss menus before we go up." He sniffed. "Banana bread?"

"Muffins, and I brewed fresh coffee."

"It'll make up for what we missed earlier." He took a seat at the island.

Gathering up honey-butter and a basket of muffins, I set the goodies on the counter, then poured coffee. I slid onto the stool next to him.

He liked my idea for a make-your-own sandwich buffet for the board meeting. At first he wrinkled his nose at my suggestion of Chicken George for the memorial lunch. Then I explained it was a rich man's Chicken á la King that would please most everyone and he relaxed. Green beans almondine, fruit salad, and cherry-upside-down cake would round out the spread.

With the menus settled, he stood and stretched. "Let's get this crazy investigation over with."

When we stepped into the hall Marc took a right while I took a left. We collided and I quick-stepped backwards.

"Why don't you watch where you're going?" Our words were the same, mine a half second behind his.

We burst out laughing.

I grinned. "Why are you going that way? The stairs are in reception."

"Ven conmigo, señorita, y voy a mostrarle el camino."

As it rolled off his tongue, Marc's Spanish loosened the rest of the starch from the air even if I didn't understand but a couple words about showing the way.

He stopped in front of a closed door I'd always presumed to be a closet and pulled out a key. "I figured if we used this, fewer would see us going upstairs together."

The tiny elevator looked no larger than a side-by-side fridge. Were we supposed to fit in there? Did Marc think this was better than being seen taking the stairs together?

He pulled back the accordion-like gate and gestured for me to enter first. I stepped in and pressed my back against the far wall. He eased in and shut the gate. "You got enough room back there?"

I wanted to say we had room to spare, but since one short step forward would send me into his broad back, I'd be fibbing. Already the scent of his aftershave was sending my heart into overdrive. I so didn't want those stomach flutters again. Not when we were told to behave, and certainly not when we were about to investigate the room where Mr. Galvez met his untimely end.

"I'm okay." I hoped my voice sounded nonchalant.

He pressed the green button, and the car jerked upward. At the rate we were going, it'd be Christmas when we got to the second floor.

The car shuddered and stopped, and so did the overhead fan.

Marc whacked the button. "This happens once in a while. There's a little trick. If I could only remember it." He fiddled with a switch.

The air tightened around me, and a bead of perspiration trickled down my back. Why did it feel like the claustrophobic box had no oxygen? Marc banged his palm on the up button, then the down.

"Marc, I hope you have a Plan B."

He wiggled around to face me, his peppermint breath tickling my nose. "It always starts again when the reset switch is toggled. No plan B or C." He rested his hands on my shoulders. Not out of affection. He needed to put them somewhere besides in the air.

43

I let out a nervous giggle. "It's kinda warm in here."

Marc tipped my chin up with his index finger. "April, you're sweating." He pulled a handkerchief from his pocket and dabbed my forehead. I had nowhere to look but into his eyes and, once there, I couldn't pull my gaze away. Good thing I didn't want to. His eyes went to my mouth and he leaned closer. I lifted my chin in anticipation. So much for Kendall.

He brought his mouth closer, and the tiny elevator started to spin. Then everything went black.

❧ 10 ❧

M y eyes popped open. Inches away from my face, Marc's frantic stare greeted me. "April, thank goodness. You must have fainted. I was about to do something drastic if you didn't wake up."

I struggled to stand, but in such tight quarters I couldn't move. Not with his left arm circling my back and my legs kind of hanging there. My last waking moment before I went into la-la land materialized. Had he kissed me and that sent me into a swoon? Tempted to make up for what I may have missed, I smiled. "Drastic? Like what?"

He pressed his lips together and colored. "Nothing. Let's see if you can stand. I want to try that switch again. We need to get you some water." He shifted a few inches, and I was on my feet.

"How long was I out?"

"A minute or two." He hit the switch.

The car shuddered and began to descend. "I want you to go to Kitty's and lay down."

Suddenly wide awake, I stood straight and lifted my chin. "No way. I'm fine. I just fainted from the heat. That's all."

He cast me a skeptical look. "I'm sure there's nothing up there. I can handle it alone." The elevator settled into a stop and Marc flung back the gate.

I followed him into the first-floor hall. "That's not how you felt earlier."

A couple minutes later we took the stairs, and Marc led me to Ramon's door. He unlocked it and pushed it open. The distinct scent of pine cleaner hit my nose.

Marc waved his hand. "Whew. Housekeeping must have been here."

I followed him inside. He went to the windows facing the lake and yanked on a drapery cord. Bright sunlight spilled in.

Except for no stray socks or underwear lying around, the place reminded me of my brother's bachelor apartment—couch, flat-screen TV, couple of easy chairs, and a recliner.

Marc stood by the television, hands stuck in his pockets, coins jingling. "This used to be the master suite. The original bathroom and dressing area were divided into a kitchen, bath, and walk-in closet when Rescaté was remodeled."

45

Spotting a small dining alcove and kitchenette divided by a breakfast counter, I headed there. Ramón had given me the impression he enjoyed cooking, but he must have done all his playing downstairs. A dwarf would have trouble in this tiny space. I opened and shut the three cabinets. The man had more boxes and bags of chips, cookies, and chocolate bars than the local warehouse store.

"Anything here?" Marc came up behind me.

"Only a ton of junk food. Let's look at the bedroom where you found him."

On our way, we peeked into a small room next to the coat closet that appeared to be a home office. Not even a stray paper, let alone a leftover snack.

Marc stepped over to the computer. "I want to make sure there isn't any confidential Rescaté business on this thing. The bedroom is just past the bathroom. Go ahead and have a look. Then we can get out of here."

On the way, I sneaked a peek in the bathroom. I half expected to find miniature samples of shampoo and lotion on the vanity counter of the hotel-like room, but all I found was a container of liquid hand soap. I moved on.

A strange aura washed over me as I entered the dark bedroom where Ramón had spent his final moments. Had he gasped for air? Tried to call for help? Cried out to God? I pushed down the urge to tell Marc the place was clean without looking. Five more minutes, I told myself. I flicked the wall switch, using a tissue. The thing didn't work. I tried again. Nothing.

"What's for breakfast?"

I turned toward the shadowy corner that the voice seemed to have come from, and held my breath. Only my heart beating a tattoo against my chest sounded in my ears.

"What's for breakfast?"

That's it. I'm out of here. I spun toward the door and slammed into a man's chest. I screamed.

Hands grabbed my arms.

Twisting one way, then the other, I wrenched out of his grasp. "Let me go!"

"April, it's me."

I nearly knocked Marc over as I collapsed against him. "Someone's in the corner."

"It's only Pedro."

"Pedro?"

"I'm surprised you'd let a parrot scare you half to death." He crossed the room, his chuckle grating against my ears, and flicked on the bedside lamp.

A green, blue, and yellow parrot peered at me from inside an ornate cage half the size of my tiny bathroom in Atlanta. As I neared the jewel-toned bird, he tilted his colorful head and continued to regard me with beady eyes.

"Karl was supposed to get him out of here Friday afternoon." Marc wrested the cage off its stand as the parrot swung back and forth on his little trapeze. He squawked out a loud complaint.

"He doesn't sound very happy."

Marc hurried past me with the startled creature. "He's not the only one. I'll be right back."

The door to the hall slammed, and I scanned the bedroom suite. With the large king bed and heavy polished wood furniture, the place could have been a model showroom. Then something caught my eye.

❧ 11 ❧

"Sorry for leaving you alone. I left Pedro with Karl and told him to check the kitchen for some crackers." Marc stepped in the bedroom and picked up the cage stand. He started for the door. "It's almost ten, and there's nothing here. Are you ready?"

"Look at what I found." I pointed at the dresser, not knowing if I should be relieved I found something ominous or dread what may lay ahead.

He set down his load and bent to peer at the *Gingko Biloba* bottle. "Ramón's smart pills. He was always boasting how two a day helped him think. Guess they won't help him now."

"While you were gone I remembered that after colliding with the orange-capped person the other morning, something dropped out of his backpack when he got to the parking lot." I stepped closer to the dresser. "A bottle that looked like that one. It was important enough that he stopped running and chased it down."

Marc expelled a loud breath. "So?"

"It's probably nothing, but I feel in my gut we should hang onto the pills just in case."

He glanced at me. "We?"

I scowled. "Marc, we can't ignore them. Pretend they weren't here. What if it's discovered Ramón was poisoned, and we ignored evidence that was later tossed out? I thought you'd want to do the right thing. Or have you changed?" I kept my gaze on him.

He shrugged. "I'm still the same guy. Do what you feel is right."

I went to grab the bottle, and he laughed. "Boy, Sherlock, you'd never make it as a detective. Even I know not to touch evidence because of fingerprints."

My face heated, and I turned toward the door. "Just testing you. I'll find something in the kitchen to use."

Several minutes later, we entered the Rescaté kitchen and he shut the door. "What will you do with the pills?"

I placed my hand over the bulge in my apron pocket, made by the pills, safely protected in a plastic bag. "They're going into hiding."

He placed a hand on each of my shoulders and regarded me with those

48

almost black eyes. "Then you're not going to tell Kendall about them?"

I shrugged. "Not unless there's a reason. Right now I have no reason."

"Galvez took those pills every single day. That's why they were sitting there. That runner could have had vitamins in his backpack."

"Exactly why the pills are going into hiding. And when these rumors go away, so will the pills."

೨ 12 ೪

I pulled my cart to a halt in the reception area, and Rosemary stepped around her desk, her plump cheeks displaying their usual natural blush. "I should only have tea, but after smelling those cinnamon rolls…"

I followed her longing gaze to the fragrant puffy rounds, cinnamon and walnuts nestled within the seams of dough, warm icing drizzling over top. My mouth watered. Who could blame her?

She scooped up an apple-walnut muffin. "My stomach wants that gooey bun, but this looks healthier."

"Oh, they are," I worked to hide my surprise at her choice. "They have apples in them, and the walnuts are good for Omega-3." I'd left a cinnamon roll in the kitchen for later, but if she could exercise self-control, why not me? My thighs would thank me later. I grabbed a muffin.

Rosemary sighed. "To think that I sat here last Friday morning while Mr. Galvez laid up there." She directed her stare up the steps. "I wonder how long he was…gone."

Poor thing must have been agonizing over that all weekend. "Why didn't someone check on him sooner?"

"Mr. Galvez left strict orders no one was to disturb him in the mornings." She affected a stern tone and lowered her voice. "I'll be down when I come down."

"Sounds like he wasn't a morning kind of guy."

She spread honey butter over a muffin half. "He wasn't, but how he loved food. At least he died happy. Too bad he wasn't more concerned about his health."

"He was definitely a foodie." I nibbled my muffin, letting the bits of apple linger on my tongue before swallowing.

She broke off a bite and popped it in her mouth. "I'm determined to lose weight. I have two beautiful granddaughters I want to see grow up. The same thing can't happen to me." She glared at her half-eaten muffin. "This is delicious, but I can't." She slam-dunked it into the garbage bag.

While she made a cup of lemon tea, I tossed my own muffin in the trash. How could I stomach it after hearing that? We said our good-byes, and I pushed off for Candy's domain.

50

"I thought you'd never get here." Candy came up as I parked the cart outside her door. "I've been, like, smelling those cinnamon rolls forever."

While she ogled the treats, I stared at her skirt. The dishtowel hanging back in the kitchen had more fabric. She bent to grab a cup from the cart's lower shelf, and it was all I could do not to stuff a napkin into her scoop-neck top. The woman was an anomaly. People trusted her with calculating spreadsheets and doing financial projections, yet she dressed like a streetwalker.

She picked up a cinnamon roll and dropped the confection onto a small plate while I plucked a packet of peppermint tea from the basket.

"Allow me to prepare your beverage, madam." I made a slight bow.

She licked icing from her chartreuse-polished fingertips. "Thanks. After the morning I've had, I could use a little TLC."

I poured hot water into her cup. "Spreadsheets getting you down? I can relate to that."

She let out a huff. "Nothing to do with Rescaté now that the wicked step-father is dead. My mom is, like, difficult in the morning. She's disabled, ya know. Got in a factory accident five years ago and needs a walker. I'm all she's got."

I dropped a teabag into her cup. "That's crummy. No brothers or sisters to help out?"

She let out a sigh that seemed to come from her toes. "Just me. Mom gets up when I do so's I can have her dressed and fed before I leave. Today, I couldn't find her favorite blouse. I told her she'd have to wear the green top and she goes, 'I want the lavender blouse.'" Candy rolled her eyes. "Turns out the one she wanted was in the laundry hamper. Then she was ticked off because I didn't do the wash last night. Well, I was too tired, and my favorite show was on."

"Who cares for her while you're at work? I can't imagine having to take care of a parent like that. You're one strong woman."

She scooped the tea bag out of the cup with a stir stick and gave the bag a squeeze. "She's okay alone once I set her up in the family room with the remote. Our neighbor comes over at noon to give her lunch. Hey." Candy's face lit up. "I'm meeting a friend at the Apple after work. Why don't you join us?" Her eyes held a hopeful sparkle. "What do ya say?"

I opened my mouth to decline, then shut it. What if there was something to the rumor, and Rosa's suspicions were true? Candy did hate the guy. Wouldn't hurt to hang with her for a while and see what I could learn—to satisfy my own curiosity. I pushed a smile to my face. If anything, supper out would provide a nice break. "Sounds like a plan. Give me directions and tell me what time to meet."

"Cool. Five-thirty okay?" Candy grabbed a pen and scribbled on a Post-it. "Here's the directions. I added my cell phone number. Text me if you get lost or something comes up."

I escaped before I caved to my conscience over accepting her invite on false pretenses and canceled our plans. Since Helen and Rosa's door was shut, I headed toward the south wing. As I approached Karl's workroom, a voice called out, "What's for breakfast?"

Karl ambled into the hall with Pedro perched on his shoulder. "What's so funny?"

"Too long a story." I laughed. "Ask the bird. What can I get ya?"

He picked up a muffin. "Do you suppose my pal can have one of these? I feel bad that I forgot him over the weekend. Guess I had that rodeo on my mind."

And not his boss's death? What's with that? "Sure, if it's okay for him to eat muffins."

"I checked the Internet. Parrots can eat lots of things." He gave me a stern look. "But never feed this guy chocolate. It's poison for parrots."

By then a small crowd had gathered.

"April, you mad?" Rosa asked.

"No. Why?"

"You skip us and we hungry."

Helen reached for a cup. "I'm more thirsty than hungry."

"I'm sorry, ladies. Your door was closed."

"It was frozen." Rosa rubbed her sweater-covered arms.

"Your door was stuck?"

"We shut it to keep the heat inside." Helen added coffee to her *Grandma* cup.

I laughed, loving Helen's patience for her coworker.

Rosa stroked Pedro's head and clucked. *"Ave bonita."* Her soothing voice seemed to calm the bird. Did the Spanish remind him of Ramón?

"What are you going to do with Pedro, Karl?" Helen sipped her coffee.

Karl hooked his thumbs into his belt loops. "Marc wants me to call the Humane Society."

"No way. Pedro belongs here." Bob Cousins sauntered up and leveled his gaze on the handyman. "Are you willing to be our parrot-keeper, Karl?"

He appeared surprised. "Be glad to. Pedro and I are already buds. But I'm not around much on weekends."

"Good. If Marc gives you a hard time, have him see me." Bob helped himself to coffee. "I'm sure someone can take weekends." He scanned the women surrounding the cart, his gaze coming to a stop at Taryn.

Silence hung in the air as we waited for the stare-down between the man who aspired to be king and the other jouster's maid in waiting.

Bob blinked first. "I'll check with Candy. Maybe she can do it."

That was all Candy needed, a parrot to watch along with her mother. I offered Bob a napkin. "I'll cover weekends since I live next door."

Pedro made a clucking sound and seemed to look right at me. Did he understand us?

I faced Karl. "How'd your bull riding go?"

He puffed his chest. "Rode two, won me a grand."

"Just for riding you get money?" Taryn reached for a bagel.

The bull rider shook his head. "You don't say you rode a bull until you stay on for eight seconds. I rode one each show. And were they rank."

I presumed rank meant the bulls were mean. "Are the rodeos always far away?"

"Nope. This weekend there's a couple over in Elkhorn at the fairgrounds." He scanned our faces. "If anyone wants tickets, let me know. I'll be lookin' for eight both events."

I tossed a dirty napkin in the trash bag attached to the cart's handle bars. "I'll check with Mar…"

Everyone looked at me, eyes wide.

Karl answered with a grin. The way Marc's name almost came out so naturally frightened me. I hung there awhile longer listening to the ladies ply Karl with more questions about the rodeo. If Bob hadn't shooed everyone back to work, the man would have stood there until closing time talking about the mean bulls he'd ridden. By the time I rolled my cart toward the other corridor, all I had to offer was coffee.

⁂

"How did the break run go?" Marc shut the kitchen door behind him.

I looked up from wiping down the cart. "I came back with only crumbs in the basket and a few drops of coffee. I'd call it a success. Have you ever gone to a rodeo to watch Karl ride bulls?"

"Not yet. Why?"

I wanted to wipe that lopsided grin off his face before I did something stupid like ask him for a date to the rodeo. I shrugged. "I just came from chatting with him, and it sounds interesting. He said when he was a toddler, he rode calves on his uncle's ranch down in Texas. That's where he got the bug."

He swaggered toward me. "Well, this cowboy suggests you take the Rescaté van into town for your supplies." He held out a key.

I straightened from my crouched position. "Van?"

"It makes no sense for you to cram all those groceries into that shoebox-on-wheels you drive."

I planted a fist on my hip. "Don't make fun of my car. It got me here from Atlanta. But the van sounds great." I wrapped my fingers around the key fob.

He rested his palm over my hand. "I appreciate you going with me upstairs, but don't let your imagination go wild over those pills you hid away. There's a million bottles like that one."

I lowered my gaze. "I know that. The more I think about it, the whole thing sounds crazy, but I'll keep them...in case. You were always a stickler for doing the Christian thing. That's one of the characteristics I always loved." I pulled my lower lip between my teeth and looked away. "Can I have the keys so I can get the supplies?"

"Sure, if you do one thing for me." He brushed a lock of hair off my face and let his fingertips linger at the hairline before reaching around and tugging at my ponytail.

I brought my gaze back to him and gulped. "I'm almost afraid to ask."

He leaned closer and whispered, "Go out with me tonight?"

His warm breath sent a delicious string of goose bumps down my neck. Wasn't he taking a huge risk? What if Kendall or anyone walked in? I stepped back. "Sorry. I already have plans to meet Candy at the Apple."

He stepped back. "It's probably better we not go out. My mistake." His hand still rested on top of mine.

"Just not a good night. Some other time?" *Sheesh. One minute I'm avoiding the guy like a kid with chicken pox and the next, I'm asking him out. Not a good way to stay away from the man or keep our jobs intact.*

His features worked into a boyish smile. "Sure." He wrapped my fingers around the keys. "Remember to use the Tax ID Number. Talk to ya later." He turned toward the door, then faced me. "I'm calling a staff meeting at three o'clock to squash the rumor mill. Try to be back by then." A second later he was gone.

Who was that masked man? Outside, I stopped to slip off my cardigan and tie the arms around my waist.

"Lovely day isn't it, April?"

I finished off the knot and looked up to see Kendall striding in from the parking lot. "It's warmed up nicely."

"Taking a lunch break?"

"Off to my aunt's before getting supplies at Sam's in Kenosha." I pushed my sunglasses to the top of my head.

"Isn't there a food service company you could order from for such a big crowd?"

"Sure. If I had more time. I need to start prep work on some meals soon."

He folded his arms across his chest. "I was looking for Marc earlier. Rosemary said you two were upstairs." His brow hiked upwards. "I presume you helped him survey the apartment?"

Bile rose to my throat. Tempted to say we went up there to be alone and neck, I bowed to my sensibilities and said, "Yes. He asked me to go as an extra pair of eyes. Those kind of rumors Rescaté doesn't need."

"And did anything seem amiss?"

"Only a forgotten parrot. Good thing we went. The poor bird was starving."

The lines on his forehead creased. "What does a hungry bird matter when we've got thousands of hungry children to feed?"

What did one have to do with the other? "Nothing, I guess. But Karl has him now."

"Well, I'm glad you went with Marc. I realized later he was the one who found Ramón. Despite their persistent conflicts, it must have been shocking to find him that way."

I could only hope my face wasn't telegraphing my surprise. "Marc has a strong faith in God, and I'm sure the Lord's getting him through this."

"Of course. I'm sure his faith must be a great source of strength." Kendall glanced at his watch. "Bob Cousins is waiting."

I turned toward Kitty's. The next time I was tempted to work for someone I once loathed with good reason, I'd remember this season of my discontent and move on.

❧ 13 ❧

ot finding Kitty in the house, I searched outside and found her sitting at the end of her pier, bare feet dangling inches from the chilly water. I plopped beside her and tipped my face to the sun. The warm rays penetrated my body, nearly pushing out all concerns, but not quite.

"Everything okay?"

I inhaled deeply. "Why didn't you tell me Kendall is Rescaté's board president?"

"I guess it didn't occur to me. I don't remember you ever meeting him personally."

"You couldn't have forgotten when he caught me and LuAnn Dodge spying on him in the boathouse?"

She tipped her head back and laughed. "I did forget. His face was as red as his hair. He called you girls trespassers, nosy, and disrespectful."

"After what I did today, I'm surprised he didn't kick me off the property again." I let go of a bottled-up sigh. "I said something to Marc within Kendall's earshot that could have implied Marc and I were...involved. Which, of course, we're not."

"That would cost you your job?"

"Most places have a rule against coworkers dating."

"Even if both of you are single?"

"Yep. All the more reason for you to drop your dream of us reuniting that way."

"Everything is okay now?"

"I guess. He got distracted because there's a rumor running through the staff that Ramón may have been murdered."

She snapped around to look at me. "Murdered?"

"Wild, isn't it?"

"Where did that come from?"

"Seems Ramón had lady problems. His sister, ex-fiancée, and a female employee were all at odds with him for various reasons. Kendall wants all the talk to stop so he asked Marc to go up to the apartment, and then let people know that the place showed no signs of foul play. He's called a staff meeting for three."

She snorted. "I wouldn't worry. Kendall may be board president, but he's not sharp as a nail like his daddy. Does he think if anyone murdered Ramón they'd leave a trail? Did you find anything?"

"The cleaning service left the place in perfect order, but they missed a bottle of Gingko Biloba capsules. Ramón's 'smart pills,' as everyone calls them."

"So?"

"Remember what I told you about the guy running into me at the door that Friday morning? He dropped what looked like the same kind of bottle in the parking lot and made sure he picked it up before taking off toward Shore Drive. Something in my gut told me to hang onto them. Marc thinks I'm nuts, and I probably am."

"Never hurts to err on the side of carelessness." She raised a hand. "Don't say it. I know it's the wrong word. Err on the side of..." She gave me a thumbs-up. "Caution."

I held up my hand and she high-fived me.

"There's hope for me yet, dear niece. Your Uncle Daniel would be proud if he were still here."

"Aw, Kitty, you know Uncle Dan loved you as you are. Change of subject. When I ran into Kendall a couple minutes ago, he mentioned Marc and Ramón didn't get along. Marc's never mentioned it."

Her eyes rounded. "I never noticed any discord. Marc is the nicest man. Considerate. Kind."

I stifled a groan. If he needed to hire a publicist, he couldn't find anyone better than my aunt. "Perhaps they chose to keep their differences private."

Kitty poked her pedicured toes into the water and flicked droplets into the air. "I assume the pills are well hidden, since it's better to err on the side of caution."

"Yes, unless someone suddenly needs a sugar fix." I whacked my forehead. "I almost forgot. I won't be home for supper tonight. I'm meeting Candy Neer after work."

"Oh?"

"Why the questioning look? She's single. I'm single. It's about time I met some people my own age besides Marc."

"Where are you meeting her?"

"You heard of the Apple?"

"It's one of my favorite places for burgers." An impish smile crossed her face. "Is Marc going to be there too?"

I laughed and shook my head. "You never give up, do you?"

"Well, it is away from work. Kendall can't tell you what to do on your own time."

"It's a girls' night out. One of Candy's friends is meeting us there." I looked at my watch and stood. "I'd better get going if I'm going to be back in time for that meeting."

❧❧

Karl waited for me with the wheeled platform cart as I drove in from Shore Drive after shopping, the van full of food supplies. He appeared more like he belonged in a corral than a turn-of-the-century manor.

With his help the cart was quickly loaded, and I stood by while he angled the overloaded dolly through the kitchen door.

"Want some help putting all this junk away?"

I grinned. "You'll soon be stuffing this so-called junk into your big mouth and asking for more. I'd love some help since we have that staff meeting in less than a half hour."

He chuckled. "I was only messin' with ya. I'll hand off, and you shelve."

Soon we had a two-person assembly line going. Two minutes into the process he said, "You believe the rumors that Ramón was done in by one of his ladies?"

"Rumors rarely turn out to be true."

"But this one makes sense. I think his sister, Isabel, did it."

And they said women liked to gossip. Marc couldn't have called that meeting any sooner. "Aren't you afraid of pointing fingers at innocent people by naming names?"

"April, I don't get you. You're the only woman in this place who hasn't loved to speculate about this. Is it gossip if it's true?"

"But you don't know it's true. Do you?"

"No, but Isabel sure had a reason from what I hear. Correction. From what I know." He handed me a bag of sugar. "She'd been hitched once before, but married up last time. Man, I'd love to spend some time on her husband's spread. The dude owns a huge cattle ranch in New Mexico. I hear he was quite a roper in his day."

It seemed if Karl wasn't busy spreading rumors, his only other topic of choice was rodeo.

"How did a roper get to be so rich? Couldn't be by winning at rodeos."

"Raising and breeding stock. Big money in genetics these days. That's my dream."

58

"How did they meet?" At least we weren't talking about Ramón's cause of death anymore.

"Through her job with an international bank. She's got old James wrapped around her finger tighter than a dally rope. She wouldn't say, 'I do,' until he built her a mansion in Albuquerque. Wanted to be in town. Now a foreman runs the operation while James sits in his office and counts his money."

"How do you know so much about her?"

He tapped his right ear with his index finger. "A guy can learn a lot simply minding his business and fixin' what needs fixin'."

A country-western tune rang out and he pulled a cell phone from his pocket. "I gotta take this." He stepped into the kitchen and pulled the door closed behind him, but it didn't latch.

"Why you calling me during work hours?" Karl's lowered voice filtered into the pantry. "You got the message right. A grand on Star to buck off the rider. And no to the other question. You know I can't play the bulls. That's my event."

Stunned, I placed a bag of sugar on the shelf.

Karl stepped into the pantry. "Sorry about that."

"No problem." No problem at all, except it appeared our resident handyman liked to gamble and didn't mind doing so on rodeos. *Should I say something or not?* It seemed prudent to wait. "Back to Isabel. Do they have children?"

"Nope. What I don't get is why she still works. Without kids she could do whatever she wants." He pushed his black Stetson back on his forehead. "If it were me, I'd be buckin' bulls all week long, get me into the PBR."

"PBR?" I came down off the step stool.

"Professional Bull Riders. Win the finals, and it's easy street from then on. "

"Some people work because they enjoy it, Karl."

He gaped at me. "I'd never be that crazy. Give me enough money, and it's bye-bye, Rescaté."

I laughed. "And on to the PPR no doubt?" I followed him into the kitchen.

"PBR." He picked up a box of shredded wheat, along with a bag of fresh veggies and fruit.

"That bird eats better than some people."

"Maybe Ana gave him to Ramón hoping he'd copy the parrot's diet."

"Ana?"

"His fiancée, or I should say, his *ex*-fiancée. Pedro was delivered two days after Ramón broke their engagement."

"But why would she do that? Didn't someone say the other day he broke up with her?"

"Maybe to drive him crazy. I'm about ready to stuff a sock in his beak if he says, 'Ana loves you,' one more time. Good chatting with ya. You're easy to talk to. See ya at the meeting."

As he left, I grinned at the image of a sock hanging from Pedro's mouth. But funny as it was, I had to wonder why Ramón kept the bird.

❧

At exactly three o'clock the entire Rescaté staff crowded into the conference room off the reception area. Kendall sat at the head of the long table, while Marc sat to the board president's right and Bob at his left. I couldn't help but inwardly laugh at the image of the king and his attendants.

Kendall stood, and a hush fell over the room. "Thanks for coming, everyone. I don't want to take up any more of your valuable time than necessary, so I'll get right to the point. Rumors have a nasty way of taking on a life of their own. All it takes is one speculation." He gave a pointed stare to Rosa, whose face reddened. "From there, if it isn't fed, it dies. But if someone else feeds the rumor by adding to it and telling the next person, it lives.

"We—that is Marc, Bob and I—want to assure you that we have taken the matter seriously. This morning I spoke with Dr. Fuller, and he assured me that all signs point to the cause of death being cardiac arrest. Also, Marc and our newest employee, April Love, inspected the apartment for any signs of a struggle. Nothing was found out of order.

"Now, we have a funeral to honor our fallen leader coming up. I ask that we can put this pointless chatter to rest and concentrate on that. Any questions?"

Everyone looked around, but no one spoke. Marc caught my gaze and held it for a split second as if to say, "Don't mention the pills." Did he really think I would? I wanted the rumors to go away as much as anyone.

"Good. Then let's all get back to work. Thanks for your time. Marc and Bob, I need to talk to you two alone, so please stay."

Except for some low whispering, everyone filed out noiselessly. I waited until the only ones remaining were the king and his court and fell behind Rosemary.

"April, thanks for helping Marc out this morning."

I stopped and faced Kendall. "Not a problem. Happy to help."

He dismissed me with his eyes and I left, glad not to be a part of the "in crowd."

❧

Kitty glanced up from her newspaper as I entered the sunroom. "I never thought you'd get here. Didn't you get my calls?"

I took out my cell and turned it on. "Sorry. I shut my phone off. It must be important if you called twice." I adjusted the instrument to vibrate and returned it to my pocket.

"It was. But when you didn't call, I figured you were busy."

Since I had exactly ten minutes to change into jeans and leave for the Apple, I sat on the couch arm. "So why did you call?"

"I've been thinking about those rumors about Ramón's cause of death. Didn't you say you overheard Ramón in an argument on the phone the day before he died?"

I slid down the arm and onto a couch cushion. How had that totally slipped my mind? "I forgot all about that."

"What did he say? Do you recall?"

My thoughts reached back through the million things that had happened since then. "Something to the effect that if money wasn't in his account soon and something happened to him, his people would know who to blame." I stared at my aunt. "No. I refuse to believe this."

She scooted to the edge of the chintz-covered cushion. "The next morning that person in the orange baseball cap ran you down, and you saw him drop a bottle of pills like those you found on Ramón's dresser."

I nodded. Coincidence. Had to be.

"Mind my asking what type of pills those were?"

"Marc called them Ramón's smart pills. Ginkgo Biloba."

"I know that. I mean, were they tablets?"

"Capsules I think."

Her shoulders tensed. "I was afraid of that."

I checked my watch. In exactly five minutes I needed to be behind the wheel, heading to the Apple. "Afraid of what?"

"When you were a toddler, someone in the Chicago area substituted bottles of poisoned painkillers for those already on store shelves. No one suspected poison at first when people started showing symptoms more related to heart attack or stroke. Several people were killed before they discovered the capsules contained poison. I can't remember what the killer used, though. If everyone knew Ramón took those Gin...Gango...however you say it, it would be a perfect way to poison him."

I slumped deeper into the couch. "You've been reading too many murder mysteries. I'm not even supposed to be discussing this. Kendall told the staff this afternoon to stop passing rumors around. Besides, Doc Fuller, who happens to be the coroner, said he died of a heart attack and he should know."

She blew a puff of air through her lips. "Coroner, shmoroner. Doc's not exactly the sharpest fork in the toolbox. He told Eileen Waddle she had an upset stomach. Last January she delivered seven pounds of indigestion. As for Kendall, I'm not a Rescaté employee, and I'll talk about it if I want to. You just listen."

My sentiments exactly, but I wasn't ready to be fired. Still I was at home and not work, and this was a private conversation. "If Doc Fuller is that bad, how come he's the coroner and still practicing medicine?"

"For years he was the only doctor in town and, for some, old habits die hard. Newcomers go to him because he doesn't lay it on the line. He probably told Ramón to cut back a little on the sweets."

"And the coroner job?"

"The last time we had an incident in Canoga County was ten years ago when Joe Blanchett shot his brother over a gambling debt. It's hard to make a mistake when the guy is full of a half-dozen bullet holes. What if Ramón mistreated a Rescaté employee, and she decided to repay him?"

"But how would that fit into the conversation I overheard?"

"It doesn't. And that's what's troubling me about the theory."

I rubbed my temples. "Well, Candy Neer was almost fired by Ramón until Marc stepped in."

Her eyes brightened. "Good for him. He's a fine Christian man. You should see him with the middle-school boys at church."

My heart warmed as the memory of him talking to the boy last Sunday came to mind. Working with kids was a nice switch for him. I wrestled my thoughts away from dangerous territory. "But then Ramón cut her hours, making her ineligible for medical insurance. She had some sort of family plan that included her disabled mother."

Kitty's eyes sparked. "What a scoundrel. I'm surprised she doesn't look for another job. Do you suppose he's been giving bad recommendations for her?"

"It's worth considering. But, really, Kitty, I think we need to table this conversation. I had one with Karl the handyman before the meeting—or rather he had one with me—discussing another possible killer. This seems to be turning into a virtual Clue game. Next thing I hear will be that it was Colonel Mustard in the ballroom with a candlestick."

Her features dissolved into a frown. "But what if it's true?"

Didn't Karl ask me the same thing an hour ago? "There's a saying that goes: Don't borrow trouble before it happens. It's good advice. Ramón's funeral is Wednesday, and after that, I'm sure his sister will bury him. This will all soon be forgotten." I stood and moved toward the door. "Right now I need to change and hit the Apple."

~ 14 ~

A large red apple outside the rustic building assured me I'd found the right place. I guided my car into a parking slot next to a Ford pickup. The lot held only a smattering of cars, but it was still early. If only I could rid myself of the ache pressing against my gut that Kitty was buying into those rumors. Kendall could try squelching them as far as the Rescaté staff was concerned, but he had no control over Kitty.

The crunch of wheels turning over gravel broke into my thoughts, and I looked to my left. A blue pickup had pulled in next to me. A man wearing jeans and a blue work shirt climbed out. As he ambled toward the entrance, I checked my image in the rearview mirror, then grabbed my purse and let myself out of the car.

Stepping into the place, I took a moment to let my eyes adjust to the low lighting. A perky redhead who looked no older than eighteen, if she was a day, asked how many in my party.

"I think three. Do you know if Candy Neer is here yet?"

"Sure is. Follow me."

We stepped into a dining area where several booths and tables were already filled. I followed the hostess, expecting her to stop next to a table, but we ended up at the bar at the far end of the space. "She's over there." The girl gestured to a far corner.

A waving hand on the other side of the room caught my attention. I returned the gesture and headed her way, stepping past a couple guys.

"Hey, you made it."

I returned Candy's grin. "Did you doubt me?"

"I wasn't sure." She turned to the petite brunette standing next to her. "Gina, this is my friend from work. April is our chef." She said the word *chef* in an affected, la-de-dah way.

A hint of a tattoo peeked over the edging of Gina's scooped-neck top she'd tucked into skinny jeans. It was all I could do not to wonder how far down that thing went. I inwardly cringed at the thought.

Her dark eyes widened. "Cool. Like those guys on TV who have to cook, like, five dishes in an hour?"

At least the girl watched quality television. "I wouldn't mind being an

Iron Chef, but I'm just starting. I'll be preparing Spanish cuisine."

"What'll you have to drink, April?" Candy asked.

"I'll wait until we go to the dining room."

She gave me a quizzical look. "Dining room?"

"Yeah. To order dinner. Isn't that why we're here?"

She tossed her head back and laughed. "I didn't come here to eat. I thought you knew that. If you want to order food for in here..."

"That's okay, I'll live." A whiff of still-sizzling fajitas tickled my nose, and I caught sight of the steaming skillet passing to my right. My stomach rumbled. Turning away, I mentally counted to five, hoping to rid the temptation to order some of my own. Hungry as I was, I didn't want to be the only one eating. I'd catch a drive-through on my way back to Kitty's. "A Diet Coke would be fine."

Her brows shot up. "Hey, girlfriend, Coke's for at work. How about something stronger?" She put her lips against the mouth of an amber bottle and took a long draw.

"Not tonight."

She eyed me as though I'd lost my senses but gave my order to the bartender.

I reached in my purse.

Candy pushed her palm against my hand. "This is on me. Next time you pay."

My stomach seized. She assumed we'd hang out on a regular basis. So far I wasn't sure I wanted that. We didn't have much in common.

Not wanting to look her in the eye any longer, I scanned the room, its walls cluttered with sports and movie paraphernalia. "Not very busy, is it?"

"Wait," Gina said. "The softball teams start up tonight. They finish around nine and head over here."

"You guys planning to stay that late?" I wouldn't last another hour without something more than diet soda. Whatever made me think I'd find some people to socialize with tonight? They were getting started at about the time my head was hitting the pillow.

"Gina might close the place. Tomorrow's her day off." Candy handed me my soft drink. "I'll be history in a couple of hours, unless something comes up." She winked at me. "No offense, but I'm not losing my beauty sleep hanging with a couple of chicks." Her eyes went toward the dining area as though she expected Prince Charming to arrive any moment. She brought her gaze back to me. "Scuttlebutt says you and Marc knew each other before. You guys date?"

So, something else had been fodder for the office grapevine besides Ramón. How comforting. I sipped my drink. The cold liquid tasted wonderful against my suddenly parched mouth. "We attended the same college and were good friends is all."

A grin split her face. "Cool. Did he get you the job?"

"I didn't know he was working at Rescaté until the day I interviewed...it was a nice surprise." *Yeah, right. Nice as in having someone spike your Coke with pepper sauce.*

Candy cocked her head toward her friend. "You should see this hunk. Coal-black hair, dark eyes. I think his mom is from Brazil."

"Argentina." I cringed at how fast I corrected her.

She shrugged. "Whatever." Her gaze went to the entrance, and her face brightened.

Prince Charming, no doubt. I turned.

A tall man stood at the entrance to the bar area, surveying the crowd. Candy raised her arm and waved. He acknowledged her signal with a lift of his head and sauntered our way.

"Boyfriend?" I asked.

"That's my goal." Her face worked into a smile that would've lit a cave a hundred feet under. "Hi, Brett."

"Hey, babe." He caught the bartender's eye. "Give me a tall draft."

I gave the Orlando Bloom in a designer suit look-alike a quick scan. By all appearances, he was no more Candy's type than Hulk Hogan was mine.

"April, this is Brett Hagenbrink. April is the chef where I work."

Brett nodded, then turned his attention to a pretty blonde who sidled up to him.

"Hi, Brett." The Barbie-doll-come-to-life dragged out his name in an accent that made me feel like I'd never left Atlanta. "Where did you get your handsome self off to lately?"

He grinned. "Oh, here and there. I wouldn't go far from you, Sherry." He stretched an arm across her shoulders, his diamond-encrusted pinky ring twinkling.

"You're so funny," she purred. "Come on over to my table and talk to me." She hooked her arm with his.

He tossed his jacket to Candy and let Sherry lead him to a pub-height table, where they slid onto a couple of stools.

Candy threw the jacket toward a barstool, missing her target. She didn't bother to pick it up. "That little—"

"I'll be glad when Ramón's service is over." I stirred my soda with the straw. "I'm looking forward to doing what I was hired to do. Cook for the corporate presentation dinners."

Her eyes flashed. "April, did you see what that no-good did?" She narrowed her gaze toward the couple.

"Kind of conniving, I'd say."

"I'll give them five minutes." Candy faced me. "If Sherry doesn't get her hands off my man, she's going to have the same fate as Ramón."

She slammed her bottle on the bar and marched up to the pair. Had five minutes passed that fast? She tapped Brett on the shoulder, then said something into his ear. He slid off his stool and they meandered to my side. His right arm still hooked loosely around Candy's neck, he mouthed something to her. She held a hand to her ear, motioning she couldn't hear.

"Did the deposit I made show up in your account?"

Candy hushed him with a scowl. He glanced in my direction, then shrugged and reached for his beer.

Like a homing pigeon, Sherry was at his side. "Come on, sugar. We didn't finish our conversation." In a flash he was gone. I'd have loved to have heard more, but sadly, what was said was enough to bring Kitty's speculations to my mind. Coincidence, I told myself. Even Mr. Hunk's reference to adding to her bank account didn't sway me. Coincidence.

"I'll get her," Candy muttered. "He's already made plans with me for later." She grabbed my arm. "April, I'm so lame. Here I invite you out, then totally ignore you. But you understand, right? I mean, if Marc were here, I'd understand."

But she didn't get it. Marc and I had no relationship. At least not the kind she meant. "No problem."

She leaned in. "The four of us could double sometime. That would be way cool."

I waved a hand. "Marc and I aren't dating. Even if we wanted to, we can't as long as we both work at Rescaté." Seeing the sulk on her face, I quickly added, "Or that would be fun."

She glanced over my shoulder and her face lit up again. "If you're meant to be together, you're not going to let a little office rule stop you, are you? No time like the present to start. He's standing behind you."

❧ 15 ❧

My pulse quickened and I turned.

Marc stood several feet away, wearing jeans and a polo. He offered me that lopsided smile of his as if on cue. "Thought I'd check out the place since you said you were coming here. I looked first in the dining room."

I bit back the warm greeting ready to come out: "If I'd known you'd follow me, I wouldn't have been so open with my plans."

He raised a finger to the bartender. "Soda water with lime, please."

Candy looked like she would burst out of her skin. "Hey, Marc. Glad you came. We need more socialization around that tomb." Her hand flew to her mouth. "Sorry. Lame joke."

Socializing was good, but not with my traitorous stomach having exchanged hunger pains for butterflies on too much caffeine. I had to get out of there. "I was just leaving." I jumped off my stool and took a step toward the door.

Marc grabbed my arm and whispered in my ear, "If you haven't eaten yet, have dinner with me."

I pressed my lips together...afraid if I didn't, I'd accept.

"Come on." He took my hand.

I yanked my fingers out of his grip. "If you want a dinner partner, there're plenty of women in this place who are willing." I stepped around him. "As for me, I'm history."

By the time I got to my car, I wanted to retrace my steps. Did I really want someone like Sherry going after Marc? But how could I go back and still save face? I clicked the lock on the key fob and grabbed the door handle.

A hand closed over mine. "What if the only woman I want to have dinner with isn't in there?"

"I guess you have a problem then."

Marc squeezed my hand and worked it away from the handle. *"Mi caramela,* we need to talk. What better way than over a nice meal? I know a great Italian place down the road."

What would a simple meal hurt? One supper a renewed romance did not make. But people fell in love over romantic dinners. My stomach had screamed for food a short while earlier. Now it only wanted a strong dose of Pepto.

I turned, forgetting his hand still held mine, and found myself in the crook of his arm. If my heart beat any faster, I could only hope Marc remembered CPR. "We are supposed to have a business relationship only, remember."

"We can talk about menus for the funeral, if you'd like."

"We already did that."

"Okay, then. We can talk about how I think you should stay on at Rescaté after the funeral. We'll carry on as Ramón wanted it." He brought his mouth within an inch of mine.

"How did he want it?"

"He always encouraged the staff to get along, socialize after hours, and be friends.'

"Did that mean a boss hugging his employee as one I know is doing now?"

He brought his mouth to my ear. "I never asked, but I'm sure he would approve." A million flutters filled my stomach. Then he kissed my ear, and my knees turned to molasses.

"We shouldn't ascribe thoughts to someone who can't speak for himself." My voice cracked.

Marc pressed his forehead against mine. *"Mi caramela,* if you don't let me kiss you right now, I'm going to go crazy."

"I can't let that hap—"

His lips touched mine, brushing them once, twice, three times, like butterfly wings. A soft moan issued from my throat and his mouth returned to my lips, this time remaining there. Good thing we were out of the neon glare of the giant red apple, because we didn't stop for breath for a long while.

We stood silent, arms wrapped around each other, enjoying the closeness. I'd only dated one man since Marc, and that had been short-lived. I hadn't kissed a man like I did since I last kissed Marc. Had it been the same for him? I had no idea, like I had no clue what had happened in California with that iron-solid plan of his to get a PhD. For all I knew, he'd been married and had a family in that length of time.

I pressed my palms against his chest and pushed him away. "We can't do this, Marc."

He quirked his head. I could imagine the bewilderment on his face without seeing it the dark.

"I'm sorry for kissing you back and misleading you. I need to get home."

He stepped aside, allowing me room to open the car door.

I slid into the opening and faced him. He hadn't moved away.

"April, you have to know that I still—"

I pressed my index finger to his lips. "Unless you're willing to tell me what happened to thwart your grad school plans, we can't have a future." When he didn't respond, I slipped onto the car seat and closed the door, then started the engine as quick as possible. The last thing I wanted was to let him see me cry, and if I didn't get out of there, he would.

∞

The following day, I rested my hands on my hips and stared at the gaping hole in the arrangement of chocolate chip cookies.

"I couldn't resist helping myself."

I turned. Why did Marc always come up behind me like that, looking so good I couldn't stay mad at him? I'd stewed half the night when I should have been sleeping. First, reveling in the feel of his lips on mine, and then angry at the silent answer to my question. Now, after one look at that crooked grin, all I wanted was to kiss him again.

His expression grew serious. "I owe you an apology for kissing you last night.

I moved the remaining cookies over to fill in the gap, then faced him. "It wasn't just you doing the kissing."

His eyes creased at the corners. "Don't think I didn't notice, but I'm the one who started it, and I'm sorry. I should have respected your feelings."

I turned back to the table and moved a spoon over a half inch. "Wouldn't it be easier to tell me what happened to the PhD?"

"Nothing more than what I said."

"That's what I thought you'd say." I edged down the table and moved the salt and pepper shakers over. Did I really want to know what happened? The more he avoided telling, the more I was afraid to know. At least his cop-out now restored some of that anger that kept me tossing around the bed all night.

"April, didn't you hear my question?" Marc had moved next to me.

"What question?"

"I said the spread looks great, but there's a ton of food. Could we put some in the break room for the staff?"

The man's rating in my book soared. Not good. I wanted to stay mad at him. "Great idea. I'll set up a table. Of course, if the volunteer you'd promised were here to help…"

He whacked his forehead. "I nearly forgot. She's coming this afternoon."

The conference room doors opened, and half a dozen men drifted in. I wanted to escape to the kitchen, but at Marc's insistence, I stood next to him at the table. As each man picked up a paper plate, Marc introduced me and bragged on my cooking.

My cheeks warmed. How could anyone judge my culinary expertise by a ham-and-cheese sandwich? A minimum-wage deli worker could throw something like this together. Although I did put out a special herbed spread and added dry white wine and tarragon to the potato salad.

To keep my head, I focused on the men. A varied assortment of ages and builds if there ever was one. Most weren't under the age of fifty and, by their physiques, I surmised they loved to eat. Well good. They came to the right place.

"We meet again, April. Your buffet looks great. How's the meal prep for tomorrow coming?"

I hadn't noticed Kendall come up. "Pretty good."

"Only pretty good?"

I nodded. "Marc has arranged for a volunteer to help, so we'll get a lot done this afternoon."

I was about to ask if he wanted to start the buffet line, but Marc approached us. "If you two are discussing tomorrow's buffet, it's all under control, thanks to April."

Kendall smiled. "And she told me you've arranged for some help for her."

"That I did." Marc looked at me. "But it's April who planned the menu, shopped, and has the prep work schedule worked out."

And will do most of the cooking. I pasted a smile on my face.

Kendall chortled. "That's why we hired her. Right?" He picked up a plate and moved on.

Marc's piercing stare followed him. "I didn't notice him around when I hired you. Did you?"

I stuffed a giggle. Sometime I'd tell Marc about the Kendall I knew. Sometimes things never look any different.

"I let the staff know lunch is on the way." Marc dropped a scoop of potato salad on his plate. "I really am sorry about last night. I only wanted to talk. Didn't intend to, ah, communicate the way we did."

I eyed the men scattered about the room. "Maybe you should have phoned it in."

"But it wouldn't have been as much fun."

"No. But it would have been a lot safer."

"Depends on your perspective."

I let my gaze return to him and gaped at his plate. "You planning to eat all that in one sitting?"

He scraped half the potato salad back into the bowl. "Just lost track."

⋙⋘

I spent the next fifteen minutes laying out food in the break room. All it took was a few calls from Rosemary to alert the troops, and they came like a swarm of wasps returning to the nest. As much as I wanted to stay and visit, I couldn't. I made myself a roast beef sandwich and carried it back to the kitchen where I sat in front of the laptop computer to open my to-do list for the afternoon. I lifted my sandwich to my watering mouth.

A loud squawk sliced the air, and I looked up. Pedro sat on the pot rack between a two-quart sauté pan and the stockpot, his little head raised, proud as a parrot.

I dropped my sandwich onto the paper plate. "How did you get out?"

The bird made a chattering sound, then launched into a glide around the room. He took a turn over the sink and came toward me, landing on my shoulder. His pointy claws dug through my shirt like needles. "Ana loves you."

I leaned back and caught his beady eye. "How come you don't have clipped wings?"

The bird fluttered to the counter and strutted toward my sandwich, his colorful head bobbing like a drum majorette.

"Oh, no you don't, buster." I scooped up my uneaten lunch and whisked it into the fridge. I had exactly three minutes to get the escapee back in his pen and eat. After I cushioned my shoulder with a towel and proffered a potato chip, I finally got Pedro to jump on board, and we set off for his cage.

With the escapee back behind bars, I found Karl at work in the ballroom setting up the soundboard. "The kitchen just entertained a feathered visitor."

His face paled. "Did the board members see him loose?"

"I thought pet birds had clipped wings. How did he get so lucky?"

"He's a retired show bird. Ramón let him fly around down here at night. I guess Pedro thinks the place is his." Karl stood. "I'll rig up a lock he can't figure out. I think one of his tricks was to escape his cage."

❧ 16 ❧

By the time I got to prepping the funeral lunch, I felt like any moment I'd meet myself coming while I was still going. With the ingredients for Chicken George set out, I arranged chicken breasts side by side in a large roasting pan, then checked my watch. Another minute without help. Marc was fast losing those points he'd earned.

"Excuse me."

I looked up and had to remind myself not to gape.

The *Vogue*-magazine-cover-come-to-life raised her voice over Beethoven's *Fifth*. "Sorry for shouting, but my knock couldn't be heard above the music. Is Marc around? He told me to meet him in the kitchen."

My adherence to my mother's admonition to never gawk having failed, I took in the quality of the woman's curve-hugging knit dress, the diamond cocktail ring on her right hand, and the shimmering black hair that fell past her shoulders like an ebony waterfall. Suddenly aware that my lips hadn't seen the business end of a lipstick since early morning, I glanced down at my spattered apron and wanted to slink under the counter.

A thought rocketed into my mind. Was this beauty what happened to Marc in California?

"Here I am." Marc came up behind the thirty-something woman and, for a moment, I expected him to hug her. He grinned over her shoulder. "This is Ana Velasco, your volunteer helper."

I gave the visitor a second assessment. This immaculate creature had no intentions of getting those French-manicured hands dirty, let alone those expensive clothes. And what about those stiletto sandals? They were at least three inches higher than the chef clogs adorning my size sevens. This arrangement wouldn't work at all.

Wait. Did he say Ana? Not the same Ana who once wore Ramón's engagement ring. I went to the iPod dock and adjusted the volume. "April Love. I'd offer my hand, but I've been handling chicken."

Expressionless, Ana flipped her hair over a shoulder. "Sorry I couldn't get here sooner. I'd better change." She set a large leather tote on a stool and took out jeans, a yellow T-shirt, and sneakers.

I grinned. "Glad to see you brought those. I was a little worried."

She uttered a laugh that sounded forced. "I wouldn't boil water in this outfit. Be back in a sec." She glided through the door and out of sight.

How did she do that? I couldn't even wear a pair of espadrilles without becoming a catastrophe waiting to happen. I glanced at Marc, who was leaning against the kitchen counter, arms folded. "Well, she wasn't who I expected."

He scowled. "What do you mean?"

"Isn't she Ramón's former fiancé?"

"So?"

"Who'll help me tomorrow? I presume she'll attend the service." I walked to the sink and held my hands under the hot water. He did bring the assistant he promised, but assistant for what? I squirted soap onto my palm. Did I have to spell out the requirements of a kitchen helper? I didn't need an ornament that gave the job a lick and a promise. I needed a worker.

"She wants to help you tomorrow."

I shut off the water. "You sure?"

"She insists on it." He grabbed a towel from a nearby rack and handed it to me. "Frankly, it's none of our business if she wants to grieve this way."

I dried my hands and tossed the towel over the rack. On second thought, he was right. For all I knew, this was her way of working through her grief. If she wanted to work the memorial buffet, who was I to complain?

Marc left, and I darted into the pantry, where I exchanged my soiled apron for a clean one, and restyled my fly-away curls into the claw clip I'd worn since morning. An improvement, but hardly enough to compete with the fashionista.

I'd dabbed on lipstick by the time Ana returned. As I might have guessed, even in jeans with her hair in a ponytail, she looked gorgeous. How could this slender beauty have been attracted to a man whose girth likely took up both cushions on a loveseat? No sooner had I thought those words than a sick feeling filled my stomach. How had I turned so judgmental? In truth, Ana was a better person than me for seeing past the exterior. Maybe if I'd done that the day Marc's good looks swept me off my feet, I'd have saved us both a lot of grief.

God, forgive me.

I got Ana sautéing mushrooms in a stainless steel pan for a cream sauce before I began mixing dried bread cubes, chopped onions, and spices together. I glanced in her direction. "Ramón's death is so sad. He seemed like a nice man."

Except for pushing her spoon through the mushrooms, the woman stood stone still.

I opened my mouth to repeat my statement.

"I told him time and time again…" She transferred the caramelized mushrooms into a bowl.

I waited until she added a slab of butter to the sauté pan and returned it to the flame. "You were saying?"

"It's not important." She dumped the remaining raw mushrooms into the melted butter.

"Did you know him well?"

She let out the tiniest of sighs. "I'm surprised you haven't heard through the gossipmongers." She stilled her hand and stared into the mushrooms. "We were once engaged."

Taken aback by her flat tone, I pushed on. "I try not to pay attention to gossip. I'm sorry for your loss."

"Ramón and I have been history for months. What do you want me to do with these things?" She indicated the bowl of cooked mushrooms.

I got her preparing the cream sauce, then added chicken stock I'd made earlier to the dried ingredients I'd prepared. "Have you lived in Canoga Lake long?"

"Only a couple years."

I waited several long moments, expecting her to continue. But it was as if someone had Krazy Glued her lips together. Should I shut up or keep trying?

"This recipe is a good choice for the lunch." Ana kept her gaze fixed on the pan in front of her. "It should appeal to most people."

I had to strain to hear her, but at least maybe now we'd have a conversation. "My thoughts exactly. I loved the dress you had on before. Is there a place around here that's good for clothes shopping?"

"I suppose. You have to nose around. I think this sauce is ready. What do you want me to do with it?"

Without further small talk, we got the chicken casseroles made and in the refrigerator, then prepped the ingredients for appetizers, finishing only a few minutes later than I'd intended.

I asked if she'd like something to drink while we went over tomorrow's agenda. Ana opted for bottled water with a slice of lemon while I went for my usual chemical-laden diet soda. By the time she left, the only thing I knew about her was that she was a good worker.

✑ 17 ✐

With Ana gone and a Casting Crowns CD cranked up, I ran a soapy sponge over the granite counters. The chore gave me time to rehash all of the ten or so words Ana had uttered in the past several hours. If I hadn't already heard about the stormy fights she'd had with Ramón, after today, I would have been happy to conclude that she didn't have enough fire in her belly to battle a mosquito.

"Good. You're still here." A shout came above the music.

I turned. Karl shut the door and settled onto a stool. He removed his ball cap.

I studied the logo on the hat and gave up trying to figure out what *Justin* meant. Didn't matter. "So what's up?" I crossed over to the player to lower the volume.

"Don't." Karl's shouted order caused me to startle.

I shot him a questioning look.

"We need to talk." He beckoned with his finger.

I approached him and leaned in—the only way to hear him over the racket.

"The music will stop anyone from hearing," he said. "Thought you'd like to know there's a new rumor going around. They think Marc killed Ramón."

"What?" I stepped back and stared at him.

Karl held up a hand, palm out. "Keep your voice down."

"Who told you that?"

"Doesn't matter. I know you and Thorne are friends. I don't believe a word of it, but I think someone's out to frame him."

Like a pair of crazed pinballs, my eyes zigzagged over his face. "Who is framing him?"

"Dunno. That's all I know."

"How?"

"Dunno that either."

"I've not seen any police around here. Wouldn't they be involved?"

"You'd think so." He picked up his cap and set it back on his head. "Just wanted you to be aware. I still think Isabel or Ana knocked Ramón off. They'll both be here tomorrow. Keep your eyes open."

76

After Karl left, I made a double-shot espresso and tried to digest what he told me. Marc may be a lot of things, but he wasn't a killer. Karl seemed to want me to warn Marc, but how could I with only a rumor? Ana had called the people around Rescaté "gossipmongers." Was I to believe the latest one or not?

A knock came at the door, and Marc stepped into the room. Worry lines creased his face. He marched across the room and cut the music. "Do you realize you've been playing the same song over and over? I could hear it in my office."

"I hadn't noticed. Guess I was deep in thought."

"Came to see how Ana worked out." He loosened his tie and let it hang free around his neck before he sat on the stool next to me.

"She was great." I touched his arm. "Marc, we need to talk...do you have a few minutes?"

"I'll walk you back to Kitty's. We can chat on the way. The board meeting is continuing at the Fin and Tail over dinner, and I need to leave soon."

We walked toward the shore path in silence—him with his hands in his pockets and me with my arms folded across my chest. We came to the boathouse. Did the memory of the day he proposed evoke any emotion for him? I chanced a glance his way. His set jaw gave me no clue. We continued toward Kitty's. Our conversation time was fast evaporating. I had to speak now or forget it. "Karl told me something disturbing."

"What's happened now?"

"He heard through the grapevine that you're suspected of..." I bit down on my lip. "Of killing Ramón."

He stopped walking and grabbed my elbow. "Tell me you're joking."

"I wish I were, but I'm not."

"Who's accusing me? The cops? Someone from Rescaté? Who started these rumors?"

"I have no idea. Karl didn't know, or he's not talking. Just said it was another rumor. He doesn't believe it and wanted to make sure you knew."

The vein in his neck pulsed. "I've had about enough of Karl Murray and his gossip. He was at Kendall's meeting. Doesn't he care about his job? Who else has he told?"

"He said no one, but that's kind of hard to believe."

"I'll say. The guy is a real busybody."

"But he did want you to know. Do you think we should call the police?"

"And tell them what? We have a rumor going around that I may have killed the boss. And, in case you hear that suspicion, it's not true."

"It's probably best to ignore it." We began the trek up the hill toward Kitty's. "Like you said, it's only rumor and lies."

"Rumor and lies that he's probably running his mouth about all over the place, letting everyone know. I need to tell Kendall."

"Maybe he's not. He made me play the music loud to mask our voices."

We arrived at the back door, and Marc squared himself in front of me, his face drained of color. He cupped a hand on each of my shoulders. "April, you need to help me quash these rumors. Ramón died of a heart attack. Period. If word gets out he was murdered, a lot of damage could be done to Rescaté's reputation. I'm afraid for the kids we support."

I stared at the pink and white tulips bordering the circular drive, then faced him and nearly crumbled at his earnest expression. "There's something you need to know that isn't rumor. I never told you that I overheard Ramón on the phone the day I had my interview with him. He was angry and yelled at the other person that if money wasn't in his bank account soon the person would pay. Then he said if he was found harmed, his people would know who to blame."

Marc's complexion paled. "And then you saw that person in the orange cap the next morning."

I dropped my gaze and studied a glop of sauce from the Chicken George splattered on my left shoe. "I don't know why I forgot about that phone conversation until Kitty reminded me, but I did."

"Now your aunt is in on the rumor." He paced a circle. "Don't you know what happens when someone tells another and that person tells another?"

Heat filled my gut. "Of course I do. I was trying to stop her from imagining Ramón was killed. But now I wonder if it's true."

"And next you'll wonder if I did it. Thanks a lot, April." He stomped across the drive toward the pines.

I ran after him and grabbed his arm. "I think no such thing, Marc Thorne. I know for a fact you aren't a killer. I was the only one to overhear that conversation and see the person running from the mansion. In spite of those two things, I don't want to learn he was murdered. But if he was, the killer has to be exposed before you get blamed for something you didn't do." I ran my gaze over his troubled face. "I'm keeping my eyes and ears open for anything that will expose the truth."

He tweaked my nose. "You know, April, your insatiable desire to help others is one of the things that made me fall in love with you." He stepped closer until the lingering scent of his cologne filled my senses. Taking a deep breath, he ran his eyes over me until they came to my mouth. "I've never found anyone who could…"

A dull pain filled my chest. I wanted more than anything to taste his kiss again, but I stepped away.

The glimmer left his eyes. "I need to get back. See you tomorrow." He turned and broke into a loping jog across the lawn.

∂ 18 ∂

I found Kitty in the kitchen preparing a meatloaf as Rosebud and Violet took turns rubbing against her legs. Focusing on the ground meat mixture oozing between her fingers seemed to calm me. I waited until she formed the glob into a rectangle and placed it in a foil-lined bread pan before I spoke.

"Remember when we talked about the rumor that Ramón was killed?"

She crossed to the stainless wall oven and slid the pan onto the rack. After closing the oven door, she turned. "How could I not?"

I plopped onto a kitchen chair as a tear escaped from my left eye and trailed down my cheek. "Now it's worse. The latest newsflash on the Rescaté grapevine is that Marc is suspected of murdering Ramón."

Her hand flew to her chest. "My word. If this is some kind of a sick joke..."

I huffed. "Funny. Marc said almost the same thing when I told him."

"What is he going to do?" She picked up a potholder and hung it on a hook near the stove. I cringed at the sight of the hand-shaped grease mark on her new knit top. I should have waited to tell her about the rumor after she washed her hands.

"What can we do? It's rumor, and so far the only thing we know is what Karl told me earlier. Kendall hasn't mentioned it, nor has anyone else. Ignoring it and moving on is probably the best."

She went to the sink and turned on the hot water before soaping up her hands. "Doesn't mean we can't be on top of things. The early bird gets the prize you know."

Even Kitty's twisted idiom didn't make me laugh. How could I when the only man I'd ever loved might be hauled off to jail? I had to remind myself "loved" was in past tense, but that didn't mean I shouldn't help him clear his name if it came to that.

I went to the fridge and grabbed a Diet Coke. "Seems to me shutting up the source is the answer. But I don't even know who started these rumors."

By now she was blotting a damp cloth on her top. "I've been thinking about the telephone conversation you overheard. Almost sounds to me like Ramón was blackmailing someone."

"Blackmail? How?"

"Didn't he say if money wasn't in his account by tomorrow and if he was harmed his people would know who did it?"

"He didn't say a specified timeframe. But yeah, he did say that other stuff. Guess it could be blackmail."

"Tomorrow is the funeral service. Let's keep our sights on people and our ears open. We know that Candy and Ramón had issues. Who were the other women you mentioned?"

"Ana, his ex-fiancée. She helped me today with food prep. And his sister, Isabel."

"How did Ana seem?"

"Gorgeous, well-to-do, mysterious, and moody."

She joined me at the table. "How mysterious?"

I shrugged. "Without her dark beauty, I'd call her distant or unfriendly. She's a terrible conversationalist. I did all the talking, trying to draw her out. But I wasn't trying to observe her from a murderer angle." I took a swig of my soda as my mind trailed back to my attempts at socializing. Was she distant because she didn't want me finding out something that would expose her as a killer? She wasn't even dating Ramón anymore. But her clothes reeked money, not to mention that cocktail ring on her finger and her diamond studs. If Ramón was blackmailing her, it was possible she could lay her hands on some dough.

My thoughts drifted to the night at the Apple. "As long as we're on this delightful subject, Candy may not make enough money to factor into the blackmail scheme, but I did hear a strange conversation between her and a guy she's hung up on. Seems he's dropping cash into her bank account. I have no idea how much or why."

"What's his name?"

"Brett is the first. The last was something long, but I can't remember."

Kitty drummed her acrylic nails on the tabletop. "The other woman was Ramón's sister. Right? Does she have money?"

"Yes, according to Karl. Or at least her husband does. She's the one Karl thinks killed Ramón—if he was murdered." I rubbed my temples against a headache. "I can't believe we're even talking about this."

"I can't either." She tossed the damp rag into the sink. "Why don't you go upstairs and have a soak in my spa tub. Run those jets on high. While you're doing that, I'll make a list of what we need to look for tomorrow."

I stared at Kitty. Did she fancy herself a modern-day Miss Marple or something? Who was this woman, and what did she do with my crazy, lovable aunt?

❧ 19 ❧

By the time the funeral began, Ana and I managed to have everything ready to go for the buffet. A feat I wasn't sure we'd achieve, considering the restless night I had worrying about Marc. Having the meal to prepare turned out to be a good distraction as it kept me focused.

Several minutes before 11:00, I poked my head out from behind the folding screen and peeked at the mourners. The shore-dwellers, as the town folks knew them, had collected in front of the window wall. Men in dark suits and the women in silk and wool. Kitty could have easily been a part of that group, but she stood in the center aisle where the townies had gathered, wearing an assortment of sports jackets, pant suits, and skirt-sets.

At the far end of the ballroom, Marc stood next to the podium shaking hands with a dark-haired woman. A craggy-faced man with a thatch of gray hair stood off to the side. By his Western-cut suit jacket and the cowboy hat he held, the couple had to be Ramón's sister, and her ex-roper, rich-rancher husband.

The animated conversation looked like it was going to continue awhile. I'd give anything to wander over and introduce myself, but my job waited for me on this side of the room. I reluctantly slipped behind the screen and surveyed the buffet table. Everything appeared in order, at least as far as it could until serving time.

Marc's voice came through an overhead speaker, asking everyone to sit. Muffled discussion and the scraping of chairs followed. He made a brief acknowledgment to Isabel and her family, and a moment later, Kendall Montclair spoke into the microphone.

Tuning out his litany of the organization's milestones for which he gave nominal credit to Ramón, I glanced at Ana, who stood at the table arranging the silverware. We'd raced through the morning prep so intently that I'd had no time to attempt another conversation. Maybe later during cleanup. I approached her and said, "I'm going for the salads. Be back in a jiffy."

Expressionless, she set down the forks and smoothed her cashmere sweater. "I'll go. You stay and listen." She grabbed an empty cart and headed toward the door. I pushed my puzzled thoughts about her detachment to the side and tuned in to Kendall's eulogy.

He droned on about Rescaté and how much he and his dad had contributed to where the organization was today. Still barely a word about the deceased. When he finally paused, I pictured him lifting his chin and running his eyes over the crowd. "I'm pleased to tell you that Rescaté's board of directors unanimously voted yesterday to keep Ramón's dream for Mexico alive. Beginning next month, we will invite corporate donors to sponsor some of Mexico's neediest children."

Spontaneous applause broke out.

"My family is proud to have a role in this endeavor..."

The man was as full of himself as he'd been in the past, and I'd had enough. I repositioned a bouquet of tulips on the table and looked up as Ana reappeared with the salads. With Kendall's dull monologue as a backdrop, we arranged the large glass bowls on the table.

On the other side of the screen, Kendall's eulogy ended, and Bob Cousins came to the mic. More boring Rescaté history. So little about Ramón as a person. Why didn't Ana go up there and tell us all the things she'd loved about him? Maybe they'd lost the romantic love they'd shared, but at a time like this, did it matter? Maybe it didn't, and Kitty was right about her being a suspect in a murder I wasn't sure happened. I signaled I was going for the green beans. She gave a slight nod and continued tossing a salad.

When I returned, a string-quartet played a soft Beethoven piece. A welcome respite from the self-serving eulogies. Across from the buffet table, Ana rested against the wall, staring straight ahead. The amount of emotion the woman displayed could have been stuffed in a thimble with room to spare. Difficult for me to understand since I couldn't harness my emotions anymore than a wild wind could be contained by anyone other than God.

I set the beans on the table and peeked around the screen. Candy sat four rows from the front, her jaw working her chewing gum. I doubted Beethoven was her music of choice, but she could have shown a little more decorum. I stifled a smile. What could one expect from a woman who wore skirts the size of dishtowels?

There I went again. I had to stop the judge act. Look for the positive. I zeroed in on Candy again and noticed the stylish navy dress she wore. Appropriate for the day.

From her seat in the back row, Kitty caught my eye and held up a small notebook before turning her attention toward the musicians. Good heavens. Was she taking notes on the so-called suspects during the funeral service? I hoped no one noticed. Edging behind the divider, I tiptoed over to Ana and whispered her name.

Her eyes popped open. "I'm sorry. Did you need me?"

"We should get the casseroles. Marc's about to speak, and he's the last one on the program." I'd never admit it to her, but I wanted to be back in time to hear him.

We each took a cart and got the chicken dishes set on the table within record time. As I lit the Sterno flame under the last of the four pans, Marc's voice filled the air. I slipped over to Ana's side. "Can you take care of the beverages?"

With hardly a nod she headed out the door. I was half-tempted to run after her and squeeze whatever she had stuffed inside right out of her. It wasn't healthy being bottled up like that. But then I'd miss Marc's speech.

"I never expected to be here eulogizing the man who believed in me when others didn't." Marc's statement pulled me out of my thoughts. "I owe a great deal to Ramón. The past year working for him has been invaluable to me." His voice cracked.

An ache pressed against my lungs, and I wanted to kick myself. I'd been so focused on our nonrelationship and the rumors, Marc's grief had blown right past me. As soon as I had an opportunity, I'd make it up to him. An empty apology didn't seem enough. Would a sympathy card be appropriate?

Wings flapped above my head. I shut my eyes, afraid to look.

❧ 20 ❧

A collective gasp came from the other side of the divider.

I darted around the screen.

Like a feathered dive-bomber, Pedro propelled his colorful body over the mourners' heads, his call reverberating throughout the room. He looped a figure-eight in the air, then arced to land on top of a loudspeaker.

Bob Cousins jumped up and scrambled to catch his balance, nearly falling over a blue-haired lady in front of him. He approached the show bird like a tomcat stalking a sparrow and stuck out his arm. "Come on, boy."

Pedro raised his beak and screeched. Bob grabbed for the bird's leg, but he was already airborne and coming my direction. "Somebody get Karl." Bob's stage-whispered order was almost drowned out by the gasps.

Pedro whooshed past me and landed on the top of the folding screen. I inched closer and extended my hand. "Come on, Pedro. Come to me."

He cocked his head and stared at me as if to say, "Last time I came to you, I ended up back in the pokey."

I glanced over my shoulder. The silent cry for help in Marc's eyes made me wish I'd kept looking at the bird. Something had to be done, but what? Would he come for a lettuce leaf as readily as a cracker?

Pedro squawked and flapped his wings. I stepped closer, using a sing-song voice, but he took off and circled the air space before coming to a perfect landing on Marc's head. He puffed out his green chest and blurted, "What's for breakfast?"

Chuckles filled the room.

Marc gripped the lectern, his clenched jaw muscle pulsing so hard I thought it would burst through his skin. Pedro chattered a string of unintelligible sounds, while beneath his claws Marc's face turned the color of a tomato. "Someone get Karl Murray."

"He's on the way." a man called out.

Bob Cousins guffawed. "Thorne, the bird definitely adds to your appearance."

Someone let out a snort. In the back row, a woman was laughing so hard she couldn't sit straight. Like a rolling tide, the wave of giggles and snickers picked up momentum.

Above the din, the bird called out, "Pedro is a good boy." Had he been able, he would've flashed a grin and taken a bow. He was a show bird. If Marc had a tiny hoop in his back pocket, the parrot would have jumped through it.

Marc chuckled as he tossed his notes over his shoulder. "Seems Pedro wants to be a part of his master's memorial."

Taking it in stride, Pedro preened himself.

I glanced at the door. Where was our bird handler?

As if reading my thoughts, a guilty-looking Karl appeared in the entrance, holding an empty cage. The room went quiet. Eyes focused straight ahead, he ambled toward Marc, his polished black boots clomping on the hardwood floor.

Pedro hopped into the cage without hesitation. Of course, the proffered Ritz cracker Karl held out helped. He snapped the door shut, then marched toward the exit as Pedro called out, "Ana loves you."

"Let's conclude the formal portion of our service by moving through the French doors to the patio," Marc said. "Everyone's invited to return at 12:15 for a buffet that April Love, our chef, has prepared."

All eyes followed Marc's gesture made in my direction. Did I actually hear someone hum that song? At a funeral? I pushed out a smile and gave a tiny wave. We needed to get those hors d'oeuvres out and circulating fast. I headed behind the screen.

Ana slammed a tray onto the table. Shrimp toast flew in every direction. "Even from the grave he taunts me."

"Ana? Are you okay?" Dumb question. I gathered the toast squares, grateful that most looked intact.

She reached for a piece I'd missed. "Ramón assured me he'd disposed of that awful parrot."

"What?"

"I wouldn't allow that thing in my house."

"Ana, everyone thinks *you* gave Pedro to Ramón."

She faced me, her dark eyes burning. "You think I'd buy Ramón a bird and teach him to say Ana loves you?"

"Why would he say you gave Pedro to him?"

"Because he was a terrible man. I'll get the other appetizers." She whacked the serving cart with her hand, and it careened toward the door. Catching the cart by its handle, she pushed it into the hall.

One bird got more of a rise out of her than anyone else had all day. As much as I wanted to tell Kitty she wasn't a suspect, how could I after that display?

❧ 21 ❧

I stood behind the serving table as a pair of little boys swooped in and confiscated the last two pieces of cherry-upside-down cake. They dashed off, their polished oxfords skidding on the shiny wood floor. Was it necessary to go for the remaining cake back in the kitchen?

I surveyed the room. Some people had left, but many still lingered, most freed of their dirty dishes. No need for more dessert unless someone asked.

Seated next to the windows, their figures silhouetted against the bright sun, Kitty held court with a mustached man. As she waved her arms to make a point, he pulled a small notebook from a pocket and flipped it open. He couldn't have jotted down more than a word because in a flash the spiralbound pad was back where it came from.

"Great meal, April."

I pivoted.

Marc stood several feet away with Isabel and her husband. A woman sporting a short, spiky hairstyle stood next to them.

"This is Isabel and James Lynch, and Flavia Hernandez," Marc said. "Isabel is Ramón's sister, and Flavia is their cousin."

I took in Isabel's upturned nose, diamond stud earrings, and the cluster of rocks on her ring finger. Her husband stood silent next to her, cowboy hat clutched in his hand like a security blanket. Seeing him close up, with his leathered complexion, he appeared much older than she. Too many days on the range must do that to a guy.

I nodded at Flavia, whose gold hoop earrings and simple black dress stood in stark contrast to her cousin. While I offered my hand to Isabel, I tried to gauge if her height was close to the same as the orange-capped person and hating myself for even thinking of it. "I'm sorry about your loss."

She laid a cold hand against my palm. "Thank you." Ana had met her match when it came to emotionless demeanor. Did Ramón do that to the women in his life?

"I see someone I need to speak to." Marc brushed a hand over my shoulder. "Carry on for me?" He headed off across the room.

My gaze flicked from one expressionless face to the next before settling on Isabel. "I only met Ramón a short time before he died. He seemed like a lovely man."

She gave a slight roll of the eyes. "My brother could be nice when he wanted—"

"April, I'm so sorry I missed that scrumptious-looking dessert." Flavia stared at the empty cake platter as though she'd missed out on a six-course meal from Spiaggia.

Isabel grabbed her husband's arm. "James, I want you to meet the Ingleharts. I can't believe they're here."

In an instant, Isabel was off, weaving between chairs with her husband in tow, not to mention my missed opportunity.

By now the crowd had thinned to a few clusters of people. Ana, with an untouched platter of food on her lap, sat next to Rosa. It didn't appear that anyone was interested in a second helping of dessert. I turned to Flavia. "I still have some cherry-upside-down cake in the kitchen. Would you like to have some there?"

Her face brightened. "I'd love to."

By the time we reached the kitchen, we were talking recipes like girlfriends and continued our chat while I cut two generous slices of cake. After pouring cups of coffee, I took a seat next to her.

She forked a bite and popped it in her mouth while I did the same.

"April, this cake is absolutely divine."

I let my own mouthful, which included a huge cherry, resonate on my tongue. If I didn't mind saying so, with this dessert I'd scored big, as Karl liked to say about the bulls he rode. I sipped my coffee. "I want to offer my condolences. Losing a cousin can be as painful as losing a sibling. I'm sure Isabel appreciates your support."

Flavia waved her fork. "Thanks, but if Isabel hadn't already been in Chicago, I doubt she'd have come and neither would I." She speared another bite and put it in her mouth. "Is it inappropriate to ask for the recipe? We have my niece's christening coming up in a couple week—"

"Not a problem." I pulled a notebook from my pocket and tore off a blank page. "Jot down your phone number and e-mail if you have one. I'll get it to you later. I'm sure Isabel will be glad in retrospect that she came today."

Flavia stirred cream into her coffee. "I doubt it. Ramón threatened more than once to reveal her past to James. It would have ruined her marriage. Ramón's death has made my cousin a happy woman." She continued to work on her cake as though it were her last meal.

This information didn't sound good, but happy didn't mean automatic murderer. "She and James seemed content a few minutes ago."

"That's because he doesn't know the truth," she said around a mouthful of cherry topping. "Isabel can't risk his finding out. Too much money is at stake. Lots of money."

"Was the secret that bad?"

"I've already said too much." She scraped her fork across the plate, gathering up the last bits of syrup. "I can't say anymore."

"I shouldn't have asked. Did you like Ramón?"

She pushed the slip of paper containing her contact information in my direction. "We didn't see much of each other. He was involved here, and I have my 12-year-old daughter to raise. Marisol is with her father today. She wants to spend more time with him, but he always has an excuse." She shook her head. "Constantly giving me a hard time. Why? You'd think he'd be glad to help his only daughter. Those boys of his always come first."

I offered a sympathetic smile. "Men can be infuriating, can't they?" Sliding off the stool, I retrieved my purse from a drawer and found an old business card. I scratched a line through its front and scribbled my cell number on the back before handing it to her. "Feel free to call if I don't get the recipe to you in time." A niggle of guilt pressed against my heart. What would it take to jot the instructions down for her? But if I did that, I'd lose my excuse to stay in contact. And it appeared she was my only connection to Isabel. As much as I hated the thought, if Marc were ever falsely accused, I needed to be ready.

She took the card and dropped it in her bag.

"So, Isabel was already in Chicago when Ramón passed. Even though they were at odds, I'm sure it must have been a comfort to have you with her when she got the news."

Flavia gathered her dish and cup and took them to the sink. "Actually, she was at a hotel downtown. I, um, wasn't with her that morning."

"Oh. Well, no doubt she'll be relieved when Ramón is buried and she can move on."

"She's considering cremation."

I willed my feet to move toward the door. "Well, I suppose that's best. I'm so glad we met."

Flavia followed and we stepped into the hall. "I'm glad too."

We parted company when we reached the ballroom. By then only a couple people remained, but not Kitty. I itched to call her, but I had no time. Ana was waiting to start the cleanup.

❧

Ana wiped her hands on a kitchen towel and returned it to the rack next to the sink. "If there's nothing more you need, I'll head home." Her indifferent tone reflected the demeanor she'd displayed all day except for the meltdown over the parrot, but I was so exhausted I couldn't have cared less if she'd suddenly danced around the kitchen with castanets.

"Go ahead. I can't thank you enough for all your help."

She slung a store bag that contained her soiled work clothes over her shoulder and headed for the door.

"Ana?"

She turned on her stiletto heel. "Yes?"

Seeing her deadpan face with only one moving part—her mouth— I felt like I was conversing with a ventriloquist dummy. "I know this week has been difficult, even if you and Ramón weren't still involved. You have my deepest sympathies."

"What happened to Ramón wasn't anything I didn't warn him about. I need to check the volunteer schedule; then I'm out of here." She disappeared into the hall with only her exotic fragrance left hanging in the air.

I wanted to shrug off her odd behavior to a personality quirk, but how could I with a remark like that? Warn him of what? Overeating, or that if he didn't watch his back, he was going to be killed?

I crossed to the pantry to put away the last of the supplies, but Marc's megawatt grin stopped me cold.

I raised my brows. "You look mighty cheerful for a guy who attended his boss's funeral."

His smile faded a few watts. "Just relieved to have gotten through the day. Thanks for all your help."

"My pleasure." I untied my apron and flung it over a stool. "And now I can't wait for a good soak in Kitty's spa tub. You must be exhausted, too."

He grabbed my hand and pulled me into a hug, pressing my head against his chest. "I should be, but I'm going on adrenalin. Kendall told me that the board has appointed me interim director."

"That's wonderful," I muttered into his dress shirt.

He repositioned us into a dance position and waltzed me around the room. "God answered my prayers. It's only interim for now, but who knows what lies down the road?" He stopped dancing and released my hair clip. My tangles fell to my shoulders in what I imagined resembled a squirrel's nest.

"There," he said. "Much better." He twirled me around and pressed his cheek to mine. I half expected him to start the Argentine Tango, but after another whirl, he stopped, a silly grin still filling his features.

Where was the grief I'd seen earlier? Or, for that matter, the vulnerable Marc from yesterday when I'd told him about the rumor? This guy seemed too much like the old Marc. The one who ended our relationship in favor of his drive for success.

"Come on." He released me and reached for my jacket where it hung on a peg. "I'll walk you back to your aunt's, and we can talk on the way. Maybe go out for a bite to celebrate."

What happened to my need for a bubble bath? "Does your promotion mean we don't need to be cautious about being seen together?"

He held my jacket open for me. "Hadn't thought about it. I didn't think he meant we couldn't be together away from the office. Did you?"

I turned and slipped my arms into the jacket sleeves. "No. But I wondered with you coming in here and dancing me around and all."

"Good." He arranged my jacket over my shoulders, then spun me around to face him.

I kept my eyes focused on a shirt button that was up close and personal with my cheek. "Marc, I think I'd rather go home to Kitty's for that soak I mentioned. I'm beat."

He stared at me as though I'd said I had a date with the latest celebrity heartthrob. "That the only reason, or are you thinking about those rumors again?"

"Mostly tired, but I don't want you to get in trouble. With the gossip, maybe it's best not to create fodder."

Marc raised his eyes skyward. *"Mi caramela,* I'm not worried, so don't you worry. It's unfounded. The funeral is over. Tomorrow we get back to normal around here."

His words hit my heart like a saber. Normal around Rescaté didn't necessarily include an in-house chef. My days could be dwindling to a precious few. Tomorrow I'd ask for clarification on my job status. For now, that spa tub was calling my name.

He pulled me back into a hug. "Go ahead on home and relax. We can celebrate tomorrow night."

I waited in the kitchen door until he rounded the corner toward his office. Over the past couple days, I'd been tempted to admit he'd become the changed man Kitty claimed him to be, but now I wasn't sure. I wiggled out of my jacket and tossed it on a stool before heading for the pantry to make sure it was in order for tomorrow. No time to mull over Marc's idiosyncrasies. I'd save it for tub time.

"April. You still here?"

I shoved a canister of Panko breadcrumbs on the bottom shelf. "I'm in here."

Ana came into the pantry. "Good heavens, after today I thought you'd be home soaking your feet. I want to talk to you."

I wanted to say, "Who are you, and what did you do with Ana?" Instead, I said, "Let's chat out there."

We stepped into the kitchen and exchanged awkward glances. I indicated one of the barstools. "Care to sit?"

Ana shook her head. "I wanted to apologize for my temper tantrum this afternoon."

What was going on? First Marc reverts to the person he was before, and now Ana shows me a side I didn't know existed. A woman with heart. I stepped over to a drawer and took out my purse. "What temper tantrum? Never saw one."

Ana's smile belied the coldness in her eyes. Scratch the heart part.

"Thanks for understanding. If you're leaving, I'll walk out with you."

"Sure." Feeling in my gut she had more to say than what was meeting my ears, I grabbed my jacket and flicked off the pantry light.

We reached the parking lot without saying a word. Her, gliding on those heels with the grace of a ballerina, and me, slogging along in my clogs. "Ana, was there something more you wanted to say?"

She stopped beside a silver Lexus and stared at it. "That's all, other than that I enjoyed working with you." She opened the door and slid onto the leather driver's seat. "Nice meeting you, April. I'll probably see you around Rescaté."

I didn't move until her red taillights disappeared behind the trees on Shore Drive. Now, if someone would show up and tell me what that was all about.

༻ 22 ༼

After my soak, I donned pajamas and a robe and padded downstairs. I found Kitty curled in her favorite chair in the sunroom reading *Poisons That Kill: A Mystery Writer's Guide.*

"Writing murder mysteries these days?"

"It occurred to me that mystery writers have to learn about poisons, and what better way to investigate Ramón's possible murder than to act as if I'm writing a story? At least that's what I led Mavis Dorfler at the library to believe."

I groaned as I settled into a chair. "It's not like you to fib."

She raised her chin. "I implied. She's always got her nose in someone's business, and the last thing I want is her meddling in mine. I thought she'd direct me to a book on poisons, but she gave me this instead. I'm only on the first couple pages. No new information yet." She let the book slide to the floor and lifted a china teapot off the maple end table. "Cinnamon Spice. Want some?" She held the spout over an empty cup.

I nodded.

She poured the tea, then set the teapot down. "Kendall was a little full of himself today, but what can you expect from a Montclaire? He certainly proves that the tree isn't far from the apple."

"The apple doesn't fall far from the tree."

She waved a hand. "Whatever."

"Getting back to the Montclaires, Parker couldn't have been all bad. He donated the property to Rescaté." I picked up my tea and sipped.

Kitty harrumphed. "And made sure his son stayed on as president."

I startled, sending my teacup rattling on its saucer. "Parker stipulated Kendall be board president?"

"You heard me."

"President forever?" I took another sip, letting the hot liquid soothe as it went down.

"Only five years. This is year two."

"Has he done a good job?"

"Would they say he'd done anything but?" She set her cup on the end table. "I'd loved to have seen Pedro land on Kendall's head instead of Marc's and mess his ever-so-perfect hair. I've always wondered if he hasn't gotten implants. His hairline used to go much further back."

I chuckled at the vision Kitty's remark conjured up.

My aunt's grin lit up the room like a spotlight. "Pedro landing on Marc's head was perfect. He got a little flustered, but after all the self-serving eulogies, we needed a little levity."

A memory of Marc's egotistical attitude a short time ago flashed through my mind. Not wanting to endure Kitty's defending him at the moment, I chose to not mention it.

"On a more serious note, did you learn anything more about Ana?"

Kitty's question drew me back to reality and those awful rumors. I shared about the former fiancée's burst of anger and that despite his saying she'd given him the bird, he'd actually bought the creature for her even when she didn't like birds.

Kitty scowled. "Why would he give Ana a bird if she doesn't like them?"

"Good question. Maybe to push her hot button. Ana made a special trip back to the kitchen after she left and apologized for losing her temper, but it seemed insincere. She's very closed. I so wanted to be able to cross her off the list, but I can't yet."

Kitty grabbed the service program from the coffee table and studied it. "What about the sister. Did you have a chance to meet her?"

"Only briefly, but her cousin, Flavia, chatted with me over dessert in the kitchen. I learned what caused the rift between Isabel and her brother. Ramón threatened to reveal a dark secret about her to her husband. Something bad enough it could cause her marriage to end. I also found out that Isabel has been staying in a Chicago Loop hotel since she's been here."

Kitty pursed her lips. "Then she had opportunity to drive up here and leave poisoned pills without her cousin knowing her exact whereabouts. The question is, does she have entry into Rescaté, as well as the apartment? She doesn't live here, and they weren't getting along."

"Aren't you making a big jump to assume Ramón was poisoned with those pills I found?"

She picked up a paperback book from the side table and opened it to where a marker had been placed. "Something similar happened in this story. The sleuth is a housekeeper and always gets mixed up in unsolved murders that happen to her clientele. A wealthy lady was found murdered, and it turned out her stepson wanted her out of the way. He was estranged from his father and had no key to the home. The sleuth discovered that he lifted a key from his sister's key ring in the middle of the night, went to one of those 24-

94

hour superstores and had a copy made. The key was returned before she even missed it."

She closed the book and lifted her chin like a proud child who'd won the spelling bee. "If she didn't have a key, Isabel could have done something like that."

"You've been reading too many of those mysteries. Whose key would Isabel have copied? Flavia wouldn't have had one. And how could she have copied a key card to get in the front door?"

She picked up her teacup and frowned into it. "I hadn't thought that far."

"Doesn't matter. Assuming your idea about the poisoned pills is true, my guess is that she did have access to the mansion and Ramón's apartment with a card and key from before they fought. If the code hasn't been changed since then, or the key, then there's our answer. *If* any of this happened at all."

"You and the person in the orange cap collided at the mansion door around six-thirty. If that was Isabel, she could have been back in the Loop without being missed."

I sighed. "With plenty of time to make a business appointment." Everything seemed surreal. Reconnecting with Marc, Ramón's sudden death, rumors of murder and Marc being accused. I felt creepy even discussing it. Was it only a week ago I got the call from Kitty about the chef job? It seemed like a year.

"So Isabel remains a suspect. What about the others?"

I gave Kitty a blank stare. "Which others?"

"The others we talked about. Do you think they would have access to the apartment?"

"I doubt Candy would have access to Ramón's apartment unless she snatched a key from his administrative assistant's desk and made a copy. Ana's the most likely since she was his fiancé." I winced. "There's one more suspect I hesitate to name because, despite his tendency to gossip, I like the guy."

"Who?"

"Karl, the handyman."

"That nice young man who came for the parrot? Why suspect him?"

"He's a bull rider on weekends. I overheard him on the phone making what sounded like a bet on a rodeo. I've been mulling that over ever since you mentioned the blackmail possibility. What if Ramón was blackmailing Karl, threatening to let the rodeo people know? It would kill his career. He has access to every room in the mansion and is about the same height as the person who ran me down. Maybe he's trapped. Had to keep betting to pay off Ramón. He's the one who told me about the rumor that Marc is supposed to have killed Ramón." I sighed. "I've gotten to know him the past couple days. He's a nice guy. At least on the surface."

Kitty chewed her lip. "Did you see Marc before you left the mansion?"

I shrugged. "Yes, and I wish I hadn't. He's been promoted to interim director, and he couldn't stop gloating. Came by the kitchen after the service."

"I wouldn't let Marc's rejoicing over the appointment bother you. It was probably a spontaneous reaction."

Irritation ripped at my gut. I knew I shouldn't have mentioned his promotion, so why did I? What had happened to the aunt who'd been so furious with Marc the day he dumped me? Now it seemed as far as she was concerned, he could do no wrong.

Her eyes sparkled. "I was young and in love once. And what a rollercoaster ride Daniel's and my courtship was. One day up and the next day down. But the bottom line was that we loved each oth—"

"I'm not in love with Marc and have no intention of being in that sorry state again."

She exhaled loudly. "Why can't you give him another chance? Eight years is a long time, April. People change."

I crossed my arms and fixated on a potted palm across the room. No way was I going to tell her how many times that thought had skittered around in my brain. No matter how often I'd tried to trap it and push it away, it returned. "How can I think about going back to him when he won't explain why the very thing that broke us up never happened?"

"Have you forgiven him, April?"

Tears teased my eyes. "I thought I did until I saw him again. It's a little hard to forgive without an apology."

"Eight years is a long time to hold a grudge."

"I'm not holding a grudge. Fact is fact. He loved his precious goal sheet more than he loved me. Now he's back in my life with nothing to show for having left me almost standing at the altar, and he's unwilling to say why. The hurt is still there."

"Seems to me I remember you saying he did apologize the other day. Even God gives us second chances. It's time to forgive him."

Her words poked holes in my defenses like shrapnel. Wounded, but not done in, I stood. "I'm going for a walk."

"In your pajamas?"

I glanced at my robe. "I'm dressed. Besides, there's no one out there."

Kitty's face revealed concern. "Sit. There's something else I need to tell you."

❧ 23 ❧

I dropped back onto the chair. "If this is about Marc…"

Kitty kept her steady gaze pointed at her lap. "I was a bit of a blabbermouth today and told Police Chief Bronson about the capsules and the speculations about Ramón's death."

I felt the color drain from my face. "Kitty, it's one thing to hypothesize among ourselves, but to get the police involved? We have no proof any of the rumors are true."

She pulled a scalloped-edged hanky from her pocket and blew her nose. I got the feeling she was buying time to formulate an answer. "I'm scared, April. What if the rumors are true, and all of a sudden Marc is framed and hauled off to jail? The Bible says to be prepared in season and out of season."

"It also says to avoid mindless chatter. The chief must have laughed when you told him you were reporting rumors."

She wiped her nose with her handkerchief. "No. He asked me why we thought the pills you found were important, and I reminded him of those murders I told you about. Then he said I was reading too many mystery novels."

Relieve washed over me. "And I'm inclined to agree. So that was that?"

"Yes. After he reminded me Doc Fuller is the coroner and knows what he's talking about and that we'd best not be adding to the rumors, I assured him the pills were safely tucked away in a bag of sugar in the Rescaté pantry."

I almost fell off my seat. "How did you know where I hid them?"

"Dear, you told me. Don't you remember?"

I shook my head. "Doesn't matter now. We got sidetracked before I could mention the other thing I learned today. Isabel is considering cremation. I was upset at first, but maybe it's for the best. If he is cremated, then there won't be any way of determining if he was killed."

She stared at me through eyes as wide as the buttons on her sweater. "What are you doing sitting there? You need to get those pills."

"Why? The only people who know about them are you, Marc, and the police chief."

Kitty flew to her feet, her fists resting on her hips. "April Love, where is your sense of right and wrong? If there was a murder, that means a killer is still out there. If there wasn't, then it's better to err on the side of...of...I still can't remember the right word, but you know what I mean."

"Caution. It's better to err on the side of caution." Maybe it would be best to get them out of the pantry and off-site. "I'm on my way."

❧ ❧

After changing to jeans and a tee-shirt, I headed next door. At the beginning of the path leading through the pines, I hesitated. Even though the sun still hung on the horizon and the sky overhead remained a bluish hue, the overgrown trail was already saturated in darkness. If a killer were on the loose...

A shudder ran down my spine. "Okay, Lord, I know I'm being a bit childish. These are only pine trees, and I feel rather silly reacting to the rumor mill like this. I don't even like watching those gossip shows on TV. I'm sure there's no killer and that Ramón died of natural causes like the coroner said. But if collecting the pills puts my aunt's concerns at rest, I'll do it."

After an uneventful trek through the trees, I stepped onto Rescaté's plush lawn. Ahead, the mansion blazed orange in the setting sun's reflection. Other than the outside lamps on either side of the entrance providing a soft glow—hardly more than a couple candles' worth—no lights shone in the windows.

The parking lot stood naked in the glare of its overhead lights. What little bravado I had earlier drained out of me. I'd never been inside the mansion alone. Maybe this could wait until tomorrow. But if I didn't bring the pills back with me, my aunt wouldn't stop pestering. What she expected me to do with them, I had no idea. It wasn't like I could test them for poison myself. I marched across the grass, key card in hand.

I'd heard the phrase "the silence was deafening" many times, but never until I entered the dimly lit reception area had I understood its meaning. Even Pedro, who could usually be heard from the front door, was quiet. Shadows lurked in every corner. I had exactly 29 seconds to enter the code into the alarm before Canoga Lake's finest converged—all four of them. Not exactly how I wanted to meet Chief Bronson for the first time.

I darted through the security light's yellowish glare to the alarm box and punched in the numbers Marc had given me. A green light blinked an okay at the same time realization flashed in my brain. Ramón had said the alarm turned off at 6:30 a.m. I'd waited until then to head over to the mansion that Friday. The person I'd seen that morning must have known the alarm code...or they'd been in the building all night.

I gave myself a mental shake. Not exactly a newsflash, after all. Marc had conjectured the person was likely a Rescaté employee. Someone who would likely have the code.

Keycard still in hand, I stole across the room on my tiptoes and turned down the hall. Another safety light beamed from a spot past the kitchen door—the open kitchen door. Didn't I lock up when I left with Ana? An act so routine it would be easy to not remember doing it. But I was exhausted, and she did distract me. Was that on purpose?

My mouth feeling like I hadn't had water in days, I crept to the door and hit the light switch. The stainless-steel fridge gleamed, the counters shone, towels hung neatly on their rack by the window. Nothing out of place. Across the room a drawer protruded about an inch, and my lungs constricted. Another drawer wasn't flush either. I checked the towel drawer. Beneath it, a half dozen or so white towels lay scattered in a heap on the floor.

I flew across the room into the pantry. Sugar granules crunched beneath my rubber soles. I didn't have to look in the crumpled bag on the floor to know.

The pills were gone.

∼ 24 ∽

I tore down the shore path, my thoughts skittering through my brain like a dozen silver balls in a pinball machine. Did the person presume the pills were in the kitchen or did they spy on me? Did someone overhear my aunt telling the police chief they were hidden in the kitchen?

Already winded, I jogged up the hill and around the house where I dropped to the grass, my breath coming in short gasps. The only car in the circular driveway was mine. Kitty had already left for her Wednesday night Bible study.

I pushed to my feet and walked on rubbery legs toward the house. My cell phone was out of my pocket before I got to the door. I pressed the speed dial code for Marc.

"Hi, April. Change your mind about supper tonight?"

"Someone broke in the kitchen and took the pills."

"What?"

"I'm sure I locked the door, Marc. No, I'm not sure. Ana was talking to me and—"

"Where are you?"

"Standing by Kitty's back door."

"She home?"

"No. She's—"

"I'll be right there."

The line went dead. I'd wait outside until he got there. I glanced around the darkened lawn.

Maybe not.

∼∽

The screeching of tires on asphalt announced Marc's arrival, and I stopped pacing the kitchen. Before he had a chance to ring the bell, I flung the door open.

His eyes herk-jerked over my face, then he expelled a breath and gathered me into his arms. In the protective cocoon of his embrace, the adrenalin that had kept me functioning evaporated. I wrapped my arms around his waist, hoping we could stay that way for at least the next hour.

He squeezed me tighter. "You okay? You sounded terrified."

"I was out of breath from running when I called. Really, I'm doing fine."

He broke the hug and stood back, running his gaze over me, his eyes full of doubt. "The way you're shaking says otherwise. Stay here and lock the door. I'm going over there to check out the kitchen."

"I'm going with you."

"You don't need to. Once I see the damage for myself, I'll call the police. I don't want you there until we know it's safe."

I gritted my teeth and pushed past him. No way was he going back there without me. Rescaté may be his responsibility, but it was my kitchen that was invaded. "The door will lock behind you when you close it. Kitty has a key if she gets home first." Or if we didn't make it back ever.

Outside, Marc slammed the door and jiggled the handle.

He wanted to walk over, but I'd had enough of those pine trees for one night. We set off in his Escape with a question nudging the edge of my thoughts: *Should I have called the police first?*

We arrived at Rescaté, and Marc slid the flashlight beam over the grounds. Nothing out of order. Once we were inside, he motioned me to wait by the door while he reset the alarm. That done, he threw the main light switch and the crystal chandelier sparkled to life. Was that a good idea? Maybe so. Evil loved darkness and hated the light.

He pointed to the hall and mouthed, "Let's go."

A moment later, my throat went dry for the second time that evening. "I left the door open, Marc." I blurted out my words, forgetting to whisper. "I know I did. I was too scared to stop long enough to lock it." My lips trembled.

Marc tugged me to his side. "Let's see what's inside." He pulled a handkerchief from his pocket and turned the doorknob. Locked. He raised his keycard to the electronic pad.

I grabbed his arm. "Maybe they're in there." I glanced over my shoulder toward the reception room. "Or anywhere in this place."

"We can't not do something." He put his ear to the door. "Nothing," he mouthed.

I pressed my ear against the wood and only heard silence. Would anyone be dumb enough to make noise after hearing people in the hall? But only an idiot would hang around waiting to be caught. The person was probably miles away by now.

He raised his brows is if to say, "Okay?"

I nodded, and he waved the card. The lock clicked, and in a slow, deliberate movement he pushed the door open and aimed his flashlight into the room. Blocked by his shoulder, I couldn't see a thing. I was about to move around him when he said, "Stay back, April." He took a step and shot the beam into the open pantry. "Hit the lights."

I flicked the switch, and the overhead fluorescent lights came to life.

Seeing nothing unusual, I stepped in, my rubber soles squeaking on the freshly mopped floor. Were we in a movie? If we were, this was one flick that would get no thumbs-up from me. "They cleaned it up."

I crossed to a drawer, taking robot-like steps, and pulled it open. Towels lay folded and stacked as though straight from the dryer. From there I moved to the open pantry door and stared at the floor. I hauled in a breath and pointed at the tiles. "The bag the pills were hidden in was right there in the middle of a pile of sugar."

I wiped my tears away with the back of my hand. Had someone slipped me a hallucinogenic drug? Was I so overtired I couldn't think straight? No. The place had been a wreck a half hour ago. "I'm not crazy, Marc. It really happened."

His arms came around me from behind, and he pressed his mouth close to my ear. "I may not have believed the rumors before, but I do now. Whoever did this knows that without evidence of a break-in, the police can't do much." He paused. "Still, we need to call them. Let's go back to Kitty's and do it from where it's safer."

I faced him and pressed my head against his chest. His heart's staccato beat belied the calmness in his voice. We needed to get out of there. This dream kitchen had morphed into a nightmare.

Despite Marc's comforting grip on my hand as he drove one-handed back to Kitty's, I couldn't wait to get inside. I led the way into the kitchen, then went to the wall phone and grabbed the receiver. "The direct number to the Canoga Police is below the keypad, but before you call, you need to know Kitty told Chief Bronson about the pills today, and the rumors."

Marc grimaced as he took the phone but said nothing. I crossed to the fridge and grabbed a couple bottles of water.

He punched in the number. "This is Marc Thorne from Rescaté de Niño. April Love, the Rescaté chef, found our kitchen ransacked about an hour ago. Some pills she'd hidden in the pantry are missing." He listened a moment. "Well, no. She found the door unlocked and drawers pulled open, their contents tossed on the floor. The pills were in a bag of sugar in the pantry." Another pause. "No. Nothing illegal. They were over-the-counter pills that Kitty McPiper spoke to Chief Bronson about. Can you send an officer out

ASAP?"

His jaw pulsed. "I don't care how many guys you have on duty. This is an emergency. The thief already has disturbed things. April came to her aunt's next door to Rescaté and called me. We went over there. Everything's wiped spotless."

He caught my gaze and shook his head. "Yes," he said into the mouthpiece. "I agree. She should've called you first, but you know how it is when you've had a shock."

He rocked back on his heels. Things weren't looking good. "Fine. We'll be in touch with Chief Bronson tomorrow." His thumb hit the *Off* button. "Nice to know how well we're protected. There's only two guys on duty—the one I spoke to and the other officer, who's checking out a domestic disturbance. Since we have no evidence of breaking and entering, he suggested I call Bronson later."

He pulled me into his arms. *"Mi caramela,* you're shaking."

I didn't realize I was until he said it. I wrapped my arms around his waist. "When are we going to wake up from this crazy dream? That's all it is, right?"

He ran his palm up and down my back a couple times. "Wish it were."

I stepped back and studied his face. "It doesn't seem we can keep laughing at those rumors or ignoring them. Someone took those pills for a reason—to scare me or to keep them from being tested."

"Who knew where they were hidden other than Kitty and the chief?"

"Only me and Kitty until this afternoon, when she told Bronson."

A frown creased his forehead. "I saw her and Bronson talking quite a bit during lunch. A lot of people milled around them. Someone could have overheard."

"Who? Do you remember?"

A moment passed. "Sorry. I don't."

I stepped back and handed him his water. "Why don't I nuke some leftover soup and throw a couple salads together? You can help by getting rolls from that bag on the counter."

We worked in silence as I got the soup into the microwave and dumped romaine from a cellophane bag into salad bowls.

Marc set a wholegrain roll on each of the wood trays I'd found. "You always did turn to food in stressful times. Don't know how I forgot that. The lasagna you usually made before finals was the best. Maybe if I'd had you around in Cali—"

I looked up from slicing a tomato. Marc's lips were cemented into a thin line. "If I'd been in California, what?"

"It wasn't important."

"Try me."

"Maybe with your lasagna I'd have done better on my master's thesis. Only got a B on that."

My stare bore into him. "If you assume I'm buying that explanation, you must think I've become the epitome of a dumb-blond joke."

He closed the space between us and wrapped his arms around my rigid body. "I really didn't do well on that thesis. Spent the night before it was due wolfing down cardboard pizza and slurping high-caffeine soft drinks. If I'd had some of your cooking, I have done a whole lot better."

My spine relaxed. "No doubt you would have, but even if Wolfgang Puck had laid out a full-course meal for you every night, I don't think it would have been enough to sway you from your goal. What did, Marc?"

He pulled me closer. "Realizing it wasn't right for me." He released me. "Come on. Let's eat."

We carried our meals to the sunroom and sat side by side on the couch. He prayed a blessing over the food, then we dove into our suppers. For a while, there was only the occasional *clink* of spoons hitting the bowls.

Then, his bowl still half full, Marc rested his spoon on the tray and sat back.

I glanced in his direction. "Finished already?"

He shrugged. "Not as hungry as I thought."

I dragged a carrot through my broth with the spoon. "What you said in your eulogy today made me realize you're grieving over Ramón's death, too. I've been so focused on the gossip, I didn't take that into account. I'm sorry."

A half-smile softened his features. "Thanks. Truthfully, I'm not sure how I feel. Ramón was a complicated guy. As long as he wasn't crossed, he'd fight for you to the end. But once betrayed, he never forgot." He dropped the remainder of his bread onto the tray. "I prayed for him all the time, but he never changed."

"So you didn't get along with him either?"

"We had our moments." He slid his tray onto the coffee table. "Before I forget, my mom's sending you some Argentine cookbooks. I told her you were Rescaté's new chef, and she's excited. She always loved you."

A warm, soothing sensation came over me. Gabriela Thorne had always called me the daughter she never had, and I'd looked forward to having such a godly woman for a mother-in-law. Although my mom and I always had a good relationship, the tension between Dad and me often put her in the middle. Avoiding Dad usually meant avoiding Mom, too. I'd only spoken to her once since arriving in Canoga Lake to tell her about Marc's working at Rescaté and that I'd gotten the job. All she said was, "Be careful." I pulled my thoughts out of the past. "I loved your mom, too. I've missed her almost as much as…" I snapped my mouth shut.

Marc reached his arm across my shoulders and nudged me closer. "As much as what?"

I inched my head away. "As much as the kids we knew at college."

"One rather dumb kid in particular?"

His breath tickled my ear, nearly sending my sensibilities into oblivion. I needed to move before we ended up repeating that kissing scene in the Apple's parking lot. Sharing supper, talking about his mom, being snuggled into the crook of his arm fit like pieces of a puzzle. Too much. I scooted to the edge of the cushion, then set my tray next to his and stood. "Want more iced tea?"

Marc let out a loud sigh. "Sure."

~ 25 ~

With drinks in hand, I returned to the sunroom and sat, leaving a cushion width between us. "How many people know the alarm code?"

He tossed the magazine he'd been flipping through onto the table. "Me, Cousins, Karl, the board, and you. Ramón may have given it to others."

"What about Ana or Isabel?"

"Maybe Ana. I don't know why Isabel would have it. She wasn't around."

"It's never been changed since Ana and Ramón broke up?"

"It's been the same since I started a year ago, but the code will be changed first thing tomorrow." He pulled his phone from his breast pocket.

I couldn't drag my eyes away as he tapped out a note on the tiny screen. The set of his jaw, the dark hair cut just long enough to allow a lock to drop over his forehead an inch or so when it wasn't gelled, the full lips, and those nearly black eyes stirred up delicious flutters in my stomach. Aside from his good looks, Marc had his faults, but there was so much more that was good about him, especially now. His interest in helping kids at church, his concern for the staff at work, and a new tenderness that hadn't been there in the past. His earlier display of haughtiness was probably a knee-jerk reaction after all the stress.

He returned the phone to his pocket and looked up. His eyes seemed to search mine as he brought his head closer to mine, his mouth coming within inches of my lips. Lips that ached to feel his once more. Another kiss would propel us even further into the kind of relationship my heart wanted, but my brain wasn't ready to accept.

I tilted away. "How many employees have keycard access to all the doors in Rescaté?"

His head shot back so fast he probably got whiplash. "Officially, the three of us who were directly under Ramón, along with Karl and Gerald Claypool."

"Gerald who?"

"Claypool. Since he's the board member living closest to Rescaté, he has access to everything."

A vision of a large jowly man I met at the board lunch popped into my mind. "I remember him. What happens if a staff member needs to work overtime? Are they given the alarm code?"

"That's up to their bosses."

"If someone uses the code, is it recorded at the alarm company?"

"Dunno. That's always been Bob Cousins' area—until tomorrow." He twisted his body toward me. "Let's change the subject. The police aren't interested in any of this, and I'm not either right now." He slipped his arm around my waist and tugged me against him. "I've been thinking how I've missed those times we'd talk after dinner, solving all the world's problems."

Not seeming to notice how, at his last remark, my spine went stiff as a starched shirt, he tousled my curls with his free hand. "Are you going to be able to sleep tonight with all the excitement?"

Which excitement was he referring to? The kitchen at Rescaté or what was happening right here? "Once my head hits the pillow, I'll be out. I'll make sure Kitty sets the security alarm tonight."

"Good. I don't want you losing sleep," he said in a near-whisper.

I grinned and quirked my head. "Why? So I can be awake enough to fix more goodies tomorrow?"

"What time you planning on starting?" He moved a strand of hair from my face, his fingertips brushing my skin like a feather. Tingles ran down my neck.

"Seven-thirty."

"I'll be there too."

"For that, you'll get an extra latte."

He nuzzled his nose into my curls. "Your hair smells like lilacs."

"It's the shampoo."

"Don't ever stop using it, babe." He pressed his face into my hair, then trailed his fingers through the locks.

My eyes fluttered shut. I'd forgotten how much I loved the sensation of him playing with my hair. Was that a kiss he just placed on my head? I pressed a palm against his chest and pushed myself upright. "We've got to stay focused."

"I am focused. On the woman I lost once and don't want to lose again."

"You won't lose me again, because I won't let you have me the way you did before."

Hurt clouded his eyes. "I'm not the same man. Haven't you noticed?"

"I've seen some change." I swallowed back the knob in my throat. Okay, so I fibbed again. Wasn't that better than being truthful and leading him to think I was ready to pick up where we left off?

"Just some?"

I shut my eyes to stop his smoldering gaze from searing my soul. "A little more than some, but it's not enough to—"

His lips brushed over mine, soft as a gentle breeze. "To what?"

"I forget."

"Good." He brought his warm lips to my mouth again, this time letting them linger. I let out a tiny groan, and my arm went around his neck as the kiss deepened. Even his kisses seemed better than before. We parted enough to breathe, lips still touching, then came back for more. He pulled away from my mouth and feathered my face with kisses. When we finally came apart, I stayed snuggled in his cozy hug, dizzy from the sudden explosion of pent-up emotions.

He tilted my chin upwards with a crook of his finger until our gazes met. "Time to stop the cat-and-mouse game, *mi caramela.* I still love you. I never stopped."

I blinked. As much as I wanted to be in the moment, say the words he was waiting to hear, my sensibilities wouldn't allow it.

He leaned in, ready to kiss me again. I strained against the pull in my heart and slid over, putting needed space between us. "This isn't very platonic."

Now it was his turn to stiffen. "I wasn't intending on platonic. Seemed for a minute there you weren't, either. Nor were you the other night."

Why wasn't he as confused as me? "I know. But we can't go there. We need to keep this to talking, or you'll have to leave."

He stared at the six inches of flowered chintz that separated us as if I'd dug a chasm as wide as the Mississippi. Maybe I had.

He raised his head and looked at me in frustration. "What's with you? One minute you act like you still love me and the next you're shoving me into the next county."

I pressed my face into my hands. "I don't know, Marc. All I know is that I can't love you. Not while I sense there's more to the California story than you're telling me. Maybe you should leave."

"I can't take off until Kitty gets home. The pill thief might still be around."

I forced a laugh. "Like Kitty could stop someone bent on hurting me." I moved to the chair. Sitting next to him only got me in trouble. Especially with the taste of his kisses still fresh on my lips. "Do you see your family very much?"

He blew air out through his nose with a loud puff. "I see Mom a couple times a year. Last Christmas, Steve and his wife came from Argentina. We had

108

a great time."

I came to the edge of my seat. "Your brother is married and living in Argentina?" I couldn't believe I hadn't asked about him until now.

"He married our cousin's best friend. They're expecting in September."

"I bet Argentina is beautiful."

"It is." Regret painted his features. "I planned to take you there, didn't I?"

"Yes." I glanced away. "Such are the dreams of youth."

Marc rested a hand on my arm. "I meant what I said before. Let's give God some time with us and see what happens."

A recurrent mental image of me in a wedding dress, walking across Kitty's lush green lawn to an arbor festooned with roses, the blue lake as the backdrop, and Marc waiting for me in his tuxedo, charged uninvited into my thoughts. Over the past several years I'd managed to tuck that vision away wherever unrequited dreams go. It was back, but without knowing what Marc was hiding, I wasn't sure I could trust him enough to love him again.

"How can I consider giving us another chance if you won't be honest with me?"

"How have I not been truthful?"

"Do I need to bring it up again?"

He rubbed the back of his neck with his left hand and stared at the floor. "I never told you how my dad drank himself to death the spring of our junior year—"

"Drank himself to death? I thought he died in a car crash."

He gulped hard and pushed to his feet before he walked to the window and stared out at the dark lake. "The car accident was his fault. There wasn't any slick spot on the road like we said. His precious bottle of whiskey was found on the seat beside him. Praise God he didn't hurt anyone else."

Talk about feeling left out of the loop. What else had he kept from me all those years we were together? And here I thought only eight years were missing. "So alcoholism retired him early, not some recurring virus like you said?"

"He did catch a bad virus in Argentina but nothing debilitating." He turned and caught my eye. "No one except my family knew about his drinking. Even then, we hardly spoke about it. The proverbial elephant in the room."

"When were you going to tell me?"

"I knew I'd have to when we married, but Mom asked me not to until then. We all wanted to believe he'd recover." His voice caught. "You don't remember the times I'd suddenly suggest we eat out instead of with my family?"

Chastened for my selfish reaction, I moved next to him and gripped his arm. "I'm so sorry, Marc. If I'd known about…"

"If you'd known, what could you have done? Dad controlled our lives, and he would have controlled yours, too." He gathered me closer, rubbing a circle on my back with his palm. "My pastor in California helped me see how Dad's alcohol problem contributed to my being so rigid and controlling with others. Those boys at church I work with—their parents attend the addiction ministry that meets there once a week. If I can help them avoid becoming like I was…"

I nuzzled my head under his chin as all the puzzling circumstances of the past resolved themselves. The times Paul Thorne didn't make it to parents' weekend or wasn't feeling well and stayed in the bedroom during my visit. Marc's vague answers one year when asked why he didn't make plans with his family for Father's Day. I wasn't the only one with a difficult father relationship.

"So, why didn't you get the doctorate?"

His hand still on my back stalled. "Does my having a PhD matter?"

I stepped back. "It did to you. Knowing about your father helps, but it doesn't explain why you didn't achieve your goal."

He edged away and turned his head.

"I have to know, Marc." By the time I said his name, I practically shouted it. "Other than God, our relationship must come first. I won't let you hurt me again."

He twisted around to meet my stare. "You didn't put me ahead of what you wanted. Made like Chicago was the only place to live. Then what do I hear a couple years later? You've moved to Atlanta. You'd go to Atlanta, but not California."

"I told you a hundred times why I needed to stay in Chicago. It was only two years. Would you have liked paying my dad back four years' worth of tuition bills? Not exactly a good way to start out a marriage, especially with you in grad school. I left as soon as the two years was up. Atlanta had a good culinary school, and it was far away from both you and Dad."

"Your dad seemed like a great guy. You have no idea what it's like to have a bad father."

Were his ears filled with wax? "My dad didn't have a drinking problem, but he was anything but a good father." I marched out of the room with the sound of my raised voice still echoing in my ears. How could someone so intelligent be so obtuse? I may as well have been talking to a stone. I was going home.

I halted in the kitchen. What an idiot. I was home. He was the one who should be leaving.

"God's been working on me, April. I'm not the same." He came around to face me.

I knew how to handle the smug expression that usually appeared when we'd fought before, but I had no idea how to handle the humility I saw now. It scared me. I didn't trust it.

"I wasn't a good listener before," he said. "I'm ready to listen now."

Tears hung on my eyelids, but I had to stay strong. "Tell me about the change in plans, Marc. Tell me what happened to bring you back to Canoga without that degree."

"Aren't the differences you see in me enough?"

"No. I can't give you my heart again until I hear from your mouth what happened."

Silence fell between us, heavy and awkward.

Headlights flashed through the windows and he turned to look. "Kitty's home. I'll see you tomorrow."

The door slammed behind him, and I moved to where I could see outside.

He'd stopped to say something to Kitty, the tender bent of his head only serving to infuriate me. How dare he act so concerned when he wouldn't share the intimacies of his past with me.

As I stalked to my room, I made myself a promise. As soon as I had assurance Ramón could rest in peace, I was leaving Canoga for good.

❧ 26 ೞ

I unwound the sheets, damp with perspiration, from my legs and squinted at the clock radio. In three hours K-LOVE would blast through the speakers, rousing me from a sleep I never had.

After rolling onto my back, I stared at the ceiling. Marc still loved me. Of course, I knew that before he ever said the words. All fooling myself aside, I loved him, too, but I couldn't act on it.

Whatever happened in California had to be awful. Why didn't he trust enough to tell me? He seemed to trust me in the past, didn't he? But if he had, would he have been so thickheaded to not believe me about Dad's tuition deal? How could he have thought I wanted to stay near home? He'd heard me say many times how my father's belittling my love of cooking cut deep. How could he not remember that? The day of my interview, he'd acted surprised when I said I was chasing my dream to be a chef. Had I been talking to a wall those four years we'd dated?

If he wasn't going to tell me, I would figure it out for myself. I flung back the covers. Without bothering to turn on a light, I padded downstairs and slipped into the chair in front of Kitty's computer.

Lord, if I don't find anything about Marc that I don't already know, I'll drop it and tell him that I'm ready to start over.

Within moments I had the computer booted and was at a search engine home page. My hands hovered over the keyboard. I took a deep breath, then typed *Marcus R. Thorne* into the search field. A new screen popped up. Dozens of Marc Thorne's, but no exact matches. I settled against the chair back, wanting to stop right then. But I needed to be sure.

I tried variations of his name and each time got new links, but none of them for my Marc. No news was good news as the saying goes. My eyelids grew heavy. Now, maybe I could grab a couple hours sleep. Tomorrow I'd tell Marc I was ready to start over. Did he still have my ring? If he did, I'd happily take it back. I manipulated the cursor to close the window and paused as I read the link at the bottom of the screen:

Don't fall into a trap like Marc Thorne. Moral failure is never good for anyone....

My stomach knotted as I clicked on the blue letters. The site for California Christian University's Graduate School forum popped up. The two-year old posting might answer the very questions that had plagued me for too many days. I read the next screen.

Moral failure is never good for anyone. Marc Thorne will be the first to tell you that. Last I heard, he's serving his sentence at SACC. Check out the archives for the complete story.

I guided the mouse with a trembling hand and clicked on the archive link. A screen asked for a university ID number and password. I had neither. Some choice I had. Weaken my stance and return Marc's love, despite not knowing about a huge chunk of his life, which was the choice of my heart. Or walk away from him, which reason told me to do. Or keep on searching until I found the answer that didn't require a password, which seemed a good compromise.

After several stabs at searching for SACC in California, the only reasonable hit I came up with was Santa Alicia Correctional Center. A shudder trailed down my back. Marc may have been a lot of things, but he wasn't a lawbreaker. Was he? How many times had I heard news reports about some Joe Anybody being arrested for a crime and his friends saying they had no idea? That he seemed like a normal guy with a job and family? The post I found earlier did say "serving his sentence."

Marc always looked hot in most anything he wore, but not in the prison jumpsuit that popped into my thoughts. A sob escaped. Serving time had to be wrong. Straight-arrow Marc and convict Marc did not belong together in the same thought. But what else could that statement mean? I'd want to cover up a past like that, too.

"April, I heard you all the way upstairs."

I whirled around. "It's Marc. He...he...I think he did time in California."

Kitty tightened the belt on her pink robe and dragged a chair up. "Where did this idea come from?"

"He told me last night he still loves me. I told him that until I found out what happened, renewing our relationship wasn't an option. He still refused. We had a terrible fight. I couldn't sleep and decided to search his name on the Internet. I read something that if it's true..."

"Show me."

I back-clicked to the CCU Forum and pointed at the post.

Kitty bent toward the screen and read. "What did the archives say?"

"I couldn't get in without a password."

"And what about this is upsetting you?"

"There's a Santa Alicia Correctional Center in California."

Kitty's features hardened. "That's a broad jump to a conclusion. You owe it to Marc to ask him what this means. If your worst assumption is true, you need to hear him out. Not every person sent to prison is guilty, and even some of the guilty ones come out restored." She closed her eyes for a moment. "Right after we married, Uncle Daniel did 14 months in prison for being in the wrong place at the wrong time."

My eyes widened. "Uncle Daniel?"

She wiped moisture from her cheek with the back of her hand. "A man at the company where he worked embezzled money and used Daniel as a front. Dan knew nothing about it, but the judge didn't believe him. It took his attorney those 14 months to prove Daniel's innocence. We decided what was done was done, but it changed both of our attitudes toward prisons and the people who are kept there."

Trying to wrap my head around the thought of Uncle Daniel in prison garb and sitting in a cell was like trying to visualize Donald Trump living in a homeless shelter. "How come I never knew?"

"Your father was still in high school when all this happened. By the time he married and you were born, it seemed almost like a lifetime away. Daniel and his friend started the firm that he eventually took over. Since he was exonerated, it seemed better to not mention it."

If ever I felt on information overload, it was now. My heart twisted, wanting Uncle Daniel back so I could hug him and talk to him. At least I still had Aunt Kitty. "That must have been hard on your marriage."

"It wasn't easy, but we managed. I worked at the business, keeping it going, and spent weekends driving to the prison to see Daniel. That's when he'd advise me on what to do with the firm. The situation could have driven a wedge between us or deepened our relationship. We chose the latter, but it took work."

"Are you saying I shouldn't be upset that Marc may have broken the law and spent time in prison?"

"I'm saying, keep an open mind, and let God show you the path to take, should it be true."

"Maybe God's telling me to not get involved."

Kitty's blue-veined hand rested on my knee. "We need to pray."

Minutes later, when my aunt finally said "Amen," God seemed as far away as the most distant star. Why, even with Kitty's words pleading for special insight regarding Marc and our future, was He so silent when I needed Him the most?

She squeezed my hand. "You've been hit hard tonight. Maybe you should call in sick tomorrow."

She had no idea how much I wanted to heed her advice, but I couldn't.

～ 27 ～

I arrived in the kitchen two hours later, finding it as immaculate as it was when Marc and I blew out of there last night. First thing on my agenda was a triple-shot espresso straight up. By the time batter was mixed for lemon-blueberry muffins, I was on my second cup and able to see a bit more clearly. I could only hope the caffeine buzz didn't wear off until I'd had a chance to face Marc. I decided against checking my appearance in the pantry mirror out of fear I'd want to stick a bag over my head and grabbed a lemon instead. I ran the yellow fruit over the grater and breathed in the fresh scent as the zest fell into the batter.

"I came to apologize."

I glanced up. Marc stood in front of me, his jacket hooked over his shoulder by one finger. Dark blotches underscored his eyes. I refocused on the mixing bowl. This wasn't where he was supposed to make his entrance. I still had to write my lines for that scene.

"Can we start over?"

I raised my head. Big mistake. How could I resist those soulful eyes? Still, I pressed my lips together.

"No one kisses like you did last night without feeling something, April. We both know the spark's still there." He closed the door and tossed his jacket over a stool.

Reason told me to pelt him with questions, but the message hadn't gotten to the icicles around my heart before they melted. I let him tug me into an embrace. With the grater in one hand and the lemon still in the other, my arms awkwardly wrapped around him.

"What do you say?"

I couldn't answer. Was I some kind of crazy woman? Wanting nothing to do with him one minute and the next, ready to fall into his arms forever, no matter what the past?

He leaned back and regarded my face. "Are you okay? You don't look good."

"I could say the same about you. I pulled an all-nighter at the computer last night. There's something I need to ask—"

The door flew open. He released me so fast I had to grab the counter for

116

balance. The grater hit the floor with a clatter.

"Yes, Karl?" Marc's impatient tone matched his tight smile.

I wanted to crawl under the sink and never come out.

Karl's questioning gaze darted from Marc to me, then back to Marc, where it settled on a lipstick smudge above his shirt pocket. A smirk formed on Karl's lips, but he quickly dissolved it. "Pedro's missing."

"Seems the cage needs a new latch," I said. "That bird's escaped his pen one too many times."

Karl's jaw stiffened. "The cage is missing too."

"Who on earth would steal that bird?" A vision of Ana spiriting away the colorful beast, cage and all, popped into my mind.

"Beats me." Karl shrugged and walked toward the door. "I've got work to do. I hope he's got a better home now. Sorry for interrupting."

After the handyman left, Marc pushed the door closed. "Are you thinking what I'm thinking?"

"That we'll be fodder for the Rescaté gossip mill within 15 minutes? How long before Kendall finds out, and we hit the unemployment line?"

"Right now I'm more concerned about Pedro. His disappearance could be connected to the missing pills."

"That's a stretch. That bird talks more than a politician the day before an election, and what would he have to do with the murder?"

"That's what I mean. No one would take him for a pet, so he has to be missing for another reason."

I made a face. "I've had too much caffeine this morning. It's hard for me to think."

Marc picked up his jacket. "I supposed we'd better treat this as two unrelated instances until we know more."

I couldn't help but chuckle. "You don't by any chance have a clean shirt, do you?"

"I keep a spare in my office in case of a last-minute evening meeting. Why?"

"Unless you like your pocket decorated with my Very Berry Parfait lipstick, you may want to change."

With the muffins in the oven, I was setting out the makings for a coffee cake when the kitchen phone rang.

Marc's commander-voice came through the connection. "Everyone's upset that Pedro's missing. Is it possible to take the break cart out early? Some of your fresh-baked goodies might help take minds off the bird."

"When they're done baking, I'll get right on it."

"Karl interrupted before we could discuss us." Mr. Wonderful was back.

My stomach tightened. No way could I answer his question until he answered mine first. "I have something to ask you, too. Do you have time to talk in private?"

"Got a meeting in five minutes. Can it wait until lunch?"

"Sure. I'll hang here until you call." I hung up and expelled a sigh that seemed to come from my knees. Time to earn some bread while I still had a job.

⁓ 28 ⁓

My head still reeling between suspicions about Marc's past, the birdnapping, and Karl walking in on our embrace, I rolled my cart into Rosa's and Helen's work area and flashed them a cheesy grin. "Ladies, you're my first stop."

Rosa scurried over. Wearing a rose-red blouse and green pants, she looked like Christmas in springtime. "I heard about Pedro. I hope he not outside and lost." Her gaze slid over the selection, then lingered on the yogurt and fresh fruit I'd substituted for the coffee cake. "It look good, but I can't eat, thinking about Pedro outside and lost."

"I doubt he's lost outside since his cage is gone too. We're hoping whoever took him wanted him for a pet. I made some lemon-blueberry muffins. Maybe if you eat one, you'll feel better."

"*Sí.* You right." She picked up a muffin.

Helen approached the cart. "I love the cute way Pedro tilts his head before he talks. If only he'd learn some new phrases. I don't know how Ramón stood the constant repetition."

Rosa swallowed a mouthful of muffin. "I love when Pedro flew into the service yesterday. I think he scared the *señoritas,* but he not mean."

Helen doctored her coffee with several packets of creamer. "Yeah. Ramón's bird wanted to attend the service while his fiancée didn't."

"*Ex*-fiancée, Helen. Besides, after I hear them argue, I'm surprised the *señorita* even serve food yesterday."

Helen brushed sugar off her maroon blouse. "What could be worse than any other argument we've heard between those two?"

"You wouldn't understood the words." Rosa rested a fist on her hip. "They speak *Español.* It was a dizzy."

I quirked my head. "A dizzy?"

"She probably means doozey," Helen said.

Before I could ask what a *doozey* was, Rosa nodded. "*Sí.* Ana was furious. She tell him, 'If I weren't a God-fearing *señorita,* Ramón, you'd be dead.' Then he say all he needed to do was make one phone call and she'd be...I don't know the word. It mean sent back to Mexico."

"Deported," Helen supplied.

"*Si*. Deported. Next I hear loud crash and he say, 'If you want to throw something, make it that ring. It's *terminado*, Ana.' Then I hear her crying and coming close to the door so I hurry away."

"Good thing," Helen said wryly. "That's what you get for eavesdropping."

It was all I could do to keep a straight face. For someone so quick to chide her friend, Helen had hung on every word, as did I.

The rest of the break run went without incident, but I didn't care. Maybe Pedro's birdnapping was a decoy—to draw attention away from the truth. If Ana had been the one to break into the pantry, she must have overheard Kitty telling the chief about the pills and then come back to the kitchen, expecting me to be gone.

I yawned. If I ever escaped from this nightmare, I might even go back to crunching numbers. At least with numbers I could figure out the answers.

❧

A little before noon, the kitchen phone rang. Seeing it was Marc, I poised my hand above the receiver. Maybe it would be better to wait until after work for our discussion, or even after supper. What about tomorrow? A vision of another sleepless night crept into my foggy brain. I grabbed the receiver before I could change my mind. "Kitchen. April Love." Not my usual "Hi, Marc" I'd been using with him.

"Want to catch a sandwich in Lake Geneva? You choose the restaurant."

He was making it sound like a date. Hardly what I had in mind. "I'm not really hungry. Can't we just meet to talk?"

"Not even Popeye's? You always liked—"

"I was there recently with Kitty."

"Okay, but I'm starved, and this is the only free time I have. You can tag along while I eat."

A half hour later, I sat in Marc's Escape with him at the wheel and me wishing I were anyplace else. I let him do most of the talking. His mom was planning a visit in July, and she wanted to have a girls' night out with me. Was he delusional? Or was I? Maybe this was a new tactic. Pretend I'd agreed to renew our relationship, and it would turn out to be the truth.

I wallowed in grief. After I asked Marc about the post, I doubted he'd still want me around. Was knowing the truth worth losing the only man I ever loved? If I left Rescaté, would Marc be accused of killing Ramón? The pretend game was beginning to look good.

I studied his profile, enjoying the maturity the lines around his eyes had given him over the past eight years. Already a shadow of his dark beard tinged his jaw line. I wanted to run the back of my fingers over it and feel the scruff. A tiny scar still nicked his right eyebrow. An injury he once told me happened when, as a kid, he fell while carrying a glass. Canoga Lake wasn't big enough for the two of us, and I sure didn't want to go near Chicago. Too close to Dad. Maybe I'd apply to cook on a cruise ship. A ship headed for Singapore. The further away from this place the better.

We stopped at a deli for sandwiches to go, then walked two blocks to the Riviera dock. Although the day had warmed to nearly 70 degrees, the grounds were free of people except for the guys readying the excursion boats for summer. We circled the structure with the deserted beach off to our right, and Marc pointed to a bench across from the *Lady of the Lake,* a paddle-wheeled replica of a twentieth-century boat. "How about there?"

We settled on the seat. The familiar fusion of fresh lake air and motorboat exhaust escorted me on a mental excursion back to a time when my biggest worry was who my roommate would be at Wheaton College. Across from us a pair of brawny young men worked behind plastic sheeting on the *Lady,* while off to the side, in front of the Water Safety Patrol office, was the infamous spot Marc and I had met.

"Aren't you eating?"

I glanced at him. He had wrapped his mouth around his sub, about to take a bite. "I was just remembering."

He moved the sandwich away from his mouth. "Good memories?"

I stared at my turkey and Swiss. "Yeah. The best." I needed sustenance, but how could a girl eat when she felt like something one of Kitty's cats had dragged in? The aroma of spices and oil from Marc's lunch wafted to my nostrils. My stomach lurched, and I closed the wrapping around my food. "I think I'll save my lunch for later. Too many samplings this morning."

"Suit yourself. I wonder who swiped Pedro?"

I rested against the bench back and stretched out my legs. "I have a theory."

"Only one?" He popped a potato chip into his mouth.

"Maybe two, but one seems more reasonable than the other."

He playfully nudged me with his elbow. "Tell me yours, and I'll tell you mine."

"Ana."

"Not her. How could she handle that cage?"

"You didn't see her hefting stacks of plates in the kitchen the other day."

"But why her?"

"Maybe she's in the country illegally and Ramón knew it. She likely has an apartment key and a keycard. What if at the luncheon she overheard Kitty telling the chief the pills were hidden in the kitchen?"

Marc sent me a look that had "Yeah, right" written all over it. "Okay, so let's say she poisoned Ramón with those pills. That still doesn't explain why she'd take Pedro."

"It would if you saw her sending the appetizers flying like tiny Frisbees when Pedro squawked out 'Ana loves you.' The woman has a temper. She could have returned to the kitchen yesterday, hoping to find the capsules. When I was there, she went to Plan B—apologizing for her bad behavior. To get me out of the building, she insisted on walking out with me. Made sure I was distracted so I'd forget to lock up. Once I'd gone home, she came back and found the pills. Then, on her way out, she took the bird as a distraction."

Marc nodded. "It's possible."

"What's yours?"

"I think Cousins might be involved. He's made no bones about wanting Galvez's job. If things like ransacked kitchens and missing birds happen while I'm interim director, it looks like I'm not in control."

"What do you know about his background?"

"He worked in the private sector until a couple years ago. He's never liked me. Guess he figured I took the job that should have been his." He let out a long breath. "Let's forget Rescaté and Ramón for now." He took a bite of his sub and scanned the dock. "Seems like old times coming here."

"Too bad we can't turn the clock back."

"No reason we can't make more memories now, even better than the old ones."

I couldn't avoid the conversation any longer. Keeping my gaze pinned to the *Lady's* bow, I said, "If we don't unpack the baggage we've created since we were last together, we can't make good memories."

"Baggage?"

"Yeah, starting with answers about your past eight years."

He put the last bite of his sandwich in his mouth and crumpled the foil wrapper in his hand. "It's pretty boring. School and work. That's about it."

I sent a prayer upward for the right words. "Last night I found something on the Internet about you. I don't want to ask about it, but I have to."

He hesitated. "What'd...you...find?"

I faced him and wished I hadn't. I could handle the washed-out complexion, but the earnestness in his eyes about did me in. I gathered up courage from somewhere deep down. "Did you go to prison while you were in

California?"

Marc stared at me as if I'd grown an extra head.

"I found a post about you on the California Christian University forum last night."

"Someone said *I* did time in prison?"

"Not exactly. The guy said you were serving a sentence for moral failure at a place called SACC. There's a Santa Alicia Correctional Center..." I tore my gaze away from his face that had gone from pale to crimson. "Tell me I'm wrong."

"You have to ask me that?"

"Sometimes Christians stumble. Marc, you can tell me the truth."

"You really think that's where I've been?" His voice sounded more robot-like than human.

"It appears that way." I brought my gaze back to him. Seeing the moisture in his eyes, my insides turned to quicksand. "I don't know."

He tossed the wadded sandwich wrapper in his bag. "Since you're so savvy on the Internet, why didn't you check the database for California inmates before jumping to this conclusion?"

"You can find out if someone's been—"

"Let's go." His left brow twitched so fast I thought it would pop off his face. He pushed to his feet and marched across the dock toward the arched exit.

I scrambled off the bench and hoofed after him. How would I know inmates' names were on the Internet? No one I knew had ever been in trouble with the law except for an occasional speeding ticket.

The distance between us widened, and I sped up. Marc wasn't getting the last word on this. He was going to tell me the truth for once. Even if it meant admitting he'd done time. But what if he hadn't been in prison? The posting didn't exactly say that he had. Would he suggest I check the database if he were an ex-con? Hardly.

I caught up to him halfway to the car. "I'm sorry, Marc. I jumped to conclusions. Can we get together tonight and talk about it?"

He halted, and his painful stare ripped through me like a serrated knife.

Filleted and chastened, I dropped my gaze. "I guess not."

"I think it's a good idea not to be involved with each other beyond work."

I lifted my chin and chopped the air with my hand. "What would you expect me to think when you've been so evasive? It was only a question."

He started walking at a slower pace. "Let's go back to work before I say something I'll really be sorry for."

ᵔ 29 ᵔ

fter a very silent ride back to Rescaté, and feeling like yesterday's leftovers, I brewed a double-shot latte.

I've always believed that nothing happens that hasn't been allowed by God, but at the moment, I was at a loss to know why my life had become a Tilt-a-Whirl ride gone amuck. I should have followed my first instincts the afternoon I laid eyes on Marc here in this very kitchen and bolted for the unemployment line. I poured my latte and booted up the kitchen computer.

As I was calling up a search screen, Kendall stepped into the room. He shut the door and settled on the other stool, resting his elbow on the counter. The pose said relaxed, but the popping vein in his neck said otherwise. I mentally added dealing with a cranky board president to my list of trials.

I closed the laptop and forced a perky smile. "I made a latte. Would you like one?"

He held up a caffeine-free Diet Coke. "I'm good with this. I heard about the kitchen being ransacked last night. Why didn't you tell me?"

Why didn't I tell him? When did I see him since last night, and since when was I the interim director? "Sorry. I thought Marc would tell you."

"He did. But he should have called me, not the police. Doesn't matter now. Chief Bronson phoned. He wants to discuss some questions people have raised about Ramón's death and the break-in last night."

I felt the color drain from my face. What would he think if he knew Rescaté's prize supporter, better known as Kitty McPiper, was the one who tipped off the chief to the rumor mill?

The skin around his mouth stretched tight. "We don't need bad publicity during this transition time."

I wanted to give him a good shake and ask what he was thinking. Bad publicity was never good, but since last night my view on everything had changed. If the reason for taking those pills and stealing Pedro was to put fear in me, the person had succeeded. The police needed to be on the case. Amateur sleuths were good for novels and TV, but not real life.

"With the chief on the case we'll get some answers," I said. "Chances are he'll find out Ramón died of natural causes, like Doc Fuller indicated, and the

124

pill theft and parrot-napping were only a couple practical jokes."

His eyes looked like they would pop out of his head. "Parrot-napping?"

"Someone took Pedro. I'm guessing the pill thief did."

He finished off his soda and crushed the can. "Good riddance to that bird. What an embarrassment he was at the service."

I bit my tongue as I looked longingly at the laptop and my interrupted research.

After a minute's lecture on why pets shouldn't be allowed in the workplace, Kendall tossed what was left of his soft drink can in the trash and left. I moved the can from the paper trash to the blue bin, then opened the laptop.

I typed Inmate Database California into the Google search field, and several hits popped up. After navigating through a couple more screens, one asked me to agree to a long list of stipulations. Finally, I came to a field asking for an inmate's name. Then I hit a roadblock. The database held current inmate data only. I ended up calling a phone number on the screen.

After traversing several layers of an automated answering system, a woman with a gravelly voice answered.

I opened my mouth to speak, but the words log-jammed. Typing would have been much easier than human contact. I reached for my coffee and sipped.

"Hello, may I help you?"

"Yes. Sorry. I need information on a past inmate at the Santa Alicia Correctional Center."

"Name and date of birth?"

I spelled out Marc's name and gave his birth date.

"Please hold."

Was it that easy? I watched the kitchen clock's second hand go around once, twice, then three times while I sipped my latte. Halfway through the fourth cycle, the woman returned.

"Did you say last name of Thorne with an e?"

My palms grew moist. "Yes. With an e."

"I have a Mark, with a k, Thorn, last name has no e, served time for embezzlement, but his date of birth is different. Are you sure about the spelling?"

"Yes, absolutely."

"That's the only Thorne I have."

I thanked her and hung up before I let out a whoop and a "Praise You, Lord."

You learned the truth. Now don't you think you owe Marc an apology?

Wasn't I the one who deserved the apology? If he'd been open from the start, I wouldn't have had to do an Internet search for his name. And, besides, I still didn't know what happened over the past eight years. What I needed was another dose of caffeine. I stood from the stool, reached the espresso maker, and stopped.

Time to admit it, Love. What you need is a big helping of humility. In spite of him still hiding behind those walls of secrecy, you did jump to a conclusion on that prison assumption.

A dull ache filled my chest. I picked up my cell and called him. It went straight to voice mail. I pressed the *Off* button then made a beeline for his office.

Taryn looked up from loading a cardboard box. "April. Hello."

I pointed toward Marc's door. "He in there?"

"I wish he were. He's supposed to be packing for the move to the director's suite. But he won't be back until late afternoon. Do you want him to call you?"

I pressed my hand on a corner of her desk to keep from toppling over and glanced at the wall clock. Only three, but my day was done. "I'm not feeling well. I'll call him later."

❧ 30 ❧

I headed back to the kitchen and gathered up my jacket, purse, and lunch sack. At least asleep I wouldn't waste time wondering if Ramón was murdered and if the killer had taken the pills and Pedro. And maybe I'd shed the guilt pressing at my heart for all but accusing Marc of having done time. Outside, a gusty wind howled through the trees along with the familiar drone of a lawn mower.

Mower? The landscapers cut the grass the other day. Why were they mowing again late on a Friday?

The racket came closer, louder, faster. I turned a 180.

Silhouetted against the sun, a figure stood at the mower's controls. Was he aiming right for me? I shifted to the left. The mower adjusted direction too.

My direction.

The motor revved. I sprinted toward the lake. Like a bull charging its prey, the mower bore down on me. I had to move before he chewed my body to bits under those megasized blades. I took off for the trees, kicking off my clogs and tossing my lunch bag. Maybe a turkey on whole wheat would tame the beast. I needed time. Precious time.

The engine screamed. I'd probably lost a good pair of clogs, but what did it matter if I didn't live to wear shoes again? I glanced over my shoulder. He was close enough to make out the man's red and white ski mask.

I zigged to the left, then zagged to the right. *Lord, keep me from stumbling.*

The motor's angry roar echoed in my ears, and I gulped in the stench of its acrid breath. Lungs stinging, I reached the tree line and dashed into the pines, their wide branches enfolding me like angel's wings. Rocks and sticks cut through my socks, but I didn't stop until I came to a large bough.

I crawled underneath it and forced myself to breathe slowly. On the path the mower idled. Had he gotten off that monster and come looking for me? Nearby, dried pine needles rustled and I jumped. A squirrel scampered away.

The mower's motor revved again. I held my breath until it faded off toward the mansion, then made a dash for Kitty's. My lungs ached, my bladder was full, and I felt like I hadn't slept in a week. But I wasn't dead, and no one was going to change that.

⪧ 31 ⪦

"Get inside!" I shouted at Kitty as she was climbing out of her car, a withered Easter lily nestled in the crook of her arm.

Her wide-eyed stare begged an explanation, but she banged the car door shut with her hip and scurried toward the back porch without a word.

Inside, I double-locked the door and punched in the alarm code. "Someone tried to kill me."

Her face as white as the bedraggled flower she carried, she slammed the plant on the table, scattering clumps of dirt across the oak surface. "Who?"

"I couldn't see because of a ski mask. The creep was on one of those big lawn mowers and chased me across the yard."

Kitty pulled me toward her and wrapped me in her arms. "You're shaking all over." She guided me to a chair at the table and eased me down.

I looked up at her still pale face. "Thank the Lord for those pines. If they weren't there, I'd be hamburger meat by now." As I replayed the horror in my mind, tears puddled in my eyes, and I didn't fight them. The hot moisture trailing down my cheeks assured me I was alive.

Kitty took my hands in hers and prayed against "the evil that has pervaded this once peaceful place." I let her plea for my protection buoy me and echoed her "Amen" as she concluded.

Exhaustion washed over me, but first things first. "I need to call the police. In fact, I'm going to call the chief directly. He needs to hear it straight."

"Why Howard?"

"Who?"

"The chief."

"Oh. I found out he's taking Marc's and my report about the kitchen break-in more seriously than the officer who answered the phone last night. He called Kendall in for an interview of some sort this morning."

"It's odd he didn't ask to speak to you or Marc, since you two are the ones who discovered the pill theft."

I shrugged. "I was too focused on Kendall's being upset with me because the police were investigating."

"Why would he be upset?"

"He's afraid of Rescaté's reputation being tarnished, only to find out later it's nothing but rumors and pranks. Some people won't hear that and the kids will suffer. He's probably right. Without the pills, I have nothing concrete. Same as with that guy attacking me with the mower."

"You're certain it was a man?"

I pulled up a vision of the masked figure silhouetted against the sun. "I guess it could've been a woman."

"Think, April. What about the build?"

"The shoulders weren't very broad, but some men have slighter forms."

Kitty grabbed the landline phone from the wall base and handed it to me. After I punched in the number, a woman answered.

"This is April Love, the Rescaté chef. Is Chief Bronson there? I need to report an attack."

"The chief isn't available. What kind of attack?"

"Someone tried to run me down with a riding lawn mower."

"A what?"

"One of those big jobs. The kind you stand on."

"And the operator attempted to run you over?" Skepticism replaced surprise in her voice.

"I was heading across Rescaté de Niño's lawn when the huge mower came around the mansion and aimed for me."

"But you got away."

"Only because I ran into some pines. Trust me, the attack was real."

"Can you describe the attacker?"

"No. He wore a ski mask. It could have been a she."

"Where's the mower now?"

"The guy headed toward the mansion. I wasn't about to follow." The woman's condescending tone lit a fuse in my gut. I raised my voice. Can you interrupt the chief? He's already familiar with the situation here."

"He's in a meeting and can't be disturbed. I'll notify patrol. What's your number?"

I let out a sigh. So what else was new? I gave her my cell number and hung up. "Who answers the phone there during business hours? She's not an officer, is she?"

"Kristy Bronson, the chief's daughter."

"She said the chief is in a meeting. I don't buy it. Kendall couldn't still be there. That was over an hour ago."

"You were almost killed." Kitty grabbed the phone out of my hand and punched in a number. "Kristy, this is Kitty McPiper. My niece reported an attack on her life. If your father can't come to the phone, I demand you send the squad over here immediately." As she listened to Kristy's response, creases formed between her eyes. "I don't care what he's investigating. Does she need to be killed before you do something?" She listened again, her fingers white in a tight grip on the phone. "Whatever."

She hit the *Off* button and replaced the receiver in its base. "I don't want you going over there anymore, April. It's not safe."

I wanted more than ever to put Rescaté on my personal list of places not to visit before I died, but how could I? "Sorry. No can do. If I cave in now, he wins. I'll be careful."

"Your life is more important than any of this." Her eyes blazed a trail over my face. "You're my only niece." She pulled a tissue from her jeans pocket and wiped her nose. "You're like a daughter to me, my best friend."

Guilt burned in my chest. Maybe I should quit the job. But I couldn't leave with my aunt next door and nothing resolved. I gathered her into my arms. "I'll be okay. Marc already said he doesn't want me alone in the building. When he hears what happened, he'll probably arrange for someone to be my bodyguard." At least he would have yesterday. Today? I wasn't too sure.

"I guess it'll be okay if you have an escort." She angled her head back to look me in the eye. "This seems almost insignificant, but were you able to clear up the question about Marc?"

"Yes, but not without causing him to blow a gasket. I can hardly blame him since I accused him of being an ex-con. I found out later I could call the California Department of Correction and get information on past inmates. He was never in prison." I blinked at my tears. "I feel like a louse. By the time I knew the truth and went to apologize, he wasn't in the office. I left a voice mail but he hasn't called."

"You accused him? What exactly did you say?"

I recounted our conversation as best I could through the sobs.

"Sweetie, I didn't hear an accusation in there. You asked a question."

I stared at her.

"He may have heard the question as an accusation, but you didn't accuse."

I mentally rehashed the conversation as I remembered it. She was right. The way he reacted had caused me to see my words as an accusation. Maybe I could have softened the question better, but I didn't accuse. Still, humility is always better than pride. I pulled my cell phone from my pocket and hit the speed dial for Marc.

After four rings, the call went to voice mail. I visualized him glancing at the caller ID screen and thinking, *Her again.* As soon as his recorded greeting ended, I blurted out, "Marc, this is an emergency. Call me ASAP." I disconnected. "That should get his attention. Now I'm taking a shower. On second thought, mind if I use the jet tub?"

Forty-five minutes later, as wrinkled as elephant hide and wrapped in a terry robe, I stepped into my bedroom. Kitty sat on the bed.

I stopped towel-drying my hair. "Don't tell me the police are here."

She offered a wry smile. "Only in a perfect world. With everything else, I forgot to mention that I had lunch at Dina's Diner."

I draped the towel around my neck and sat next to her. "So?"

"LuAnn Dodge was our waitress."

I smiled for the first time that day. "My childhood spying partner in crime?"

Kitty nodded. "I never realized what a beautiful girl she is. She's styled her hair now and wears makeup. I teased that she must be in love. When a girl blushes like—"

"Did you mention I was in town?"

"Yes. I told her you were staying with me."

"Did she say anything about us getting together?"

"Before she could, we got to talking about Ramón's passing. She said quite a few Rescaté people come in there. Then I realized that maybe someone had been there that morning wearing the same jogging outfit that person who bumped into you wore." She quirked her head. "Wild idea, but it didn't hurt to find out. I asked if any Rescaté employees had been in there the morning of the death."

"What'd she say?"

"A huge family sat at one of her stations. Well, her station and Dorry's. The other waitress. They had to put three tables together. I never got another chance to talk to her." She worked her lower lip. "I'm sorry."

I waved a hand. "You tried. At this point it wouldn't hurt to pursue that idea. Maybe I'll stop by the diner myself. It'll be fun to see her again." Sheesh. There I was, trying to act like Nancy Drew or something. But if we didn't turn over every rock to be sure...

"I'm glad you're not upset. You've had enough with that terrible scare."

A vision of the monster mower flashed into my head. Coming closer, angry, belching fumes. Then my futile attempt at stalling him by kicking off my clogs. He ate them like a hungry dog going after a bone.

"That's it." I bolted across the room to my dresser.

Kitty was beside me in two seconds. "What are you doing?"

I pulled out my jeans. "If my shoes are still there and torn to shreds, I have proof of the lawnmower attack."

"It's gotten dark now and you're exhausted. You're going nowhere but to bed." She tugged at my jeans, but I was stronger.

I stepped into the pants and fastened them under my nightshirt. "I won't be able to sleep until I've done this."

Kitty raised her hands in surrender. "Then I'm going with you."

✑ 32 ✐

Kitty turned her Mercedes into Rescaté's vacant parking lot and pulled up to its edge, the headlights aimed straight across the lawn. "Is that about right?"

"Can you move a little more to the left? I think I was closer to the trees."

She backed up, then angled the car. "Better?"

A swath of light illuminated the grass ahead. During the short drive over from Kitty's, I couldn't wait to find what was left of my shoes, but now that I was here, I wanted to stay in the locked-up Benz. What if that monster was sitting in the shadows waiting for me? Ridiculous. Even a fool would know to get out of there.

I wiped my hands on my jeans, then lowered the window a smidge and listened to the eerie silence. "Everything looks different in the dark. I guess it's okay." I opened the glove compartment and pulled out a flashlight, then took a swig from the water bottle I'd brought along. I stuck the bottle in the cup holder. "Wish me luck."

"Better than that, I'll pray." She held up her cell phone. "And I'm ready to call for help."

"Unless you've got a direct line to Superman, you may as well put the phone away. I'll take the prayers. He's our ever-present help in times of trouble and if this isn't trouble, I don't know what is." I climbed out of the car. A soft *click* assured me the door was latched.

The hair on the back of my neck rose to attention. Once I stepped into the light anyone could take a potshot at me. Assuring myself that so far there'd been no guns involved in this caper, I took off across the grass, my eyes trained on the ground. All I needed was one scrap of sliced leather, half a rubber sole. Anything. Grab it and run for the car.

I ran my light beam over the parts of the lawn Kitty's headlights didn't reach. Grass, grass, and more grass. All of it looked mossy green even in artificial light. I had to find out what they fed the stuff and tell Kitty. Something brown caught my eye. I scampered over to my lunch sack. Other than being more crumpled, it appeared no different than when I last saw it.

I snatched the bag up and turned toward the car, skimming the ground with the flashlight. Halfway between the parking lot and the lake, I paused to get a fix on the trees. The moments right before I kicked off the shoes played in my mind. The stand of trees had been ahead, green and welcoming—except for one brown bough.

Adrenaline surged through me, and I skimmed the pines with the light beam until it landed on the dried-up branches. Taking a couple steps to my left, I stopped. Without a doubt, this was the spot I kicked off my clogs.

I circled the area, enlarging the circumference of each lap like rings in a tree trunk. Not one rubber sole. Not one scrap of leather. Was I crazy? A sob escaped, and I dropped to the ground. I had proof—the missing shoes, same as the missing pills. How can something missing be hard evidence if you have no proof they existed? Well, I sure didn't go to work this morning in my stocking feet.

My insides burned. I couldn't fool myself any longer. There was a killer, and whoever he or she was, they were trying to mess with my mind. But why? They must think that if the trail turned cold, the cops would stop investigating. With the coroner's report already filed and no proof of foul play, the police would go back to nailing unsuspecting drivers as they came off the highway into a speed trap, and Ramón's cause of death would always be seen as heart attack. I could ignore the rumors, too, except for one.

❧ 33 ❧

Friday morning, my cell chimed from my purse as I was shrugging into my jacket. I snagged the phone and checked the caller ID. Finally. I hit the *Accept* button. "Marc. There's so much I need to say—"

"What are you trying to do, April, wreck my life? Did you tell the police you suspected I'd done jail time?"

"No. I—"

"Then why'd they ask me to come in for a little heart-to-heart, as the chief called it?"

My stomach felt like I'd swallowed a brick. "Stop shouting, and I'll start at the beginning."

"So you *are* in on it."

"The chief is following up on what Kitty told him, but I almost got kill—"

"Great. Now I not only have you wrecking my life, but Kitty, too. Both of you do me a favor. Leave me alone."

"Suit yourself." I threw the phone in the waste can and stomped out to my car.

❧❧

At Rescaté, I mixed batter for muffins, brewed coffee, and made an apple coffee cake. It was still too early for the break run, so I whipped up a batch of raisin-bran breakfast cookies. Some people wouldn't be able to boil water after dealing with the kind of stuff I'd been going through, but thankfully, cooking always helped me get past the worst moments in my life. Today was no exception.

Of course, it helped that Marc was off the premises. If he had shut up long enough this morning, he'd have heard my apology and how I almost was creamed in a lawnmower attack. With every ingredient I added to the recipes, a prayer left my lips for Marc's protection. Maybe the chief was following up on the pill theft report and nothing else. My worst fear was that he'd heard the rumor about Marc's being responsible for Ramón's death and was taking it to heart. What hurt worse was that, with Marc so angry at me, the moment he got back to the office, he'd whip out his pen and write me a pink slip.

Unless you counted numerous thanks I received for my fresh-baked goodies, the break run was unremarkable. Office chatter mostly centered on who would be the next director. Marc was the favorite, but several thought Bob Cousins had a shot. If it weren't for the fact that Marc would probably issue me my walking papers as soon as he arrived, I'd have been rooting for him, too.

Back in the kitchen, since I had nothing left to cook, I started wiping down everything in sight. At least I could depart head high, leaving the kitchen as gleaming as the day I first saw it.

I glanced at the clock. Almost noon. I had nothing left to do but take inventory for the next person. At least with me gone, maybe the killer would feel safe and everything would settle down. How comforting to think that someone who got away with murder might be daily rubbing elbows with everyone.

Lord, please cause justice to be done here. Protect the innocent.

Armed with a legal pad and pen, I stepped into the pantry and counted the sacks of flour.

"April? You here?"

I braced myself. "In the pantry."

The door flew open and whacked against the shelves. Condiment and jelly jars rattled. Marc stared at me, his jaw muscle throbbing as though plugged into an electric socket. "We need to talk, but not here."

"Sure."

He stepped into the kitchen.

I followed, tossing my pad on the counter as I passed it.

He led the way to his new digs. The same desk Ramón had used still sat in front of the window. Only now a nameplate bearing Marc's name occupied its polished surface. We stepped out a side door and onto the flagstone patio.

"Let's go to the boathouse, where we won't be overheard."

Why pick the boathouse of all places? Any place but there. Side by side, we walked down the grassy slope, me taking two steps for each of his single strides. I crossed my arms against the cool lake breeze and prayed for control of my tongue.

"Chilly?"

"I can deal with it."

No offer of his wool sports coat or suggestion to have the conversation inside. I gulped back a mass of sadness. Today wasn't the time to wallow in my pity pot.

The screen door to the boathouse porch creaked in protest as he pulled it open and waited for me to enter. He gestured toward the wood bench. I sat to one end of the worn seat. At least in his anger he hadn't forgotten his manners.

He stood several feet away, hands jammed in his pockets.

"You can sit here. I won't bite."

He turned and faced the lake. "It's better I remain standing." He jingled the coins in his pocket, then faced me, his left brow twitching. "Thanks to you, the police suspect me of murder. How is it that the loving and supportive woman I once loved has become a liar?"

I flew to my feet and came to within a foot of him, hand raised. "When have I ever lied to you?"

"Not to me, to the police."

"For a man so well educated, you aren't very bright. I checked with California Corrections. You never did time. If you'd returned my call yesterday, you'd have heard me apologize for causing you to think I was accusing you. I've never said a word to the police about you or Ramón's death. They won't even talk to me when I call them. I'll pack my things and be gone in ten minutes."

I marched to the door and yanked on the handle.

My behind hit the floor with a thud.

It would have been an exit not to be outdone by any drama queen if the door hadn't stuck.

Marc hunched beside me, concern replacing the anger in his eyes. "Are you okay?"

I brushed away his offered hand and scrambled to my feet. "Of course." This time the door popped open with the slightest of tugs. "See ya around."

A hand grasped my shoulder. "Don't leave."

"Why? So I can stay and take more of your accusations?"

"I'm sorry. Guess I'm guilty of jumping to conclusions, too. The rumor about me being suspected of murdering Ramón is true. Someone's framing me."

My shoulders sagged as I turned to look at him. "It's probably the same person who tried to run me over with a lawn mower yesterday."

He flinched. "Are you serious?"

I nodded, and he opened his arms. "C'mere, *mi caramela.* I'm so sorry."

I gladly stepped into his embrace. Nuts to the rumor mill. I much preferred hugging to arguing any day.

"We're quite a pair, aren't we?" His voice cracked. "What's this about being run over by a mower?"

I tipped my head back and looked him in the eye. "You first. Did the chief actually say you're a suspect?"

"He and another officer named Hogan pulled the good-cop, bad-cop routine." He plopped onto the bench. "Where was I on Thursday night? What about Friday before dawn? Did I have an alibi? Did I have a key for Ramón's apartment? Did I own an orange cap? Do I know how to operate a commercial lawn mower? You know how hard it is for me to kill anything."

I settled beside him and took his hand, trying to rub some warmth into it. "I remember junior year when you insisted your roommates release a mouse they'd trapped in the bathroom."

He uttered a sardonic chuckle. "The poor animal probably died from trauma minutes later."

"Did the police say anything else?"

"I'm not to try any funny business like leaving the country. Bronson wanted to ask for my passport, but Hogan advised unless I was officially named a suspect they couldn't. Guess I need to call a lawyer."

"They can't know how Ramón died, and they don't have the pills."

"They're gonna autopsy the body. I thought it'd be in New Mexico by now."

"Isabel was considering cremation so she left the remains here until she decided."

"How do you know that?"

"Flavia."

"Who?"

"Isabel's cousin. We had a good chat over dessert after the service." I gave him a weak smile. "Nothing like gourmet cooking to forge a friendship."

He turned his hand so our fingers naturally wove together. "Tell me about the mower."

I summarized my afternoon of terror, ending with how, when I went back for what was left of my shoes, they were gone.

"That's why they badgered me about knowing how to operate a mower." He pulled me into his arms. "I can't have you at Rescaté until this mess is over."

I leaned back and met his eyes. "We don't want this creep to win. I drove to work this morning. If I do that from now on, I'll be fine."

His cell rang out, and he put the instrument to his ear. "What's up, Taryn?" He paused to listen. "I'll meet him there in five minutes." He hit the *Off* button. "Claypool wants to see me. Let's go."

"Wait. We need a plan."

"A plan?"

"To prove your innocence."

Marc nudged me closer. "I don't deserve you," he said, nuzzling my ear. "Let's discuss it over dinner?"

"Okay."

"Tonight then."

"Tonight?"

"I may not be a free man tomorrow."

～ 34 ～

At the Lakeshore Inn, the host led us around a huge fireplace to our window-side table. Marc waited until I was settled, then sat across from me. Between us, a bronze lantern cast a romantic glow. He ordered for both of us, and by the time our iced teas arrived, so did a basket of warm breads. The inn's position on a bluff gave us an unmatched view of the lake, and we watched the sun's pink rays stretch across the water.

"Beautiful scene." Marc's voice cut into my thoughts.

"When my job in Atlanta bogged me down, I'd daydream about this place." I felt an easy smile drift over my lips. "So many good memories."

He broke off a piece of roll. "Like the day we met in Lake Geneva?"

"When you sent me into the drink, bumping into me like that." A giggle burbled. "The look on your face was priceless."

"Only my usual focused self bent on getting to the boat for lake patrol. Thought I was going to have to do a rescue right there, but before I could, you were climbing back on the pier."

"Just another day at the office for me." I laughed. "I must have taken an unexpected swim at least a half-dozen times delivering the mail." I chuckled. "I still found you irresistible, especially when you insisted on taking me to dinner to make up for my surprise dunking."

His features softened in the candle glow. "I'm not sure about the me-being-irresistible part, but you were the cutest girl I'd seen in a while, especially after you climbed out of the water."

I raised a dinner roll as if to throw it at him.

We shared a laugh, and then he grew serious. "As young as we were, I was sure you were the one God had for me."

A dull ache spread across my chest. "For one so certain, why weren't you willing to flex when I said I couldn't move to California after graduation?"

His head jerked back. "Seemed the other way around to me."

Before I could respond, the waiter appeared with our salads. After what seemed countless minutes of adding ground pepper and making sure we had the dressings we wanted, the server left.

I pushed my words through clenched teeth. "You may recall I couldn't leave."

140

"But we were engaged."

Heat filled my gut. "We've been over this road before, Marc. It's starting to get potholes. We needed to live in Chicago for two years, so I could fulfill my end of the deal with Dad. There are no loopholes in his world."

"Why would he do that?"

"He hoped that in the end I'd want to work for him, and we could become business partners. If I didn't give him two years, I'd have to reimburse him for my tuition. He thinks cooking for a living is menial work. Culinary school was not an option."

Marc's jaw slackened. "You said that, but I thought you wanted to stay near your family and that agreement thing was merely an excuse."

"Are you kidding? Even now, Dad is on me to come back and work for him. I hate staying away because it means no time with Mom, but…"

"Why didn't Brian have an agreement?"

I chuckled. "Can you see my brother analyzing financial reports?"

Marc busied himself buttering a roll. "I was pretty obnoxious, wasn't I?"

"Obnoxious is a start. I can come up with a few more adjectives."

"I really thought you didn't want to leave Chicago. I'm sorry, April. I guess I didn't listen."

I moved my gaze to the fireplace across the room and studied the flames. "If we'd talked then like we are now…"

"Mi caramela."

His melodic tone lured my gaze back to him.

"I'm sorry for hurting you," he said. "Can you forgive me?"

"Forgive you as though the hurt never happened?"

His Adam's apple bobbed like a Red Delicious in a tub of water. "You were never far from my thoughts these eight years."

He expected me to believe that? What did he take me for? "Not one call, one e-mail…nothing."

"Didn't think you wanted me to contact you."

A familiar pain pierced my heart, but I pushed it away. "If you'd only explain what happened." I stabbed at the baby greens in front of me and lifted the fork to my mouth. Despite the spicy dressing, I tasted nothing.

"Let's step outside for a moment."

I met his dark-eyed gaze. How had he slipped out of his seat without me realizing it?

On our way to a patio directly off the dining area, he caught our waiter's attention and told him we'd be right back.

Outside and out of view of other diners, Marc sheltered me in his arms.

"April, I ache to think how my stubbornness deprived us of eight years. Please forgive me."

How could I forgive when he still hid secrets? But wasn't Jesus ready to forgive me before I'd repented of my wrongdoing? I'd lived long enough in bitterness over what had happened.

I thought I'd described the deal with Dad so clearly. What exactly had I said? With my gift for gab, Marc had probably tuned out half my words. What was done was done. and I couldn't change it, nor could I blot it from memory. What I could change was my heart. He needed to hear me say I forgave him as much as I needed to say it. I looked him in the eye. "I forgive you, Marc."

I felt him relax. "Sure?"

"Yes. Maybe I didn't communicate my dad's edict very well. It's time for us to bury the past." The weight that had pressed against my chest for eight long years suddenly dissolved and our lips found each other in a gentle feathery kiss that left me yearning for more. He didn't disappoint me.

Well into our third or fourth kiss, an upbeat version of a Christian worship song sang out from my evening bag hanging from my shoulder.

I retrieved the phone and checked the caller ID. "It's Flavia."

"Why is she calling you?"

"Because I didn't send her a promised recipe. I'm sorry, Marc, but I should take it."

He stepped back, and I opened the connection. "Hi, Flavia. I know I forgot to send the recipe."

A muted laugh came into my ear. "I wouldn't bother you, but we're having a bridal shower for my cousin."

"I'd send it right now, but we're at a restaurant. I'll do it first thing in the morning."

"No problem. I know Marisol will love the cake. She's going to be in a school play next weekend. She has the lead. It's been difficult for her to learn the lines."

I looked over at Marc and pointed at the phone and gestured.

"April, I think our steaks are coming."

"Okay. I'm hanging up," I mouthed as I glanced in the restaurant window. At least we weren't lying. The waiter was setting our plates at our empty places. Normally I loved talking on the phone, but Flavia couldn't have called at a worse time. I'd make it up to her by sending her several dessert recipes.

While devouring our filets, we filled in the blanks of the long years apart. Yet, he managed to skirt the information I craved. I didn't want to burst the bubble of joy I'd felt over the past hour, but if I didn't say something soon, we'd be on our way home.

"April."

I jumped.

He pushed his chair back. "Ready to go?"

I shook my head. "One more thing must be discussed."

ᦰ 35 ᦱ

Marc glared at me. "Don't you think that's better discussed in private?"

"You don't even know what I'm talking about." I glanced around the crowded room. No one was paying attention to us. I was tired of the runaround.

"Let's go. It's better discussed in the car." He stood.

It was all I could do not to stumble in an effort to keep up with him. We climbed into the Escape, and Marc started the motor. The David Crowder Band CD we'd listened to on our way to dinner blasted through the speakers. He hit a button, and the cab became silent. I'd have much rather listened to the music than the thumping of my heart.

He turned out of the parking lot and headed toward town. The words were on my tongue, but they wouldn't come. Silence hung in the air like a heavy winter blanket.

"The floor is yours," Marc finally said.

I needed to say it. Not think about it. "What happened in California?"

"I was right about the question."

"Then you've had time to compose an answer."

The blanket had lifted, but now the air felt like a rubber band on the verge of snapping.

"Marc?"

"It's not a big deal. I realized the doctoral program wasn't right for me, so I came back here to regroup. Heard about the job at Rescaté, and here I am."

The story had more holes in it than Sponge Bob Square Pants. "That's all?"

We rounded a curve, tires squealing. My body strained against the seatbelt, and I grabbed the bar on the door.

He slowed the vehicle. "When I quit the program, I worked at the Santa Alicia Country Club for a couple months. That's what the post meant by SACC." He halted at a stop sign and glanced at me. "I wanted to explain the day of your interview, but after hearing how you persevered to reach your goal without making a mess of things, I couldn't."

"Persevered?" I uttered a sardonic chuckle. "I loved my cooking classes but lacked the guts to follow through. I'd still be doing tax returns if I hadn't been laid off. Come on, Marc. There's something you're not telling me."

"If you're saying that to make me feel better."

My gut twisted. "Do you think I'd use trickery to get you to talk?"

"You pretended to be Candy's friend when you agreed to go to the Apple with her."

I stiffened. "I really hoped I could be her friend."

"You know as well as I do, that wasn't why you accepted her invite."

Nothing like someone naming your sin and having to own it. "I couldn't sit by and hope those rumors would go away. She hated Ramón and everyone knew it. I thought if I could assure myself that she had nothing to do with the death...that situation has nothing to do with ours. I'm in love with..." I clamped my mouth shut.

"You're in love with who?"

I kept my gaze to the windshield.

Behind us a horn honked.

Marc drove into the intersection and turned right. A short distance down the street he pulled over to the curb and cut the motor. "Once you hear the truth, you may not want to finish that sentence."

I slowly faced him.

He sat rigid as the nearby streetlamp, staring straight ahead. "I falsified data on my dissertation and was expelled from the doctoral program."

His words fought their way into my brain. Cheating and Marc didn't go together anymore than an enchilada with teriyaki sauce. My voice finally untangled itself. "Did you say what I think you said?"

After a long pause, he spoke. "I'd been offered a position with His Helping Hands, contingent with getting my PhD by June. The data I needed for my dissertation had already been delayed a couple of times, and I'd been forced to ask for extensions. If I didn't get my doctorate then, I'd lose the job offer." He gripped the steering wheel. "When the researchers announced another delay, I fudged the numbers on the paper and turned it in."

"Why?"

"The position was in their Buenos Aires office. I thought by living down there, I'd be able to erase the memories of us. The ministry wanted me, being fluent in Spanish and half Argentinean, until they found out I was a cheat."

"How'd you get caught?"

"My advisor and the researcher were grad-school buds. Within a week, I was out of the program, and a short while later the job offer was rescinded." He slumped against the seat. "It's doubtful I'll ever get my doctorate."

Despite his horrible confession, sweet relief washed over me. What he did was so out of character with the Marc I knew, but it could have been much worse. With the truth out of the way, we could finally move forward. If that was the direction we were to go. "I'm speechless."

"No words are necessary. I thought I knew better than God what was right for me and took matters in my own hands." He grasped my hand, giving it a squeeze. "I messed up everything, including us."

"What happened when you got caught?"

"I worked with my pastor out there and mowed the golf greens for about six months. Then I came home. Pastor Shay set me up with a mentor."

The mower attack flashed through my mind. "That's why the police drilled you about knowing how to operate a large mower. They should've asked me. Your shoulders are much broader than the guy who tried to run me down."

"They seem to know everything about me from the time I was a Cub Scout."

"How'd you start working at Rescaté?"

"For a couple months, I waited tables at my uncle's restaurant. Then one day at church Kitty mentioned the Rescaté job. Ramón said he believed in second chances. Of course, it was God giving me a second chance, not Ramón." He released my hand and gripped the ignition key. "Did you mean what you started to say? The part about being in love?"

Moisture filled my eyes. There we'd been, two refugees from difficult relationships with our dads and neither of us willing to share the sordid details.

"I guess the answer is 'no.'" Marc began to turn the key.

The tenor of uncertainty in his voice made it clear. We both needed to be transparent.

I placed a palm over his hand. "Don't you dare start that engine."

146

ಱ 36ಳಿ

"I've loved you, Marc, even when I wanted to hate you." I squeezed his hand, surprised that we'd intertwined our fingers.

He pressed the release button on my seatbelt, and it fell away as his arm went around me. "Come here, you."

I stretched over the center console, ignoring an upturned map poking through the thin fabric of my dress, and nuzzled my nose into his neck. The heady scent of aftershave and man teased my senses. At last I was home. No more grabbing a hug or kiss and feeling like I shouldn't.

"Babe, I promise to make up for all the hurt I've caused." He gently cupped my face in his hands, then trailed kisses over my face until our mouths connected. Kitty was right after all. Never again would I scold her for matchmaking, because there wouldn't be another time.

There wasn't anything left to say except, "Ouch."

He jolted back. "Did I pinch you?"

"No, but this did." I pushed down the seatbelt clip. Like a Jack-in-the-Box, it popped up.

Marc chuckled. "Probably just as well we were interrupted." He placed a tender kiss on my forehead. "We'd better leave before the chief comes along and arrests us for public display of affection."

I giggled. "You don't think he would be sympathetic to our story of long-lost love reunited?"

"Not when my back has a large target painted on it. Ready to go home?"

I fastened the seatbelt. "Let's stop at Dina's for coffee and see if LuAnn Dodge is working."

ಱಳಿ

I recognized LuAnn the minute we stepped into the diner. Slim, with carrot-red hair caught in a ponytail, she stood next to a booth jotting down an order. We sat in an adjacent booth.

A minute later, she sauntered up with a half-filled coffee pot and laid a couple plastic-covered menus on the table. "Hi, Marc." She turned her gaze to me, her facial expression asking why I looked familiar.

147

I grinned. "Hi LuAnn. Long time, no see. I'm April Love."

She slid the coffee pot onto the table, barely making her target, and stared at me. "The same April Love I played with while my mom cleaned the Montclaire mansion?"

I nodded. "One and the same."

"How long has it been?"

"Oh, probably since we spied on Kendall Montclaire down in the boathouse."

LuAnn giggled. "We sure gave that know-it-all a hard time. I wonder if that girl ever saw him again. Hopefully we saved her some grief."

I answered with a laugh. "And to think I'm now the new chef at Rescaté."

"No way." Her eyes rounded. "Did he remember you?"

"Eventually. So, how are you?"

She shrugged. "I'm good. Never did make it to beauty school. But that's okay. Life goes on. What about you?"

"Worked for my dad for a while, then moved to Atlanta. Bookkeeping by day and culinary school at night." No use flaunting my college education.

"Haven't seen you in a while, LuAnn," Marc said. "How's it going?"

"Same old, same old." She pulled an order pad from her pocket. "What can I get you guys? Fish fry is good tonight."

After the meal we'd finished, I doubted I'd eat again for at least a day. I caught Marc's eye and shook my head.

"We'll just have coffee," he said.

She snapped her pad closed. "Decaf okay?" She indicated the pot where it still sat on the table.

I nodded.

LuAnn turned over our mugs and splashed the dark brew into the cups. The telltale smell of old coffee floated to my nose. I reached for the creamer, then looked up at my childhood friend. "The other day you mentioned to my aunt that you worked the morning Ramón Galvez died. Would you have time to clear something up?"

Her smile dissolved as she glanced over at the next booth. "I have another table. What's my working that morning have to do with anything?"

"I'm not sure it does. But do you remember if anyone from Rescaté came in here for breakfast that morning, say around six?"

"I think that was the morning Candy Neer and her friend Gina came in." She rolled her eyes. "That woman has a body to die for and eats like there's no tomorrow. It just isn't fair."

I laughed. "My sentiments exactly. She didn't happen to have on exercise clothes, did she?"

"Candy? In exercise clothes? That woman thinks exercise is lifting food to her mouth. Another reason she's so disgusting." She laughed at her own joke, then flicked her gaze between Marc and me. "So, you two dating or something?"

I offered a coy smile. "Something."

"Dating," he answered, his words chasing mine.

LuAnn smirked. "I'll leave you two alone so you can figure out what you are." She stepped over to the booth behind us. "Can I get you guys anything?"

Marc fixed his eyes on me. "Something?"

I sipped my coffee and made a face. Even the extra dose of cream couldn't mask the burnt taste. "I didn't know what to say."

"How would you define us?"

Words raced through my head. *Reuppers?* Was that even a word? *Reconnected. Re...re...* "Restored and growing?"

"How about restored, committed, and growing?"

"Are you committed?"

"All the way."

"But don't we need some time?"

The smile on his face faded. He pushed his untouched coffee to the side and took my hand, rubbing his thumb across its back. "How much time?"

With the warmth exuding from his touch sending chills up my arm, my heart wanted to suggest we elope tomorrow. But reason won out. "Can't we take it day by day?"

"Sure, we can, sweetheart. You take all the time in the world, because I'm not going anywhere."

The delicious quiver filling my stomach suddenly turned sour. "I guess if I want to be sure of that, we'd better make sure the chief doesn't interfere."

Marc's expression went from a lopsided smile to serious concern. "Why'd you have to remind me?"

❧ 37 ❧

At seven the next morning I climbed out of bed and floated downstairs, chasing the fragrant aroma of fresh ground coffee. After filling my mug, I headed for the sun porch.

Kitty lifted her eyes from her Bible reading. "What are you doing up so early on a Saturday?"

I sat on the couch next to Rosebud and set my freshly poured brew on the table in front of me. "Couldn't sleep."

"From that goofy smile on your face am I to surmise the dinner date went well?"

"More than well." I laid my head against the cushion back and grinned at the ceiling while scratching behind Rosebud's ears. "Marc and I are back together again."

She let out a whoop, sending the cat flying off the cushion. "I knew you two were meant for each other."

"And you'll never stop gloating about your manipulating the situation to make it happen. I'm doomed."

She eased her Bible to the floor and rested her elbows on her knees. "So I presume he finally told you about California?"

I drew in a breath and held it. She was my confidant, but not everything was meant for others' ears, including hers. "Yes. But it's up to Marc to tell you, not me."

Disappointment registered for a split second, then she sat back and picked up her coffee mug. "Fair enough. The important thing is now you know. So when's the big day?"

I held up a hand. "Whoa. It's only been a couple weeks. I'm not ready to jump to that conclusion."

"I don't know why. You love each other and were engaged before."

"We also need time together as a couple again. Besides, there's more than our personal relationship to deal with."

Her smile dissolved. "What do you mean?"

"Yesterday, Chief Bronson and another officer interrogated Marc. He's been advised to stay close. From the line of questioning, it sounds like they're making tracks to charge him with murder."

150

Her cheeks colored. "What evidence do they have?"

"We don't know. Of course he's being framed, and whoever is doing the framing must be laying out a convincing case. We need to find out who ASAP since the police appear to think the information is believable." I sipped my coffee. "We talked on the way home about the possible people who could have killed Ramón."

"But do they even have solid proof he was killed?"

"We don't know that either. May have been a bluff to get him to confess, but they implied to Marc that they were about to autopsy the body." Helplessness washed over me. "If only we had those pills."

Kitty shook her head. "Even if you did and poison is found in Ramón's system during the autopsy, I'm afraid it wouldn't get Marc off the hook."

The creamed coffee in my stomach curdled as a vision of Marc being sent to prison erupted in my thoughts. How ironic that the thing I'd presumed to be the problem of his past was now becoming a real possibility in his future. Where were we to turn?

"Have you prayed about this?"

I lifted my shoulders and let them drop. "I have been for the past couple hours, and it feels as if my words are bouncing off the ceiling. How could God have allowed us to come back together, only to have us possibly be ripped apart?"

She picked up her Bible and flipped through the pages. "You know as well as I do that nothing with God is an accident. This was going to happen, with or without your being at Rescaté. God wants you here, maybe to give Marc the support he needs, or to help him dig out the truth so justice can be served to the right person."

She placed the glasses that had been hanging around her neck on her nose. "Listen to this: 'Two are better than one, because they have a good reward for their toil. For if they fall, one will lift up his fellow. But woe to him who is alone when he falls and has not another to lift him up!'"

The words from Ecclesiastes seeped into my being. How many times had I used them in the past to encourage friends who were struggling? I needed to be there for Marc to lift him up. I reached for the Bible, and Kitty handed it to me. I read the words she quoted and the following verses. "It also says that two fighting against a foe can prevail, and three is even better. With God in there with us, we can beat this."

My aunt beamed. "I think we need to pray."

Fifteen minutes later, feeling fortified spiritually, I stood. "That book on poisons you were reading the other day. Did you find any that emulate heart attacks?"

"Cyanide. I remembered that it's the one that was used in those killings down in Chicago. There were other poisons, but cyanide seemed the one most easy to get. The substance is put in rat poison, and they use it to develop film."

I huffed. "Who develops film anymore. Isn't it all on digital?"

"I bet there are some die-hards around. I still have a Brownie upstairs somewhere."

Somehow I knew that she didn't mean something you bake in an oven, but I bit back the question on the tip of my tongue.

We'd been tiptoeing around too long. Time to get serious. "I need to call Chief Bronson. I know you told him about the person in the orange cap running me over that morning. Did you mention the conversation I overheard before my interview?"

She pressed her lips into a pout. "I'm such a ditz. How did I forget that?"

"Doesn't matter, but he needs to know. I'll be on the kitchen phone."

I almost wished the chief were out chasing down a speeder on Canoga Lake's only major road. Unfortunately, the cop who answered the phone put me right through. I used the first minute or two of our conversation to introduce myself as Kitty McPiper's niece and the interim chef at Rescaté.

After agreeing with him that Aunt Kitty was indeed a very nice woman who was involved in every fundraiser that benefited the lake and village, I cut to the chase. "In light of your investigation into Ramón Galvez's death, there's something I need to tell you that may shed light on the situation."

The chief cleared his throat. "And what would that be?"

His clipped tone annoyed me, but I had to keep my cool. I raised my chin and launched into a blow-by-blow report of Ramón's telephone conversation. "Then the next morning at dawn—"

"Ms. Love, I don't know where you're going with this, but the team and I are on the case and gathering the evidence."

"But what I heard could be important. Can it be a coincidence that he had an angry conversation with someone he could have been blackmailing? The person had to have a source of money—likely a lot of money—and he or she may have killed him. Maybe with the pills I found in his bedroom, which were stolen from the Rescaté kitchen."

I paused for a quick breath and charged ahead, afraid he'd interrupt if I gave him opportunity. "It's possible those pills contained the same poison that killed Mr. Galvez. And the person who took the pills is also the same person who plowed into me the morning Ramón died, then tried to run me down with a lawn mower yesterday. "

A cynical chuckle came through the connection. "Sounds to me like you've been watching too many police shows. Thanks for the call, um, Ms...."

"Love."

"Yes. Love. I got another call coming in."

A *click* sounded in my ear. I pressed the *Off* button and slumped against the wall. If the man intended for his brusque attitude to put me off, he had another thought coming.

By the time I met Marc for lunch at Popeye's Restaurant in Lake Geneva, I had several pages of notes in a steno pad tucked into my purse. The hostess settled us at a table with a view of the Riviera and the water. After she left with our drink orders, I tossed the notepad on the table. "There's the info I gathered. What did you find out?"

He glanced around the crowded dining room, then leaned over the table. "Maybe we should talk later." He pointed at the window with his thumb. "Outside, away from ears."

I nodded and slipped the pad back into my hobo-style handbag.

Neither of us ate much of our burgers, and when we stepped outside it was a welcome relief from the loud conversation and music.

"Let's walk over to Library Park. We can talk there." Marc took my hand and intertwined our fingers. A perfect symbol of what God had shown me that morning. A bond, woven together by His presence. We'd beat this thing.

"So, what did you learn?" I finally asked as we passed in front of the prairie-style library off to our right.

"I spent nearly two hours digging through Rescaté files but couldn't find anything that showed Candy had been manipulating the records. Bob either. I think that theory is shot down. The volunteer data shows Ana was assigned a key card the same year Ramón started working there. I presume he gave her an apartment key without noting it. And I was surprised to see that Isabel was given both a key card and pass key to the apartment two years ago when she was in the area while Ramón was visiting Rescaté sites. Apparently she used his apartment as home base. Neither were turned in after the visit.

"And with Ana's apparent connections to money and Isabel's marrying into wealth, Ramón could have been blackmailing either woman." I glanced at him. "Question is, how do we find out if that's true?"

A long silence fell between us.

"So what's in your notepad?"

I pointed at a park bench. "Let's sit so I can read them."

Over the next several minutes, I showed Marc my notes on cyanide and speculations on timing for Isabel to have made the trip to Canoga Lake from

Chicago and back that morning without missing a beat. I also read my jotted quotes from my fruitless conversation with Chief Bronson.

I flipped the notebook shut. My heart all but broke at his expression. "Marc, don't look so glum. The chief is a small-town cop, feeling like he's about to score big. But we're going to prove you didn't do it. We have to."

He settled his arm over my shoulders. "I don't deserve even a minute of your support after the way I treated you."

I stretched my arm across his chest and kissed his cheek. "Hush. That's all under the bridge. God's done a healing in you and me both. We're not looking back, but ahead. It's time we had some fun. Karl mentioned he's in a rodeo at the fairgrounds in Elkhorn tonight. Do you want to check it out?"

❧❦

That evening, wearing Kitty's pink boots and the authentic Stetson I had no idea she owned, I answered Marc's knock at the door.

He caught sight of my outfit and flashed me a grin.

I pirouetted. "Don't you think it's a bit much? Kitty dressed me."

His trademark smile threatened to undo me. "If all the women at rodeos look like that, I wonder how the cowboys pay attention to their work."

I laughed. "Flattery will get you everywhere." I stepped back and checked him out. He wore jeans, but the navy polo, light windbreaker, and Packers cap did not say rodeo. I loved him anyway and let him pull me into his arms for a hug.

He brushed my lips with a kiss. "You lost your hat, pardner."

"Ah right don't care 'bout that, mister." I brushed the Stetson aside with my foot as he planted another kiss on the tip of my nose. A giggle came from behind me, and he looked up. "Hi Kitty."

I turned. My aunt stood in the door, grinning like a proud matchmaker. "Don't let me interrupt. I'm simply enjoying seeing you two back where you belong."

I stepped out of Marc's embrace and snatched the hat from the floor. "Want to come with us tonight? I'll even give you back your boots." I glanced at the pink toes peeking out from under my jeans.

She pushed away from the doorjamb. "Nope. Tonight's your night. Go and enjoy. I have a movie I've been dying to watch." She walked away.

"Guess that settles that." Marc opened the door. "Let's go. Elkhorn is a good half-hour's drive."

At Marc's vehicle I stopped walking. "A thought occurred to me while I was in the shower. Is it safe for you to go to something like this?"

"I was thinking the same thing, but about you. The police are only watching me. You're the one who was attacked by the guy on the mower."

I considered his words. I was the killer's target, not Marc. "No one is going to bully me into staying home. But maybe we should stop seeing each other until this is over. I don't want you being hurt."

Marc's face contorted as he released the lock with his key fob. He yanked the door open. "I don't think either of us will get hurt sitting in the bleachers at a rodeo. Too many witnesses."

I slid onto the passenger seat. That much was true, but we still had to make the drive over to the fairgrounds and back.

In spite of Marc's bravado, as we sailed down the highway I kept checking the road behind us, almost waiting for headlights to bear down. When the fairgrounds parking lot came into view, tension left my stick-straight body. At least for the next couple hours I could relax. I hoped.

Marc had called Karl earlier, and he said he'd meet us at the gate. We scanned the milling crowd. Karl had always been easy to spot, being the only one wearing a cowboy hat. Here half the people had them on.

"April, Marc. Here I am."

I turned as Karl ambled up wearing jeans and a dark blue shirt with the names of several companies embroidered on the sleeves. As we walked along the back of some bleachers, a pungent odor assaulted my senses, transforming me back to high school summers when LeAnn and I went horseback riding at a nearby camp. We were more interested in the boy that led the trail rides, and when he quit working there we stopped the rides and spent our money on movies instead.

"The contestants have a special place for families and friends," Karl was saying. "It's the best viewing for the bucking events. I want to take you guys behind the chutes before you go to your seats."

Behind the chutes? Was that like going in the pits at NASCAR? We followed the bull rider around the end of the bleachers.

Ahead, several calves stood in a small pen. Next to them, horses munched on the grass in another pen. "So where are the bulls?" I asked.

Karl pointed off to the left. "Over there."

We walked with him until he stopped in front of a large pen. My gaze flicked from one horned animal to the next. These were the bulls Karl always boasted about riding? Although large, not one displayed flaring nostrils, and none pawed the ground.

Disappointed, I turned to Karl. "They don't look very mean."

He laughed. "Don't let them fool ya. They know what to do when they get in that chute. See that black and white dude over there in the corner?" He pointed to one of the larger bulls, whose horns reminded me of elephant tusks. "That's Rough Rider. My ride to first prize tonight."

"That's the way, Murray. You need a positive attitude to get on one of those bad boys." Marc looked at Karl, respect written all over his face. He placed his hand at the small of my back. "Well, hon, you want to find our seats?"

I almost flipped at him calling me *hon* in front of Karl. We may have reconciled, but we still needed to keep our relationship under wraps. If he heard the euphemism, Karl didn't react. He was probably too busy telling himself what a wonderful bull rider he was.

"The bull riding is the last event," Karl said. "Wish I could sit with you and explain stuff, but I guess you'll figure it out. I need to catch someone before the rodeo starts. Can you find your way to your seats okay?"

Behind us, a man's voice called out, "April!"

I startled and was about to turn when Marc grabbed my elbow. "I'll look."

I obeyed his whispered direction and loved him for his bravado in my defense, but I stepped out of his grasp and angled myself enough to see a cowboy hug a young woman wearing jeans and a cowboy hat."

Karl chuckled. "That's April Dunning. Best barrel racer on the circuit."

I forced a laugh. "I wondered who else here knew me."

We assured Karl we were fine and he strolled off, passing by my namesake now deep in conversation with her cowboy friend.

"Well, he's a little full of himself, isn't he?" I grabbed Marc's hand as we walked toward the bleachers.

"Just self-talk. I did the same thing before football games back in high school. I bet inside he's nothing but nerves. Getting on the back of one of those brutes takes a lot of guts. "

"Thanks for explaining. I wasn't liking Karl so much at the moment."

Off to our left I heard someone say Karl's name and looked over. Huddled under a building built on stilt-like poles, several guys decked out in chaps and cowboy hats passed folded bills to Karl. As though sensing my stare, his gaze met mine and I held it. Time halted. One second, two seconds, then three—

"Earth to April." Marc tugged on my hand. "Let's find our seats."

I jerked my gaze away from Karl and let Marc guide me toward the bleachers. Over the past several days I'd convinced myself I'd misunderstood Karl's phone call that I'd overheard, but now I couldn't deny it. Gambling was bad enough, but had Ramón been blackmailing him? Did he make enough betting on small rodeos to pay off a blackmailer? Maybe he didn't have the money, and that's why he got rid of the blackmailer. He was about the height of the orange-capped person, but was he the same height and build of the mower operator? Hard to say.

My bottom hadn't been settled on the hard bleacher more than a couple seconds when a deep voice barreled out of a loudspeaker above our heads, welcoming everyone.

I scanned the cowboys standing on a catwalk behind the chute area. Karl wasn't there. What was he doing? Squirreling away the cash he collected?

I felt a tug on my elbow. A woman's soprano voice warbled "The Star Spangled Banner" through the PA system. I jumped to my feet. Enough speculating on facts I didn't know. I needed to get a grip. The National Anthem ended, and the announcer followed up with a prayer for the event. He'd barely uttered "Amen" when a chute gate opened.

A gray horse with a cowboy on his back jumped into the arena. He leaped one way and then the other, each time the rider leaning further back. How the guy stayed on without a saddle was beyond me. A horn blew, and a couple more men on horseback came up alongside the horse and helped the rider get off his mount. A tricky deal since the horse was still bucking.

I tried to pay attention to the calf roping events and trick horse riders, but all I wanted was to find Karl. Ask him what he was thinking. If he did kill Ramón and was framing Marc, he needed to do the right thing and turn himself in.

Intermission came, and Marc convinced me I was hungry.

At the food stand, he gave our order for hot dogs and drinks, then leaned down so I could hear him over the din. "You're awfully quiet. Having a good time?"

I raised my shoulders and let them drop. "Just in a mellow mood, I guess."

"Still worried about us being stalked?"

Should I tell Marc about Karl's gambling? Tricky question now that Karl reported to him. If the cowboy had nothing to do with Ramón's death, I wanted to help him with his gambling problem, not cause him to lose his job. Until I knew better, I should keep quiet.

I shrugged. "Guess I wish this whole business was behind us."

The guy behind the counter handed Marc our orders, and we headed back to our seats. The hot dog hit my stomach like a dead weight, but I was able to keep it down with the soda. I wanted the evening to be over so we could go home. After a women's competition called barrel racing came the event we'd been waiting for—bull riding.

"In Chute One we have Karl Murray of Canoga Lake, Wisconsin." The voice crackled through the speaker overhead. "A local boy who's destined for the NFR finals if he keeps up his winning streak. He's got his work cut out for him tonight, though, with Rough Rider. Let's give our home state cowboy some encouragement."

A huge whoop erupted from the stands.

The chute gate opened, and the black and white bull Karl had showed us earlier leaped into the arena. Looking smaller than life on top of the animal, Karl sat straight, his left arm raised in the air. The bull's back end bucked up at the same time he turned, then on the next jump turned the opposite direction. Ropes of snot spewed from his nostrils. The man next to me cheered. The horn blew, and Karl leaped to the ground. He ran to the side and climbed the fence while a couple guys in crazy get-ups cajoled the bull toward the open gate. The ride was over before it got going.

"That was a 91.25 ride tonight, folks." The announcer's strong voice filled the air. "Karl Murray has raised the bar for the other bull riders. He's going to be a hard one to beat."

Karl emerged out onto the dirt and raised his hat to the crowd. Even in the lights he managed to find me and hold my gaze. A shiver ran down my spine.

❧ 38 ❧

Against Kitty's protests that I shouldn't drive to work alone, I arrived at Rescaté on Monday without a problem and began gathering ingredients for muffins. With Marc's and my relationship restored, I should have been walking on air, but how could I after what I witnessed with Karl? I had stuck with my decision to not mention the gambling issue to Marc. If the guy had an addiction, he needed help and not an appointment with the unemployment line. But I hoped my decision wouldn't come back to bite me later.

Yesterday, other than church, we'd stayed indoors at Kitty's watching DVD movies and cooking. Together, the three of us made steaks over the gas grill embedded in Kitty's cook top, twice-baked potatoes, and a tossed salad. A Sunday I would have enjoyed, had I not been dreading what the week could bring.

While I sifted dry ingredients for the muffins, I convinced myself I was as safe in Rescaté's fortress-like building as I was at Kitty's, as long as I didn't take any strolls across the lawn. Besides, would the killer reveal himself in the very building he'd done the dirty deed? Especially with so many people around?

I got the muffins in the oven, then set out cream cheese to soften. Later, with extra minutes to spare, I started lattes for a break with Marc.

A thud sounded behind me, and I jumped. Heart racing, I made a slow turn. "You sure know how to scare a girl."

"Sorry. Didn't realize you were so jumpy. That box is heavy." Karl indicated a cardboard carton sitting on the island counter. "It has your name on it. Figured it came here."

I eyed the box. "What's in it?"

"Dunno. It was in Marc's office. I'm moving his stuff to Galvez's suite for him."

I resisted the urge to charge over to the carton to investigate and said instead, "You won big this weekend. Congrats are in order."

He offered a vacant stare. "Good thing you guys came Saturday. Yesterday, I couldn't stay focused. Bucked off in 2.5. Didn't even place for the weekend."

And I had a hunch his bet hadn't paid off either. "Wow. Talk about a roller coaster couple of days." I held up a mug. "Want coffee? You can have first crack at a new muffin recipe I tried."

"No to the muffin. Sure to the coffee."

I poured his brew while he settled onto a stool at the island.

As I placed his mug in front of him, his troubled eyes searched my face. "Do you have time to talk?"

I took a seat next to him, praying he wasn't about to confess to murder. "Um. Sure."

He wrapped his hands around his cup. "The reason I didn't do well yesterday...I bet money on a guy to ride a saddle bronc. He bucked off. Lost everything I won legitimately on Saturday and more."

"You bet on the rodeo?"

"You saw me. Stop acting like you didn't."

"Gambling on a rodeo could end your career, right?"

He pushed his coffee away and nodded. "It started out as something fun to do, to add more excitement, but then I won a few times and wanted more. Now it's not only the rodeos I'm in, but finals in Vegas...football..." He shook his head. "I about lost my shirt last year. You'd think I'd learn."

"What are you going to do?"

He pulled his mug toward him and hunched over it. "Dunno. I can barely make my rent. Had to hit my brother for a loan."

"Does he know about your problem?"

He shook his head.

Where did I go from here? "What about an addiction support group?"

He straightened his shoulders. "I can do it on my own."

"There's a group that meets at Canoga Community Church on Friday nights."

The right corner of his mouth drew up. "Fridays are bad. A guy I know goes to a Wednesday night group. Maybe I'll call him."

"I'll hold you to it, cowboy. And don't worry. I won't tell anyone."

He peered at me. "Doesn't Marc already know?"

"No. And I don't plan on telling him—unless it starts interfering with your work." I pulled the box toward me. "Let's see what's in here." I opened the flaps and pulled out a book. A purple Post-It stuck to its colorful cover. 'Marc, these are for April. Give her my love. Mom.' I ran my hand over the cookbook. "Marc's mom sent me these."

Karl grinned. "You move fast. Already in good with the future mother-in-law."

160

Did my face look as red as it felt? "We have no plans."

He chuckled. "Yeah, right. Everyone around here knows you two have it bad."

I set the book down. "Bad as in good?"

"You guys have been giving each other lovesick stares ever since you landed here. We're waiting for the wedding announcement."

So much for acting indifferent. Did the "we" include Kendall? "Since you already know so much, I suppose it's not news we were engaged back in college."

Deep dimples formed in his cheeks. "I thought that, but Rosa and Helen said no, that you probably knew each other from summers on the lake."

I nearly spit out the coffee I had sipped. Didn't these people ever work? "Right on both counts, but let's keep it quiet around here." I reached inside the box and touched what felt like tissue paper. Marc's mom used to tuck little surprises in packages she sent to him at school. Had she done the same for me now? I eagerly snatched up the bundle and tore at the blue paper.

The tissue fell away, and a sour taste rose in my throat. I flung the thing to the floor.

Karl jumped off his stool and picked it up.

I stepped back until my rear hit the counter. "How long was the box in Marc's office?"

He tossed the baseball cap on the counter. "Can't say."

I forced my eyes away from the orange monstrosity and shot him a venom-filled stare. "Ridden any lawn mowers lately, or only bulls?"

"Mowers?" He edged toward the door. "You're not making sense."

"Don't run away now, cowboy. You're about the right height, build. Have access to all the rooms. Pay Ramón a little visit the morning he died?"

A chill filled the air and ran down my spine. I glanced at the chef's knife on the counter. In one movement he could shut me up for good. Who did I think I was? The lead character in a thriller novel? I wanted my boring life back.

He grabbed the door handle. "You think I did Galvez in all because of some cap Thorne's ma sent you? You're crazy." He opened the door.

Was he leaving? Good. As soon as he's gone, I'm calling the police.

If Karl is the killer, he'd never leave this room with me alive. I know too much.

"Karl, wait. I'm really losing it here."

39

Karl's eyes went wide as I summarized what had gone down the past couple weeks. I ended with the mower attack and Marc being framed.

"Man, I can't believe all that happened under my nose."

I gave him a wry smile. "Do you know if Ramón blackmailed someone, and if so, who it may have been? Someone has to be feeding the police information beyond the rumors that implicates Marc. But what? I'm scared we're running out of time before Marc is arrested."

"Or you're killed." He pursed his lips. "There wasn't any love lost between him and Isabel or Ana."

"What about Candy?"

He shrugged. "No cash. The other ladies have resources."

I filled him in on what I overheard Brett saying that night at the Apple about dropping money into Candy's bank account. "What if he's financing Candy?"

He chuckled. "Hagenbrink is a small-town nobody who sells insurance out of a strip-mall office. Whatever the reason he's throwing money in her bank account, trust me. It wasn't enough to make anyone commit murder."

"Good. The last thing her mother needs is a jailbird for a daughter. Any more ideas?"

"Not now." He tapped his ear. "But I'll keep my ears open."

Feeling better, I sent Karl off. If anyone could dig up new information, it was him. Now to tell Marc that Karl was on his side...or was he? A minute ago I'd reasoned that he wasn't the killer, but what if he had me fooled? Risky still, not to shut me up when he had the chance. I had to trust him.

At Marc's office, I swept past Taryn, the hat in a brown envelope tucked under my arm. I shot her a look that said, "Don't try to stop me."

I tapped on his door, and he looked up from packing a moving box and grinned. "Time for our break already?" His voice echoed off the barren walls.

I shut the door. "The killer strikes again." I dumped the hat onto his empty desktop.

The smile slipped from his face as he picked up the cap. "Where'd you get this?"

"In the cookbooks your mom sent. Karl brought me the carton a couple minutes ago when he saw my name on it."

He paled. "I hope you don't think I put it there."

"What I want to know is how long has the box been in your office?"

"Since Friday when UPS brought it."

"You were in here Saturday. Did you look inside the carton?"

"The only time I glanced inside was when it came on Friday after we'd talked in the boathouse. I was here Saturday morning for a while when I researched information about the keycards, but I never paid the thing any mind and never saw any indication anyone else had been here." His eyes creased at the corners. "A curly-headed blonde preoccupied me the rest of the weekend. Work was the last thing on my mind."

I couldn't help but chuckle.

"At least this takes Karl off the hook." He turned the hat over in his hands. "He couldn't have planted this, then brought it straight to you. He's smarter than that."

"I agree. But can we trust our gut instinct?"

"We have to."

On the other side of the door Taryn laughed, and I lowered my voice. "Here's the name of a lawyer Kitty recommends." I handed him a business card. "Before you call him, best we nail down all you remember about your activities that Friday morning."

He tossed the hat on his desk, then sat and studied the card.

I sat across from him. "You had a breakfast appointment that Friday morning. Right?"

"Yeah. At a restaurant over on the South Shore. But we didn't meet until seven-thirty. Before that I went for a run and showered."

I groaned. "How does someone who lives alone have an alibi?"

"You don't."

"How long does it take to drive to the restaurant from your place?"

He shrugged. "About 15 minutes."

"You could've stopped here first, exchanged the bottles, and then run me over on your way out."

He stiffened. "Whose side are you on?"

"I'm only trying to think like the chief would."

The lines around his mouth softened as he grasped my hand. His skin felt cold against my palm. "Sorry. I'm not thinking clearly."

"Did anyone see you during the run?"

He huffed. "A bit hard in the dark."

"Was your car parked outside?"

"In the garage."

An odd feeling came over me. Here we were talking about a possible future together, and I had yet to see Marc's condo. That would have to change—soon. "A garage used by others too?"

"Each unit has a private garage." He stared at the ceiling. "It's hopeless."

Taryn and Candy's voices filtered into the room. I pointed toward the door and whispered, "I'd feel better if we could discuss this away from here."

He nodded. "Let's have lunch. I'll swing by for you at noon."

I left Marc and headed to the kitchen, the envelope containing the cap under my arm, our ticket to Marc's freedom.

❧ 40 ❧

Marc called right before noon. Kendall wanted to meet him for lunch. I was to wait at Kitty's for his call, and we would meet at his condo for sandwiches after I dropped the hat off at the police station.

I loved how I'd just thought about not yet seeing his home, and without my mentioning it, he suggested we meet there. Not one who looks for hokey signs that say, "We were meant to be together," I tried to temper the warm feeling the thought evoked, but I couldn't. We *were* meant to be a couple. Period.

When I pulled into Kitty's circular driveway, a plain sedan greeted me. I studied the empty vehicle for a second, then decided it must belong to one of my aunt's lady friends. Grabbing my purse and the envelope containing the hat, I climbed out of the car.

From the service porch I heard a man's voice, and my curiosity rose. Kitty had few male callers. Maybe it was the guy who worked on her computer the other day. Through the door I caught sight of the back of a tall, gray-haired man in a rumpled suit. I stepped into the kitchen.

"Here she is now," my aunt said. "April, I'd like you to meet Chief Bronson. He is on his way back from court and dropped by to see you."

I was supposed to go to him, not him to me. A trap door beneath my feet would be nice. "Chief, glad to meet you in person." I stepped in further and looked up into his steely gray eyes. Funny, his rather monochromatic appearance—gray hair, gray eyes, gray mustache, gray suit—matched the even-toned voice over the phone the other night.

"Likewise."

At his hardened stare, I hugged the envelope to my chest. Bad move. The pressure from my arm forced the bright orange cap bill through opening at the top of the envelope. The lines on his face tightened, and I shifted my gaze to a row of trivets hanging on the wall behind him. I may have been standing in my aunt's kitchen, but right then he held all the marbles.

He rocked back on his heels. "I don't want to presume you're withholding evidence, so why don't you hand over that envelope?"

At his harsh tone, I took a step back.

"Now, Howard, I'm sure April intended to give you whatever she has."

Kitty pinned a stare on me. "Isn't that right, dear?"

"I was planning on dropping this off within the hour. Seeing that you're here, it saves me a trip."

"See? There's no hurry." Kitty patted his arm. "After all, we don't even know for sure Ramón was murdered."

"That's not true, Mrs. McPiper."

"Then you autopsied the body?" The words flew out of my mouth.

He swiveled his glare back to me. "If you'll tell me how you came to have that hat you're trying so hard to hide, I'll forget how you were suppressing evidence."

"April, maybe I should call Dutch Vanderveldt."

I blinked at Kitty.

"She doesn't need a lawyer."

The name on the card I gave Marc that morning. No wonder the name was familiar. I turned my attention back to Mr. Personality. "I only found the hat in the Rescaté kitchen this morning."

"Where in the kitchen?"

"Inside a box." Sweat beaded on my forehead.

"Do you know who had the box last?"

"Yes, sir."

Kitty's gaze jumped from me to the chief's haughty expression. "Would you like some coffee, Howard? I wish I'd known you were coming. I'd have made your mother's shortbread recipe."

A sudden softness came over the man's face. "Of all the cookies Mom made, those were my favorites. Do you think before I leave you could jot down the recipe?"

Who would've thought the guy would crumble at the mention of his mom's cookies?

We settled around the kitchen table while Kitty started coffee brewing and found the recipe. The respite gave my nerves time to settle.

The chief pulled a small notebook from his pocket. It looked like the same one I saw him use at the memorial service. He flipped it open and printed the day's date in bold capital letters across the lined paper. "Okay, start at the beginning. We'll get to the hat later."

I gave him a point-by-point timeline of each event, starting with the overheard telephone conversation and ending with how Marc was being framed. At his insistence, I told him who I thought might have reason to kill Ramón and why. I inwardly winced as he jotted down Isabel and Ana's names. After his third "anyone else?" I added Candy, stressing she was a long shot.

166

He caught me in the bull's-eye of another intense stare. "No men?"

Karl's face popped into my thoughts. But he'd proven to me he wasn't a suspect not an hour ago. I shook my head.

"Who had the box of cookbooks before they arrived at Rescaté?"

My cell phone vibrated inside my pocket, its buzz sounding like a giant bee. If the chief heard it, he didn't let on. "Had to be Marc Thorne's mother, unless you count the delivery man."

He poised his pen. "She live nearby?"

"Florida."

While he jotted on his pad, I gazed longingly at the sink faucet. I'd give anything for a drink but didn't dare ask.

"So Thorne had the hat."

The man shifted gears faster than a racecar driver. Was this a taste of the interrogation Marc had gone through?

"He didn't have the hat, didn't see the hat, or touch the hat until I took it to his office after I opened the box. Whoever is trying to frame Marc planted the cap in the books after the box arrived in his office."

"So Thorne gave you the box."

My stomach soured. I had to tell the truth. "Karl Murray, the handyman, delivered the box to me because it had my name scribbled on it." I caught the man's hard gaze in my own. "Karl didn't put the hat in the box. I'm convinced of that. Someone else planted it there over the weekend." I shoved the envelope toward the chief.

His moustache undulated. "How are you so sure it was planted, missy, and how are you so positive Thorne or Murray didn't mess with the box?" He pulled the hat from the envelope.

"The box arrived Friday, but Marc was with me all weekend. And I know Karl didn't do it." I tried to swallow, but my throat felt coated with sand.

"What makes you so sure?"

"He told me he didn't, and I believe him." Oh boy, now I'd done it. Poor Karl.

A silver brow rose as he jotted another note. "Love with suspect Friday to Sunday. Did you stay at his place or did he stay here?"

My face heated.

"Howard," Kitty cut in. "All weekend didn't mean sleeping together."

"Let her answer the question."

"We each slept in our own homes. He was here until about midnight Friday night, and we were together from about noon Saturday until 1:00 a.m. Sunday. He returned here to go to church with me at eight-thirty Sunday morning, and was here until ten that evening."

"So he had plenty of time to plant that hat in the box."

I inwardly cringed. Had I unwittingly dug a deeper hole for Marc?

"So there's more than a working relationship between you and Thorne. No wonder you're covering for him. "

"I've known Marc a long while." Kitty set a steaming cup in front of him. "He's a good Christian man."

He smirked at her. "A good Christian man who was tossed from grad school for cheating."

"If that were true, he would have told my niece."

I didn't dare look at Kitty. "I do know about that. But what he did in grad school has nothing to do with Mr. Galvez's death. Someone is trying to frame him." I croaked out the words, "Marc Thorne is not a murderer."

The chief scraped his chair back and picked up the envelope. "You know that old saying. If it looks like a duck, smells like a duck, and walks like a duck, then it's a duck." He held up the envelope. "This adds the last piece to the puzzle. Sorry I couldn't stay for the coffee. It smells great."

"I'll see you out." Kitty gave the man a stiff smile and handed him a card. "Here's your recipe."

Their muffled voices drifted off toward the door. I pulled my phone out and checked voice mail.

"April," Marc said. "Call me. I'm at home."

❧ 41 ❧

After quickly answering a flustered Kitty's questions about Marc's cheating, I headed for his place. Halfway through the village, my phone rang. I pulled it out of my purse and glimpsed the caller ID. As much as I wanted to let it go to voice mail, I pressed *Accept*.

"Hi, Flavia. You still need that recipe and I forgot. I'm so sorry. If you knew how hectic—"

"I think maybe Isabel is involved in Ramón's death."

I tensed. "Why?"

"The police chief up there wanted her permission to autopsy Ramón because there's a suspicion he was killed." She sniffed. "At first she balked, but when they mentioned a court order, she relented."

"That doesn't mean—"

"The morning Ramón died she planned to drive up to Rescaté to have it out with him. She said she had car trouble and never made it there. What if she's lying, setting me up to tell them what she said, and she...I can't say the word. She was so angry at him."

Cradling the phone with my shoulder, I dug into my purse for pen and paper. "Do you know where she had the car worked on?"

"Fox Lake."

Red lights blazed in front of me. My foot hit the brake, then everything went black.

~ 42 ~

An acrid odor filled my nostrils, and I pushed the airbag away from my face. Something was burning. I groped for the door handle, but my hand tangled with the deflated bag. The door flew open. Cool, clean air blasted into the car. I hauled in a precious breath.

"Do you know how much dough you just cost me?"

My gaze lifted to a pair of the broadest shoulders I'd ever seen and, above them, bulging nostrils that I expected to smoke at any moment.

Afraid of being singed, I looked away and stared through the windshield. My stomach squeezed. Dad would blow a gasket if someone rear-ended his '55 Vette like that. I really did it this time.

I peered up at the guy, who didn't appear any less menacing than a second ago. "Totally my fault. I'm so sorry."

"You better believe it's your fault, sister. Get out."

A siren sounded in the distance. "Let me give you my information. It'll only take a sec." I reached for my purse where it had landed on the passenger side floor, and a sharp pain torpedoed through my chest.

A loud screech split the air. I looked up as the Corvette shot down the road and rounded a curve. A minute later a squad car pulled up. Chief Bronson climbed out, this time decked out in his police uniform, all pressed and creased in the right places.

He swaggered toward me, wearing a gleaming badge on his chest and a smirk on his face. "What were you doing? Chasing down Galvez's killer?"

Too bad I didn't have one of his mother's shortbreads on me. "No. But you may want to look for the guy I hit. As soon as he heard your siren, he took off. Big man in a red and white vintage Corvette, wearing jeans and a faded blue T-shirt. His license tag is *Lucky.*"

"Wait here." He stepped aside and spoke into the radio affixed to his shoulder.

I seized the moment and called Marc.

"April, where are you?"

"I rear-ended someone at Lake and Main. But I'm okay."

"I can jog there in two minutes."

"Bronson is here."

"I don't care."

"No, Marc."

Next to me, someone coughed.

I disconnected.

"What's Thorne gonna do? Come rescue you?"

"I had to tell my boss I'm going to be late for a meeting."

"Step out and tell me what happened."

I detailed the crash, after which the chief happily wrote me a ticket.

He tore it off his pad with an extra flourish and added a lecture about not talking on a cell phone while operating a moving motor vehicle. Strolling back to his car, he called over his shoulder, "Hope you got insurance. Bumpers cost a bundle."

I slipped behind the wheel and studied the deflated airbag. It had to be moved off the steering wheel if I were going to drive it to a repair place.

"Ms. Love."

I peered out the door I hadn't bothered to close.

The chief tossed me a thin smile through his open window. "Sergeant Hogan radioed. They caught the guy you hit. He was driving a stolen vehicle."

I bit back a snappy retort and mumbled, "Good to hear."

He drove off as Marc ran toward me from across the road. My knight in blue jeans never looked better.

He helped me out of the car, and the instant I pressed my face into his chest as his muscular arms cocooned me, tears erupted. "I hit a stolen vintage 'Vette. The guy was fuming. If he posts bail, he might be looking for me."

Marc patted my back. "Sweetheart, I'm sure the only thing he'll want to do is keep his nose clean, not go looking for more trouble. Are you hurt?"

I assured him that except for the bruise from the seatbelt I was fine. When he suggested he drive the car back to his condo, I gratefully handed him my keys and slid into the passenger seat. Let him deal with that bag.

Ten minutes later, after Marc had folded and maneuvered the bag's remains into a position that allowed him to steer the car, we turned onto Cliff Drive, one of my favorite roads in the village thanks to the half-dozen antique Victorians that lined the street. He made a turn into his condo complex and parked in front of a brick building. "It's driving okay. Nothing out of alignment." He cut the motor and handed me the keys.

After a quick stop at his mailbox in the lobby, we went to his condo a couple doors away. On legs that suddenly felt like rubber, I headed straight for the suede-cloth loveseat and sank into its deep cushions.

"What do you need, babe?" Marc's concerned gaze fixed on my face.

"Come sit with me."

Without a word, he plopped beside me and pulled me close.

I snuggled up and pressed my face into his shoulder. The familiar scent of Downey tickled my senses, offering a strange sort of comfort. Mom always used that stuff. But I couldn't wallow in childhood memories. This was now, and we had a hot police chief on our tails. "Does Bronson get elected around here?"

"No election, but his contract comes up this summer. I heard that a citizen group is challenging it."

I huffed. "Nothing like a big arrest to make him look good. He was at Kitty's when I got there. He couldn't have planned it better. He jacked me around, insinuating I was withholding evidence because I hadn't turned the cap over and made sure I knew about your trouble with the doctorate. I don't know how he thought I could turn it in any faster, given I'd only discovered it that morning."

He tensed. "The man seems to operate in a parallel universe. There's a big stretch between cheating in grad school and committing murder."

"I said as much to him."

He sat forward. "What next?"

"I was talking to Flavia when I had the accident. She's scared Isabel may have killed Ramón." I summarized what she said about Isabel's car trouble the morning Ramón died.

"Her car problems should be easy enough to prove by calling repair places in Fox Lake. If she has an alibi that only leaves Ana, we've no more suspects."

I grabbed a red throw pillow and hugged it. "Same for the chief, whether he wants to admit it or not. I told him the person I saw was no more than five-eight, not six-foot-one, so why are they looking at you?"

"Probably figures you're protecting me."

I snorted. "He said that, too. They can't arrest you without solid evidence."

"Think about it. The chief knows Ramón and I didn't get along. He threw that in my face the other day. And he knows I had access to Ramón's apartment. Now the cap was in my possession. Next thing you know poisoned pills are going to show up in my back pocket."

I tugged his arm. "Sit back and tell me what happened between you and Ramón."

He grabbed my hand, weaving our fingers together. "Six months ago, the board recommended making me V.P. in charge of operations. He sabotaged the promotion by informing the board about my past." Marc shook his head. "I thought they already knew, but he never told them. Ramón and I got into an argument. Kim was at her desk outside his door and heard everything. Guess she didn't keep it to herself."

His cell phone jangled. He grabbed it and studied the screen. "It's Chief Bronson."

"Maybe you shouldn't answer."

The intrusive ring continued.

"If I don't, I'm putting off the inevitable. Best I take it." He pushed the answer button. "Thorne." His jaw tightened. "Not yet. I just took it out of my mailbox. Okay." He closed the phone. "The chief wants to talk to me again day after tomorrow and says I should bring my lawyer. He suggested I check out this week's *Chronicle.*"

"If he's so anxious to slip a noose around your neck, why wait two days?"

"He has to be in court tomorrow." Marc went to the dining table and snatched up the weekly newspaper. He stared at the front page, and color drained from his face.

❧ 43 ❧

I hunched forward. "What is it?"

"Look for yourself." He flung the tabloid-style paper. Pages flew into the air and spewed across the floor. "Talk about getting no respect in your hometown." He stomped down a hall and a second later a door slammed.

I dove for the front page and stared at the two-inch-high headline: *GALVEZ DEATH DECLARED MURDER.* Pulse racing, I continued to read:

Canoga County Coroner, Reginald Fuller, was forced to change Rescaté de Niño Director Ramón Galvez's cause of death to murder. On a tip from a civilian, local police sought and received permission from Galvez's sister to autopsy the remains.

Police Chief Bronson announced today that a lethal amount of cyanide was found in Galvez's body. Authorities suspect Galvez ingested the poison through vitamin capsules containing the deadly substance. Bronson revealed they are investigating a person of interest. They expect to make an arrest soon. Pressed for more details, he declined, saying he didn't want to compromise the case.

Marc wasn't a killer. Tears pressed at my eyes as I glanced down the hall. The man stewing behind that closed door meant more to me than anything. I covered my face with my hands and wailed, "Lord, help us. We don't know what to do next."

A hand gripped my shoulder. "April, are you okay?"

I stared into Marc's stricken face. "Yes."

"Liar." He sat beside me.

"Really, I am." I sat up and palmed the wetness from my face. "Are *you* okay?"

"Yeah."

"Liar."

"You don't have to be in this battle. I wouldn't blame you if you got out while the getting is good."

I gripped his hand, stunned at its lack of warmth. "I'm going nowhere."

"They've got me pegged, and nothing is going to change their minds."

"They may have made you their target, but we'll find the killer and prove them wrong."

He brushed a kiss on my lips. "I've got to think of your safety. The more we keep investigating, the more danger you're in. I'll call that attorney and go to the appointment with the chief."

"By all means, get your lawyer, but meanwhile we've got tonight and all of tomorrow. Let's make some notes."

Marc found paper and pencil and we settled at the small dining table next to the kitchen. After going over the timeline of events, we moved next to the suspects.

I drummed my fingers on the tabletop. "We can dismiss Candy altogether after what Karl said."

"Karl?"

"Once I knew he was in the clear this morning, I told him what was going on. He's a good guy to have on board."

Marc crossed his arms and shot me a wary look. "Are we so certain he's in the clear? After all, the guy's knee-deep in gambling debts."

I felt my brows rise. "You know that?"

"I've heard him on the phone a couple times when he thought no one was nearby. At the rodeo the other night I saw him collecting money, and that confirmed it. I've been talking to Pastor Helmuth who runs the addiction ministry at church about doing an intervention and getting Karl some help."

My heart had to enlarge to make room for the expanding love for this man. "And here I was afraid to tell you because you'd fire him."

"Ramón would have fired him. I look for a solution. Taking his job away would only force him into more betting to try to make up for a lack of a paycheck." He ran a hand over his hair. "If you're convinced he's not involved in Ramón's death, I'll trust your instincts."

"After seeing his face this morning when I accused him of the crime..." I paused. What if I was wrong? No. I could see it in his eyes. He told me the truth. "I'm convinced he's innocent. We need him. Marc. Think about it. The guy can be in places we can't without drawing attention. He gave me great insight on Candy, Ana, and Isabel."

Marc nodded. "You're right. But be careful how many more people you draft. What did he say about Candy?"

"Brett is likely trying to be a big shot. We don't know what the deal was with the money, but neither he nor Candy has enough to be blackmailed. Karl says Isabel has the bucks, and it appears that Ana has enough moola as well."

"That's for sure. She lives in a penthouse in Lake Geneva and is always taking expensive vacations."

"Have you heard anything about her being in the country illegally?"

Creases formed between his dark eyes. "Never. Why?"

"Someone overheard Ramón threaten to oust her during one of their arguments. He said she'd find herself back in Mexico before she knew what happened."

"Interesting. Scuttlebutt around the office has it she comes from a wealthy family that made their fortune in Acapulco hotels."

I tapped my pencil on the pad. "Ramón seemed to have a fetish for exposing people's secrets." I looked at my watch. It was already past business hours. "I'll call auto repair places in Fox Lake tomorrow morning and see if Isabel's story matches up."

"I feel in my gut it was an inside job, and I have just the thing to smoke out the killer." Looking more animated than he had all afternoon, Marc reached in his jeans pocket and pulled out a rusty key.

❧ 44 ❧

"I remember her well," the service manager at Fox Lake Motors said to me the next morning. "Tall, dark-haired lady. Good looking. Came in at 7:32 according to my computer. Had a busted serpentine belt. Got a little huffy when she had to wait for us to get a replacement."

I tapped my pencil on my notepad. "Did she wait?"

"She had no choice. All the loaners were out."

"Did she make any calls?"

"Don't pay no attention to the customers in the wait area." He paused. "Hey, who did you say you were? I'm not sure I should be giving out this information."

"You've helped a lot. Thanks." I pressed the *Off* button on my cell phone and put it in my pocket. Marc's plan had to work. We were fast running out of time. Visions of a jailhouse wedding had been creeping into my thoughts since yesterday, and each time it became harder to quash them down.

I crossed the room to the snack wagon and gave the assorted breads, coffee, and fresh fruit one last inspection. The cart complained with a loud creak as I pushed it through the door and into the hall. At the entry to the reception room, I heaved the front wheels over the floor molding. They hit the wood planks with a thud. A basket somersaulted to the floor, tea bags skittering in every direction like hockey pucks. I dropped to my knees, wincing as a painful reminder of yesterday's accident shot through my chest.

"Looks like you've got yourself quite a load there." Gerald Claypool bent at his rounded waist, his coat sleeves pulling at the shoulder seams. He snagged a packet of green tea from under an end table.

"Thank you, Mr. Claypool, but I can manage."

"Nonsense." He huffed a breath then knelt to pick up a Lemon Zest. "Gerald. Please call me Gerald."

"Okay." I stood and tucked my handful of teas into the basket. Across the room, the conference room door remained closed. "Has the board's break already begun?"

"I had to, um, see a man about a horse." He rested a pudgy hand on his knee and pushed himself up.

Whoa. That was more information than I needed to know. What was I supposed to say to that? Nothing.

I managed a smile. "Gives you first dibs. Help yourself."

He huffed a few more times, then stabbed a plastic knife into the maple-flavored cream cheese. It didn't take a Mensa membership to realize this man had no place on the suspect list.

I straightened the tea bags. "I suppose everyone has heard the big news."

He applied spread to his bagel. "About Ramón being murdered? Awful. Simply awful. I had no idea they suspected murder."

"There were rumors, but I never believed them. Boy, was I wrong."

He narrowed his eyes. "Marc mentioned you two are involved with the investigation. How so?"

"A conversation I overheard the day before Ramón died. We've got several suspects in mind." Did crossing my fingers behind my back really absolve me from lying? But what if one's hands were full? Did mentally crossing one's fingers count? What if the lie was for the greater good? I'd have to talk to God about that later.

His gray brows lifted. "Isn't it a little irregular for civilians to be involved in a police matter?"

I shrugged. "Maybe in a large city, but it makes sense. We're right here where it happened. Know the people. We think the lower level of the boathouse is involved. It's been locked up and unused for years. We intend to keep a tight eye on it tonight."

"A tight eye?"

"I think it's called a stakeout," I whispered. He didn't seem to buy the story. Was it too out there? Marc insisted it would work. It had to, or he'd soon be wearing a number on his back.

"Sounds dangerous."

"We'll be fine. It's kinda exciting." I smiled as sweetly as I could. "Who'd have thought that old boathouse might give us the answer?"

"Isn't the key to the boathouse missing?" Kendall approached the cart.

I swooped up a muffin and dropped it on a paper saucer along with a scoop of honey butter, his usual choice. Tucking a checked paper napkin under the plate, I handed it to him. "Mark found the key in Ramón's desk."

Kendall waved off the food. "Thanks, but I have an alumni banquet tonight in Madison. Should watch the old waistline." He patted his trim stomach. "Gotta support the old alma mater, you know." He jammed his hands in his pockets. "What were you saying about the boathouse?"

I lowered my voice. "We think it's connected to Ramón's murder, and we plan to stake it out tonight."

Kendall filled a cup with decaf. "You and your aunt?"

"Marc and me. Didn't he tell you in the meeting?"

"I had to step out." He tore open a packet of sweetener then shook the granules into his brew. He sipped his coffee before giving me a stern look, then whispered, "You two haven't forgotten what I said before about office relationships have you?"

I mentally crossed my fingers for the second time. "Of course not. This is strictly office business. The sooner we can expose the killer, the better it is for Rescaté and the kids."

He stared into his coffee cup and swirled the dark brew with a circular motion. "Have you any idea who the police's person of interest is?"

My heart celebrated. The chief hadn't blabbed to Kendall, but how could I not answer and still tell the truth? The old saying, "Oh, what a tangled web we weave when we endeavor to deceive," ran through my mind. "I'm not certain, but—"

The conference room door opened, and the rest of the board, along with Marc, streamed into the reception area. Kendall waved them over. As the hungry men attacked the cart, I scanned the group, finding it difficult to imagine any one of them a murderer.

Marc motioned me to a far corner with a cock of his head. I scooted over.

"Everyone's concerned about Rescaté's reputation," he whispered. "I let them know that was our concern as well, and we hope to have answers after tonight. I told them I couldn't say more than that it involved the boathouse, because we don't want to jeopardize the case."

I brought my mouth to his ear as he leaned down. "I mentioned the boathouse key to Kendall, not realizing he didn't know about it."

"He got a call on his cell and left before I explained."

I inhaled the scent of his aftershave, wishing I could stay right there and enjoy the atmosphere, but I stepped back, gave him a wave, and hurried over to the cart.

When I arrived at my next stop, it was all I could do not to gape at Candy's to-the-knee skirt and suit jacket, a white button-down blouse underneath. Even stylish closed-toe pumps covered her feet. I glanced around, half expecting the crew from *What Not to Wear* to be lurking in the corner, crowing over their handiwork.

"Some news, huh?"

Candy looked up from examining the offerings. "News?"

"Yeah, in yesterday's *Chronicle*."

"All the *Chron* reports is who got traffic tickets and which kid was in a piano recital this week." She dunked a teabag into the hot water she'd poured.

"As for the big city papers, if the news isn't bad, it's boring. Like I care if the Dow is up or down. I read *People* magazine every week, though. What news you talking about?"

"The police announced that Ramón was poisoned."

Her eyes rounded. "As in someone knocked him off?"

"I guess you could put it that way."

"Man. As much as I hated that jerk, I couldn't imagine puttin' out his lights like that. It creeps me out to think a murderer is on the loose."

"Me, too. That's why Marc and I plan to keep an eye on the boathouse. We think the old building is connected, and something big is going to happen there tonight."

She tilted her head and winked. "Karl told me about you and Marc finally getting together. I say you go, girl." She held up a palm.

I gave a half-hearted high-five slap. "We're trying to low-key our status around the office, if you get my drift. We're only old college friends who've gone on a couple dates."

"You expect me to believe that, then I'll tell you I'm dating Karl Murray. He's a little young for me, but a girl can dream. I'd love to date a cowboy." Her voice lowered. "I've got a job interview later. Do you think the bosses will figure it out?"

I pushed the unreal visual of Candy and Karl as a couple out of my mind and gave her a once-over. "You look nice."

She laughed. "I feel like a librarian in this interview suit. But if I land the job, I can stop borrowing money from Brett to pay for health insurance."

I kept my face as expressionless as possible. "That's really nice of him to loan you money."

A huge grin filled out her face. "Brett's the best."

"You two been dating long?"

"We usually meet at the Apple, then head to his place for a while before I have to get home to Mom." She winked. "He's quite a guy."

Didn't she know she was looking for love in all the wrong places? She and I would have to have a good talk once this was all over.

I got out of there before she asked any more questions about Marc.

As soon as I stepped into Karl's workspace, my eyes went to the empty birdcage stand. I hadn't given Pedro more than a passing thought for days. A wave of guilt washed over me. Annoying as he was, I missed his antics. Was it too much to hope he was still alive?

Karl let out a whistle. "Sure don't look like you've been in a head-on. You okay?"

I tossed him a cheerful smile. "Glad to see the Rescaté rumor mill hasn't lost its steam. It was a rear-ender and, other than a left-hook from the airbag, I'm okay. Can you believe I managed to run into a stolen vintage Corvette?"

He blew another low whistle through his teeth and sauntered my way. I looked him over while he studied the cart. Although a little short, he wasn't a bad catch for someone. But Candy?

As usual, he selected a plain bagel and plain cream cheese. I'd have to work on expanding the cowboy's palate. While he ate, I told him about the guy I ran into having a license tag that said *Lucky*.

We had a good laugh, then Karl lowered his voice. "Not Marc's lucky day. I heard the news. I hope we can zero in on the real killer, or else Marc better be lawyered up."

I grabbed his arm and pulled him away from the open door. "I'm trying to get the word out to everyone that Marc and I plan a stakeout on the boathouse tonight. We need your help."

His eyes filled with apprehension. "Do you want me to come, too? That sounds risky."

The guy had no fear getting on a two-ton angry animal's back, yet quivered at the thought of staking out a building in hopes the bad guy would show up? Crazy. "We think it's better we watch the boathouse alone, but we're wondering if you could be our point person here in the mansion. When the killer shows up, we'll call your cell, and you can notify the police. Maybe if the call comes from you, they'll pay attention."

"Just tell me what time." He selected an apple juice and drained the bottle in one long draw. He bent to inspect a corner of the cart. "You have a loose screw. I'll fix it for ya."

I grinned as I drew out my pocketknife and popped out the tiny screwdriver. I made two quick turns. "All done."

"You're gonna put me out of a job with that gadget."

I dropped the knife into my pocket. "I can't fix a toilet or build a cabinet with this thing. You're safe."

We set the time for the stakeout then I headed off to refill the coffee urn.

Back on my rounds, Rosa and Helen ambushed me like a couple of clucking mother hens. They'd heard I was in a car crash and in the hospital with multiple injuries. I assured them I was fine. Of course, they also asked if it was true about Marc and me being a couple.

"I knew from the way you look at each other," Rosa gushed. "I love that you are together. But we wonder one thing."

I was almost afraid to ask. "What's that?"

"When you marry Marc, you won't be April Love anymore, unless you are like Mexican women and keep your name. We love your name."

Good grief. What was next on the grapevine? Would they have Marc and me eloping? If Kendall got wind of all this, neither of us would have a job, and we wouldn't be able to clear Marc's name before he could even give it to me. The old Elvis tune "Jailhouse Rock" floated into my thoughts.

I gave a dismissive wave. "You know the way stories get around. We're only old friends from college. Best not to talk about it. Rules against office romances and all. Speaking of stories, did you see the one in the *Chronicle* about Ramón's being murdered?"

"I been scared ever since I heard." Rosa's eyes darted toward the open door. "Is it even safe to work here?"

Helen gave her friend a sympathetic look. "I hardly think the bad guy would still be around. Not with the police looking for him." She turned her attention to me. "Isn't that right, April?"

"Marc and I think it's possible the killer might be keeping tabs on things." I beckoned them closer and kept my voice low. "We think the boathouse may be his or her center of operation. We're keeping a tight eye on it."

"His or her?" Rosa's eyebrows shot up. "You think a lady kill him?"

"Why not? He had enough women mad at him," Helen said.

Rosa fanned herself with her hand. "This is terrible."

If I didn't get them focused on something else, I'd have to run for smelling salts. I gestured toward the cart. "Nothing like a fresh-baked muffin to calm your nerves."

After they'd selected their treats, I moved on. At every stop after that, thankfully Ramón's murder was the hot topic and not Marc and me. I added fuel to the chatter by dropping hints about Marc's and my plan to watch the boathouse. By the time I rolled my cart in front of Taryn's desk, she was telling *me* the news.

❧

Back from the cart run, I popped a pair of muffins into the microwave, then started a fresh pot of coffee. Marc wandered in and sniffed. "Smells like I'm in time."

I scrunched my nose. "You've already had a muffin."

"But who can eat only one of anything you make?" He nudged the door shut with his elbow and pulled me into his arms. "Did you get the word out?"

I wiggled out of his embrace. "Tongues are wagging, and not only about murder. Remember how Karl walked in on us the other day?"

He pulled a face but put some distance between us.

"Karl agreed to be the point man." I glanced at the espresso machine. "Have time for a cup of heavy-duty?"

"The board is reconvening. I'll have to take it with me."

Sudden regret washed over me. Despite our breaking the no-office-romance rule, I still had a job to do. "I'm sorry, Marc. It never dawned on me you may have wanted lunch prepared."

"I didn't think of it either, so we're going out." Unease flashed from his dark eyes. "Besides, I want you safe at home with Kitty until we make our next move. You have the afternoon off."

His concern warmed me to my toes. "The insurance man is coming to look at my car in an hour. I'll stay put."

He gathered me close, squeezing me so tight I could barely breathe. "I'm having second thoughts about involving you. Maybe I should ask Karl to do the stakeout with me."

I stared at him. "Not on your life. I intend to be there with you right to the end."

His jaw twitched. "That's what I'm afraid of."

❧ 45 ❧

I pushed a couple of juniper bush branches apart and peered at the boathouse door's unhinged rusty padlock. Regardless of the fading light, I had a perfect view. I ran my gaze along the shoreline—what I could see of it in the deepening twilight.

Now that I was there, not waiting for Marc seemed foolish. But I'd about gone stir crazy in the house, not able to discuss our plans with Kitty. If she knew, the woman would be sitting here beside me right now. It was crazy enough for me to do this. If anything happened to her because of my boldness, I'd never forgive myself.

But wasn't I basically doing the same thing to Marc? Several times he'd expressed regret at involving me in his idea. I tamped down my guilty feeling. Now was not the time to deal with such matters.

I pulled out my cell and pressed March's speed-dial button.

"I'm almost there. Stay home until I call you."

"I'm already on site."

The connection went silent. "I wish you'd go back to Kitty's. I'm still a good five or six minutes away."

My heart constricted. The old Marc would have ordered me away like an army general. He really was trying.

I lowered my voice to a bare whisper. "I'm armed with my pocket knife. Karl's in the mansion on speed dial. I'm okay."

"Stay down. I've got another call. Back at you in a sec."

I slipped the phone into my pocket, still amazed at how quickly our lives came back together. As much as I'd been regretting those lost eight years, God had used them to mold us into the people we'd become. Without those growing times we'd have been at loggerheads on a regular basis.

Now we needed for this mess over Ramón's death to be behind us so we could move forward. I couldn't imagine life without Marc, and I didn't intend to spend it visiting him in prison.

Several minutes passed.

I glanced at the inky sky, then pulled out my phone to check the time. Marc should have arrived by now. Maybe he was in the parking lot finishing up that call.

Darkness settled around me as if tucking everything in for the night. I yawned and reached for the thermos I'd brought. Didn't expect to hit the caffeine this early.

Running footfalls pounded on the path behind me. Wasn't that like Marc, racing to get here so I wouldn't be alone? Even if we never nabbed the killer, we'd have fun just being together.

Something hard smashed into my head.

Light flashes zigzagged through my brain, and then there was nothing.

❧ 46 ❧

I tried to open my eyes, but the lids felt like ten-pound weights. Not to mention the monster headache slicing through my brain. I struggled to sit up, but my limbs wouldn't move. I forced an eye open, then the other one. White nylon rope looped around my wrists and ankles in a tight figure-eight binding, finished off with perfect sheet-bend knots—the kind I learned in sailing school years ago. I struggled to connect the dots but some numbers were missing.

"About time you woke up, Sleeping Beauty."

I hoisted myself onto my elbow, then pushed to a sitting position and stared in the direction of the falsetto voice. The single bulb hanging on a chain offered a little light, but I couldn't turn far enough to see anyone. A few feet ahead, an old dinghy bobbed in a boat slip. Okay. I was in the boathouse. Why?

A shadowy figure slid into view.

"Who are you?" My voice sounded hollow.

"Wouldn't you like to know?" He stepped closer, but thanks to his flannel shirt and baggy jeans I couldn't make out his build. Shadows covered his face.

He took another step toward me, and I stared at the red and white ski mask. I'd seen this dude before. On the back of a mower. A couple dots connected. Apparently he'd captured me.

I surveyed the part of the boathouse I could see without turning my head. In all the times I'd been in the upper level porch, I'd never been in the actual boat storage part. I squared my shoulders the best I could. "You're not going to get away with this."

Inside my pocket, my cell phone vibrated. I grunted and pulled at the bindings, hoping the sounds covered the buzzing.

The man hefted a canvas duffle bag from the shadows and dropped it to the cement. "If you think your boyfriend's gonna rescue you, think again. He's a little busy."

He had to mean Marc. "You're bluffing."

His evil high-pitched laugh sent shivers crawling down my spine. "Not hardly. You two thought you were so smart announcing to the world about your stakeout. Did you really think I'd show up and introduce myself so you could turn me in to that sorry excuse of a police chief?"

He opened the duffle and stuck his hand inside.

The rest of the dots connected. Had he done something to Marc before he clobbered me? How long had I been out?

Please help me, God.

Across the room, curse words filled the air.

"Forget something?" I called out, surprised at my daring.

"There she goes, getting all nosy again." He scrambled to his feet and held up a Hershey bar. "You're gonna help me get that infernal bird down."

"What bird?"

He waved the candy bar toward the ceiling. "Him."

In the rafters above my head, Pedro returned my stare. He let out a squawk, then fluttered his wings and launched off, swooping within inches of the man's head.

He swatted the air, the large sleeves of his flannel shirt flapping as if he had wings of his own. But Pedro was already sitting on a crossbeam, chattering in celebration of his prowess. He charged the guy again and made a perfect two-point landing on the man's head. The cocky bird puffed his chest as though waiting for applause. Sadly, this wasn't a show.

Our captor wrapped his hands around Pedro's body, his long fingers circling the bird like a grappling hook. I cringed. Pedro's talons curled through the knit mask and into the man's scalp. Cuss words filled the air, and the fingers straightened. Pedro took off for the crossbeam.

I glared at the low-life. "Now you've got two kidnappings on your rap sheet."

"Huh?"

"Murder, kidnapping, and birdnapping."

With long fingers, he ripped the brown wrapper off the candy. "Get him down and feed him this." He held out the chocolate.

A long ago conversation about parrots and chocolate filtered into my memory. This wasn't Karl, was it? Couldn't be. His fingers were short and rough from his bull rope. "That's poison to him."

"Better dead than alive." He tilted his masked head toward the rafters. "Get that no-account bird down."

I inhaled a breath of clammy air. Did he realize he forgot to fake his voice? "Why don't you leave me and Pedro here? Escape while you can."

"What do you take me for? Call the bird down." The disguised voice was back, sounding like a shrieking demon in a horror movie.

"I can do better with crackers."

"Use the candy."

"He won't come for something he's never tasted before. There are some wheat crackers in my bag outside."

He came closer and grabbed me by both shoulders, his fingers digging in like claw hammers. I kept my scream bottled in my chest.

Inside my pocket my phone vibrated, but he was too busy manhandling me away from the door to notice. "Stay here."

"Like I'm going anyplace?"

The door slammed right before my cell phone chimed. One second sooner and the dummy would've realized he hadn't bothered to frisk me. I still had my phone and my knife.

Thank You, God.

I looked up at Pedro. How could I have messed up so much? The murderer had flown completely under the radar. We should have had Karl wait where he could see the boathouse, not in his workroom. How dumb was that?

"Lord, I need Your help now more than ever—"

The door whipped open, missing my shoulder by inches. He charged toward me. "You liar. There's no crackers out there."

I squeezed my eyes shut and braced myself. *Good-bye world.*

He forced my chin upward with his hand.

Hot garlic-laced breath hit my face, and my stomach heaved. Served the monster right if I barfed all over him.

"Look at me," he barked.

I opened my eyes to his cold stare laser-beaming through the mask's eye holes.

"Call that bird down!"

"Why don't you just shoot him?"

"Don't like guns."

Pedro's voice shot through the air. "What's for breakfast?"

"So it was you I saw that morning coming out of Rescaté."

"I'm smarter than that." He turned abruptly and marched to the duffle. "Leaving this here should help point the finger at Thorne." He reached in the bag and pulled out the gold and navy tie Marc had worn that morning.

"How did you get that?"

He uttered an evil chuckle. "Thorne's habit of pulling off his tie came in handy. He never noticed when I swiped it from the meeting table this afternoon."

"It'll take more than a tie to explain my death, Kendall."

His head snapped back. "Figured it out, did ya? Think you're so smart, but you've only sealed your fate." He gripped the mask with both fists and ripped it off.

Seeing his ruddy face and the faded red hair spiking up like a punk rocker's, I averted my eyes. Any other time I'd have laughed.

"Dead women tell no tales," he muttered. "Who's gonna think that Kendall Montclaire, Rescaté Board President, would murder anyone? In a little more than an hour I'll be enjoying drinks with my college buds, and you won't be found for years. Perfect alibi, don't you think? Same way I happened to be in New York when Galvez bought it."

The guy had to have help. But who? He could've been in cahoots with any of the women, I suspected, although none fit the picture. But Kendall as the killer didn't fit either—until a few minutes ago.

"I don't know what you're planning, Kendall, but kill me and the next minute I'll be with God."

"Don't start that religious mumbojumbo with me." He slam-dunked the chocolate to the ground. The bar skittered across the cement and dropped into the murky water. "Looks like the bird's having a luckier day than you."

I closed my eyes and told God I was ready to die. A loud ripping sound came, and my eyes flew open as duct tape was slapped across my mouth.

"I'll have to hope Galvez didn't plant information on that bird like he threatened." He gripped my arm and jerked me to a standing position. "Let's go."

I took a faltering step, feeling like I had leg irons wrapped around my ankles rather than rope bindings.

One shuffling step at a time, I inched over the cement and stopped at the boat slip. The dingy looked as seaworthy as a leaf. He surely didn't expect us to travel in that.

"Jump."

Certain I would crash through the vessel's rickety bottom, I hesitated. Cursing, he climbed into the boat and yanked me onto one of the seats. He then grabbed the duffle bag. It hit the boat bottom with a thud. The vessel wobbled. Whatever was in that thing, it had to weigh a lot. A vision of cement blocks being attached to my legs crept into my mind.

As Kendall pulled a black hood from the duffle, a loud crack of thunder shook the old building.

"Perfect." He dropped the shroud over my head. "Just perfect."

❧ 47 ❧

Up near the bow, Kendall tinkered with something. He must be certain Marc wasn't going to show up or he wouldn't be taking so much time. What had he done to my man? I held back angry tears. The possibilities racing through my mind weren't pleasant.

The dinghy shuddered, then righted itself. Kendall was back on the cement deck. Wasn't he afraid someone would come? Had he left a trail of bodies on his way here? I pushed those thoughts from my mind and focused on one thing: getting free. Kendall's retreating footfalls faded toward the outside door. Another rumble of thunder, and the door slammed.

I strained at the bindings, but they wouldn't budge. He couldn't have left me there for good. I had to break free before he returned. I pressed my wrists against the ropes.

The large barn-like door to the lake rattled open, and damp air buffeted my bare arms. Goosebumps erupted. What I wouldn't give for my sweatshirt, probably still neatly folded on the grass where I was sitting.

A rumble of thunder shook the building and I startled. Was he crazy? Maybe he planned on sending me out to the middle of the lake on my own. Maybe there was only enough gas to go so far. Maybe he hoped lightning would strike the boat and he'd win the gamble. But if it didn't, I'd eventually drift toward shore. Strike the last "maybe."

Soon the boat wobbled, and Kendall settled behind me next to the outboard motor.

The engine sputtered to life then died.

He grunted and another sputter came, followed by a curse word. I imagined him yanking at the pull-start for the third time. The outboard roared to life.

Tears misted my eyes as everyone I loved came into my thoughts: Kitty with her twisted sayings. Mom with her kind words for everyone, even those she didn't like. In his own way, Dad wanted only good for me. If I met my end in a watery grave, I'd never have the opportunity to come to peace with him. My brother, Brian, with his dimpled grin and good-natured attitude. And, of course, Marc, if he weren't dead by now. Eight wasted years.

The boat lurched, and a stiff rain-drenched wind plastered the hood against my face. Kendall revved the tiny motor, and I felt the hull rise up as it pounded the swells. He was going with me, but where? Was his accomplice waiting on the other side of the lake with a car? Did he have a hideout somewhere? I was no use to him alive, unless he planned to ask a ransom from Kitty. More comfortable than some her age, she wasn't as well off as one might think. That I knew, since Dad did her taxes every year.

Take courage. It is I. Don't be afraid.

I had no idea where in the Bible those words came from, but it didn't matter. God hadn't deserted me. The boat slowed as an inboard motor came portside and reversed gears.

A woman's voice shouted out, "I was ready to head back to the dock. Why didn't you answer your cell?"

"I figured it was you," Kendall shouted. "No time. Had to get out of there. Fussed over that bird too long."

"You don't have your mask on."

"Got recognized. Doesn't matter. She's toast."

He brushed past me toward the bow. If he'd been alone, I'd have pitched against him and sent him flying. The chick could have a gun.

"Will this take long? The storm is getting worse. We're prime targets out here for that lightning."

The voice, the voice. Who did it belong to? My mind raced over every woman I'd been in contact with the past couple of weeks.

"It's raining harder, sweetheart. Please hurry. You know I don't like storms."

My stomach twisted. She didn't like storms either when we were kids. What was LuAnn doing with this monster?

A lightning flash exploded through the hood, and LuAnne yelped. I thought Kendall would burst a blood vessel as he screamed an expletive and yelled at her to deal with it. I hunched over, letting the rain pound my back. If it were possible for bones to have goose bumps, mine did.

"You couldn't leave well enough alone, could you?" Kendall's complaint came through the hood. "Wouldn't be scared off by the missing pills or an attacking lawn mower. Couldn't lead you to believe that Thorne was the killer. But that sorry excuse for a cop, Bronson, bought it."

A motor came to life, and Kendall uttered a wicked laugh. "This old dinghy's gonna look like Swiss cheese." The boat lifted and dropped as the aroma of fresh wood shavings hit my nose. My heart sank. The man was drilling holes in the boat.

I pushed my right wrist against the bindings, and the knot slipped a bit.

My pulse whipped into high gear. Kendall the sailor hadn't finished off his knotting properly.

"Sweetheart, the storm. Isn't that enough?"

I tensed. Had LuAnn noticed me messing with the ropes?

My cell phone vibrated. Was Marc still alive?

Please, God, let us have another chance.

The vibrating halted as icy water lapped at the tops of my tennis shoes.

"Won't Marc be surprised when he finds out he's never gonna see his happy cooker again. Two counts of capital murder should put him away for a long time."

My muffled cries disappeared into the duct tape. What did Kendall have against Marc? He didn't deserve what this evil man had dumped on him. Surely God would intervene, even if I didn't live to see it.

"I figure you've got no more than five minutes." Kendall's voice came from a distance. He must have transferred to LuAnn's boat. "Hit it, baby." Her motor revved then faded off.

I inched my hand toward my right pocket, and with my fingertips made out the pocket's edge. Lightning sizzled nearby. I strained against the knot, and the rope gave way. I shook off the bindings, then loosened the cord from around my waist.

Icy water hit my rear end.

Have courage, it is I. Don't be afraid.

Gripping the hood in both hands, I yanked the thing off my head and let the rain wash my tears away. A lightning bolt zigzagged across the sky, and I rejoiced. I was alive—seeing, hearing, feeling. Frantic, I used the next flash of lightning to survey the lake. No sign of a boat. No sound of a motor. I dug my nails under the tape and yanked. Precious air filled my lungs, but I had no time to celebrate. The water had reached above the seat.

I pulled out my pocketknife and popped the blade. My hands went numb as soon as I plunged them into the water, but I went to work anyway, sawing at the cord around my ankles. The rope split, and the bindings fell apart.

Over on shore, lights from Rescaté glimmered through the rain like a miniature house in a Christmas display. Next door, Kitty's sunroom lights gleamed brightly.

I took out my cell. Water dripped from its seams, but a faint light emanated from the screen. Thankful I'd left the phone on my favorites contact list, I pressed Marc's name.

"April. Where are—?"

"Kendall tried to drown me. He may be on his way to Madison with

LuAnn. I'm gonna swim for Aunt Kitty's from the middle—" The connection dropped off and I hit redial. Dead. Better the phone than me. I threw the thing in the lake, took a deep breath, and jumped in.

The frigid water squeezed the air out of my lungs. I held what little was left in there and listened. The thunder rumbled off to the east. If Kendall and LuAnn were still around, they'd cut the motor. Already numb to my bones, I turned toward shore and began to swim.

Stroke, kick.

Stroke, kick.

My arms felt like a pair of medicine balls. I wanted to stop. But I couldn't. Not now. Marc was still alive, and I had to live, too. I swam a bit more, then checked my bearings. Kitty's house was off to my left at least half a mile, and I didn't seem to be any closer to the shore. The current must have carried me.

Have courage, it is I. Don't be afraid.

"I'm not afraid. But my courage could fill a tablespoon about now. All I want to do is sleep. I'm so tired."

A motor's hum came from the middle of the lake. Closer, louder, closer.

A search beam skimmed the water's surface. I raised my arm, then jerked it down. *What if it's Kendall?* I dove under the water and flutter-kicked away. The shaft of light slithered over my head, the lake no longer my enemy but my protector.

My lungs strained, and I broke the water's surface and gulped in air. The awful light headed back my direction. I prepared to dive.

"April! *Mi caramela!* Are you out there?"

Marc?

The beam hit my face and moved on. "Here. Marc, here I am." The light reversed itself. Blinded by its welcome glow, I raised an arm. "Marc, I'm here. I'm here!"

Adrenalin flowed through my veins, and I set out toward the boat, arms working faster than a pair of propellers.

"Hang on, April. We're coming."

The inboard reversed its motors as it glided up beside me. I gripped Marc's strong forearms and looked up into his wonderful face. "It's about time you got here."

❧ 48 ❧

I climbed out of Kitty's spa tub and glanced at the crystal clock that sat on the vanity. Only ten-fifteen? It should at least be past midnight, shouldn't it?

I pulled on sweats, then reached for my makeup case. Staring at the jumble of bottles, brushes and eyeshadows, I couldn't motivate myself to move. It wasn't as if Marc hadn't already seen me at my worst. Like about an hour ago, when he dragged me out of the water.

I fingercombed my curls into place, all the while smiling at the memory of how, after Marc pulled me into the patrol boat and cocooned me in a thermal blanket, I jabbered away, saying how Kendall thought he'd finished me off, but I did him one better. Mark finally planted a kiss on my lips to shut me up, causing the sheriff at the controls to crack up. Nothing like a little levity in the midst of being left for dead. I flicked off the light and headed for downstairs.

I found my handsome man waiting on the living room sofa, eyes closed and stroking Violet behind her ears.

"Here I am."

He leaped to his feet, sending the startled cat flying. His gaze swept over me as if taking inventory. Then his eyes connected with mine, and a broad grin erased the tightness in his face.

He crossed the room in three long strides. I let him take me into his arms and relished the scrub of his jaw against my cheek. We didn't move for several moments. At last we stepped apart, but our hands were still intertwined.

I soaked in his wonderful face. "I thought I'd never see you again this side of heaven."

"I kept thinking the same thing, *mi caramela.* To think I almost lost you again." He led me to the couch, where we snuggled under a fuzzy afghan. "I'm proud of you, hon. You're one tough cookie."

"I'm not so strong." I gave him a disjointed recital of the entire incident, ending with how stunned I was to hear LuAnn's voice out there.

He brushed a curl from my forehead. "I was as startled as you to find out she was involved. Chief Bronson called a short while ago. The state police spotted Kendall's car outside Madison. They chased him a couple miles before he took an exit onto a state route, then made a wrong turn into a cornfield. LuAnn was with him. Bronson and another officer are on their way to get them."

I sat up and stared at Marc. "I'd like to know what that creep did to entice her into helping him. Kendall better not get away with any of this."

"He won't. You'll probably be the star witness."

A sudden vision of me being badgered by a defense attorney exploded into my mind. Ordinarily, such a thought would send my head spinning. But after tonight, a trial would be nothing. Especially if it put Kendall behind bars for life. He must have promised LuAnn the moon. My gut ached for her. God had been showing me a lot about forgiveness, and it wasn't going to stop with Marc.

"While I was out there with that hood over my head, counting the drill holes, part of a verse kept running through my mind: *Take courage! It is I. Don't be afraid.* I can't remember where it comes from."

Marc tugged me back against him. "Jesus said those words when He walked to the disciples on water in the middle of a wind storm."

I chuckled. "How appropriate is that? God knew the exact words I needed." I leaned back so I could look into his eyes. "How did Kendall sidetrack you?"

He dropped his gaze. "He was the other call that came in when you and I were talking. He insisted on putting the final touches on my contract immediately because he had to leave town. He said if I didn't sign tonight, the offer might be in jeopardy because a couple board members were against the appointment. I was to meet him at the Grand Geneva." He ran his tongue over his lower lip. "I looked for a place to turn around."

My heart wrenched. Marc hadn't changed after all.

"Then I thought of you and the commitment we'd made. How you were at the boathouse and in possible danger. I told him if he couldn't wait until tomorrow, I wasn't his guy. He shouted something I barely understood. All I caught was that I'd be sorry."

My spirits rose, only to be tempered by another thought. "But you didn't come."

"As I drove toward Rescaté, a huge weight lifted. So what if I lost my job, and got accused for a crime I didn't do. I had God and you. I needed nothing more. Then I rounded a curve and came to a detour. I figured the old bluff had dropped rock since I'd gone home, so I turned on Bonner Road. I tried to call but got your voice mail.

"When I got to Rescaté, the storm was heating up. Karl and I searched for you. Then I called Kitty, and she said you had left to meet me in town. I had to tell her the truth. I'm surprised you didn't hear her scream." A tear trailed from his left eye, and he swiped at it with the back of his hand.

My breath caught. Never had I seen him cry before.

"I should never have let you stay at the boathouse alone."

I took his face in both my hands. "Marc, it was my decision to go there on my own and to stay. A bad one at that."

He grabbed my hand and kissed the palm. "We were about to contact the police when you called. I thought you were dead, but here you are." His damp eyes searched my face. "You are so beautiful."

"Without a stitch of makeup on? You must really love me."

He answered with a kiss that sent tingles clear to my toes, and I happily kissed him back. Both wounded and yet surviving, we'd make it now.

I snuggled against his shoulder. "So what happened next?"

"Karl relayed the information about Kendall to the police while I called the county sheriff and asked for a patrol boat."

"I was afraid you didn't hear me because my phone died."

"We'd been searching for at least fifteen minutes when we spotted you. You were moving parallel to the shore."

"I felt like I'd been swimming forever."

"Probably delusional from the cold. Do you remember the deputy wanting to take you to the hospital to check for hypothermia?"

"No. Why didn't he?"

He chuckled. "You insisted you weren't going anywhere but here. And you'd soak in Kitty's tub. We decided with the thermal blanket around you and a hot bath, you'd be okay."

I settled against Marc's chest, then bolted upright. "Pedro's in the boathouse. We need to get him."

He tugged me back to him. "Karl has him safe and sound, and you're going nowhere but to bed for at least a day or two."

"I'll go to sleep, but I'm going to work tomorrow."

"As your boss, I order you to stay home."

"As your rebellious employee, I refuse."

He chuckled. "I know better than to argue, but no alarm."

A couple minutes later, I was jostled awake as Marc carried me up the stairs. Kitty met us in the upstairs hall and led the way to my room. I have to presume that once he settled me on the bed, Kitty shooed him away and cut the light, because I was gone before my head hit the pillow.

196

ᴂ 49 ᴈ

The next morning, I wandered into Rescaté's kitchen an hour later than normal and stared at the huge sacks of bagels and sweet rolls piled on the counter. But the red roses sitting next to the goodies almost caused me to lose it. I picked up the note scribbled in Marc's handwriting.

Mi caramela, the flowers are to say how much I love you, and the bagels and sweet rolls are for the gang. Fresh fruit is in the fridge. Let me know when you get here.
Love, Marc

I buried my face in the blossoms and breathed in the heady fragrance. Had it only been two weeks since we reunited in this very room? My sensibilities said to slow down, but my heart said otherwise. It wasn't as if we'd just met, didn't have a history.

So I ground Arabica beans and set up the espresso maker. Marc would get the best latte I could hope to make. As I poured steamed milk into one of the drinks, the kitchen phone rang. I set down the pan and answered.

"My, April, you sound happy. I tried your cell but got a recording."

"Hi, Flavia. I haven't had a chance to call since we got cut off. Sorry I didn't call you back right away. My cell phone is history, but I have good news about Isabel—"

"I already know. Isabel didn't kill Ramón."

"How'd you find out?"

"She called last night and said she wished she and Ramón could have made peace before he died. She feels awful that he passed while they were on the outs. I'm sure she didn't kill him."

Flavia then launched into a new story about her daughter. I was waiting to get a word in when Rosemary came to the door.

I covered the phone with my hand and mouthed, "What's up?"

"Chief Bronson is on the phone and wants to talk to you ASAP."

He was the last person I wanted to speak to, but I excused myself from Flavia with a promise to e-mail the cake recipe, and then waited for Rosemary to put the call through.

The phone rang, and I answered with a more subdued greeting than the one I'd used with Flavia.

"What are you trying to do? Get into the detective business?" The chief punctuated his words with a laugh, but the ever-present sarcastic tone remained.

"Not hardly. I almost got killed last night."

"But you got away after he left you for dead." Was that a note of respect I heard in his voice? "I hate to admit when I'm wrong, but for once I'm glad I was."

I almost dropped the phone. "I don't know how much I contributed."

"Thanks to Montclaire's cleverness, we came close to arresting the wrong man."

"Kendall confessed?"

"I'm not supposed to divulge this kind of information. But since you had a hand in nailing him, I can tell you that Montclaire told LuAnn that her usefulness to him was over, and he had intentions of killing her. When he realized the girlfriend had already confessed to us, he started talking. Good thing the state police spotted him when they did, or he'd have another murder one count against him."

"Whatever led LuAnn to this? He must have promised her something big."

"Greed. She and Montclaire had been having an affair for months. He said she'd be mistress of the mansion once he got Rescaté out of there. Too much temptation for a small-town girl on a waitress's salary. She's the one who ran you down that morning. He got her to exchange the poisoned Gingko Biloba capsules with Galvez's while he was in New York, creating an alibi."

I let the information sink in. "Kendall thought if Ramón died, Rescaté would vacate the mansion?"

"It's a bit more complicated. I always had a hunch Darlene Montclaire had been murdered, and now we know."

"Darlene Montclaire?"

"Montclaire's first wife. Fifteen years ago he poisoned her after she told him she wanted a divorce and threatened to take him for all he had. He buried her in Rescaté's dirt basement. She's been on a missing persons list all that time."

I stared at the floor, thankful I'd had no reason to visit the cellar.

"When his father willed the mansion to Rescaté, Kendall panicked. Galvez made a surprise visit to the mansion and found Montclaire digging up her body. To buy Galvez's silence, Montclaire promised to donate a million bucks to Rescaté. Galvez agreed, but when the money didn't materialize, he threatened to call the authorities. That's when Montclaire convinced LuAnn to help him poison Galvez. He counted on Doc Fuller's not realizing the man died of poisoning which, of course, happened."

"That explains the phone call I overheard, and I suppose he set up that roadblock for Marc last night."

"No, rocks fell at the bluff last night. We confirmed it. He figured if he couldn't lure Thorne away by that contract talk, he'd at least have more time if Thorne had to take the long way to Rescaté. Had LuAnn do that while he took care of you."

I stared at the floor again and my neck hairs stood on edge. "Chief, I have to ask. Is the first Mrs. Montclaire...um....still buried here?"

"No. Montclaire says he actually convinced Galvez to help him, and they moved the remains to a woods on a nearby farm. Some officers are digging over there now."

Marc and Karl entered the room, Marc wearing a grin and Karl wearing Pedro on his shoulder. I waggled my fingers at them. "Let me know when you want me to make my statement, and I'll be there, Chief. Are there any more questions you need answered now?"

"Nope. I'll give you a call later and set up an appointment. We'll probably have Thorne come in at the same time for his statement."

I hung up and grinned at the men. "What's this all about?"

Karl came forward. "Hold out your arm."

I did, and the bird hopped aboard. "What's for breakfast?"

"Not chocolate. I think we're buds for life." I stroked the bird's head. "Aren't we, pretty boy?" I lifted a wing and peeked under it, seeing nothing but green feathers.

"What are you doing?" Marc's voice held a tinge of wariness.

"Kendall seemed to think Ramón hid information on the bird, but I don't see anything."

Marc lifted Pedro's other wing. "Nothing here either."

I shrugged. "Guess Ramón had the last laugh on Kendall."

"I'd say you did," Marc said. "He left you to die, and here you are."

The bird bobbed his head. "Pedro is a good boy."

I looked at the bird still perched on my arm. "You sure are."

"I'll take him back now." Karl patted his shoulder, and Pedro hopped on.

"Hey, Karl, I'm cooking my to-die-for chili tonight at Kitty's. Why don't you join us?"

Marc's eyes widened in surprise. Who could blame him? I didn't know I was cooking either until the words left my mouth.

Karl thought for a moment. "Sounds good, but I can't. I'm going to that meeting with my buddy."

"No problem. We'll do it another time." I tossed him a wink.

Marc shut the door after the pair left and gathered me off the stool and into his arms. "You were inviting another man to dinner?"

I scrunched my nose. "I intended to invite you, too."

"Then I accept. If your chili is still as good as it was before…"

"It's even better." I glanced at the flowers. "Thank you for the roses and food."

He kissed my nose. "Did you look inside the flowers?"

"I rubbed my face in them."

"Look again."

I stepped over to the roses and spotted the small burgundy box nestled among the stems. Was I getting my ring back? With shaking hands, I flipped the case open. A silver heart-shaped pendant decorated with a tiny diamond glistened against a dark velvet background.

Marc came up behind me and wrapped his arms around my waist. "Recognize the stone?"

"From the ring?"

"I wanted you to have it, but as a promise for another ring to come. One I hope you'll never throw at me."

I ran my fingertips over the small stone. "Will you put it on?" I handed him the necklace, then turned and waited for him to hook the chain.

He closed the clasp then brought me back around until our lips found each other.

I was kissing the boss, and I didn't care one bit. Let the rumors fly, because they'd all be true.

Chicken George
ৎৎৎ

As prepared by April Love in *Thyme for Love*
Recipe Adapted by Pamela S. Meyers

Ingredients:

Extra virgin olive oil
10 oz. Sliced Baby Bella mushrooms
One medium chopped onion
1-1/4 cup sour cream (can use nonfat or low-fat)
1-1/4 cup low sodium chicken broth
½ cup regular sherry (not cooking sherry)
6 boneless chicken breasts
8 oz. sliced Swiss cheese
8 oz. herb stuffing mix (or make your own dry seasoned bread for stuffing)
¾ cup butter (can use margarine or spread such as Smart Balance)

Set oven for 350 degrees.

1. Sauté sliced baby bellas and chopped onion in olive oil.
2. In medium bowl blend sour cream and chicken broth with either a handheld electric blender or mixer until smooth.
3. Add sautéed mushrooms and onions, along with the sherry, and mix together.
4. Arrange the chicken breasts on bottom of 9 x 13-inch pan.
5. Layer the sliced Swiss cheese over the chicken.
6. Mix herb stuffing with the butter or margarine and drop in large spoonfuls over the layers.
7. Cover and bake at 350 degrees for one hour. Remove cover and bake an additional ½ hour.

Coming Soon...

On the Road to Love
Pamela S. Meyers

❧❧

Love Will Find a Way
Book Two

When April Love opens her new eatery and catering business in an old Victorian in the village of Canoga Lake, Wisconsin, trouble is afoot. During renovations, she discovers evidence that the home had once been the hideout of a famous gangster. When several break-ins and an attempted arson fire threaten the grand opening, April and handsome fiancé March Thorne wonder if some of the gangsters are still around.

www.pamelasmeyers.com
www.oaktara.com

About the Author

❧ڡ৯

Take a Sentimental Journey
Pamela S. Meyers

PAMELA S. MEYERS, raised in Lake Geneva, Wisconsin, in the same area as the fictional Canoga Lake, has told stories most of her life. When she was a child, her characters came from the huge collection of paper dolls that kept her entertained for hours. As a teen, daydreams sparked by the love of reading motivated her. Now, as an adult, armed with prayer, a laptop, and a myriad of ideas, stories flow onto her computer.

"I've always desired to set a story in the beautiful area of Wisconsin where I grew up," Pamela says. "As the plot for *Thyme for Love* emerged, I decided to incorporate the flavor of Lake Geneva and its many nineteenth-century mansions into the fictional Canoga Lake, set a few miles to the east."

Pamela brings her interest in cooking and tweaking recipes to the story. April's *Chicken George* is a recipe Pamela adapted from one passed on to her by a coworker.

Pamela has published articles in *Today's Christian Woman, Christian Computing Magazine, Victory in Grace Magazine, Ancestry Magazine, Christian Fiction Blog Alliance Ezine*, and the ACFW Ezine, *Afictionado*. Her true story, *Like Son, Like Father*, appeared in the compilation book, *His Forever*, published by Adams Media.

Pamela received her Bachelor of Arts Degree from Trinity International University, Deerfield IL. In her church, as a sign language interpreter, Pamela interpreted the church service and special concerts for many years, and currently serves in the church's outreach to the Japanese community. She also facilitates a women's Bible study.

Her author tag, *Take a Sentimental Journey,* exemplifies her stories, which take her readers to the small towns of the Wisconsin, and sometimes beyond. She resides in Illinois.

www.pamelasmeyers.com
www.oaktara.com

CPSIA information can be obtained at www.ICGtesting.com
Printed in the USA
LVOW112228210212

269828LV00003B/48/P